A Novel

CALEB ALEXANDER

SBI

STREBOR BOOKS

NEW YORK LONDON TORONTO SYDNEY

Strebor Books
P.O. Box 6505
Largo, MD 20792
http://www.streborbooks.com

ISBN-13 978-1-59309-127-9
ISBN-10   1-59309-127-3
LCCN 2007940440

First Strebor Books trade paperback edition January 2008

Cover design: www.mariondesigns.com

10 9 8 7 6 5 4 3 2 1

Manufactured in the United States of America

For information regarding special discounts for bulk purchases, please contact Simon & Schuster Special Sales at 1-800-456-6798 or business@simonandschuster.com

This book is dedicated to my sons, Curtis and Caleb,
and to my daughter, Cheyenne

Acknowledgments

First and foremost I want to thank the Almighty Creator. It would take an entire novel for me to list all of the blessings that have been bestowed upon me. I know that it was during some of the darkest moments of my life, that He carried me. I am a living witness to His kindness, forgiveness, charity, and compassion. He's real, and His mercy and greatness is bottomless.

I want to thank my brother Theron, for giving me my imagination. He helped to develop and foster my creativity. He has an imagination and wit that is uncanny. If he ever picks up a pen and starts writing, the world is in for a treat. I want to thank my grandmother, Lillie. There are no words that could even begin to convey my feelings there. She is my heart. I want to acknowledge my wife, Jennifer; my sons, Curtis and Caleb; and my daughter, Cheyenne. My mother, Gwen; and my dad, Charles.

I want to say thank you to Zane, and Charmaine, and to the best agent in the world, Tracy Sherrod. Big ups to Keith Saunders for the cover design. Thanks to Shayla Cobb for her typing skills.

Shout out to: Stacey Wynn, Cornell Cleaver, Syidah Shaheed, Omar, Maleek, Momma Robinson, Big Lou (Sheffield), Greg Palmer, Wayman Goodley, Bart, Twin, Fresh Reggie (Williams), Magic, Stag, Unc, Tuck, Tyrus Foster, Charles Deese, Mo-Mo (Elmo Johnson), JP (James Peters), Terance Spellmon, Quentin Henry, Wynell, Stephen, Theron Duncan, Edward Brown, Timmy, Skibo (Dashawn Batts), Chrissy Barefield, Baby Ray Mathis, Dimebox, Charlie Hustle, Buggy (Albert Gistard), Shawn Butler, Smoke (Keith Theus), Ron Johnson, Ced Quigley, JR, Keith

Franklin, Black, Jesse Brooks, Fred and Sharonda Carter, Tyshea Wagner, Julon, Jarveon, Low Life (Stacey Robinson), Nick Clay, Nikki Smith, Monekka Smith, Jo Ann Smith, Dwayne Pleasant, Ernie and Valerie LaCour, Mike LaCour , Brian Green, JV Green, Can't Get Right, Kenneth Macracken, Shawn Macracken, Staci, Denise, Erin, Polly, Cibon, Greg, El ijah, Kennedy, Arboni, Janice, Devean, Kelvin, Michelle Monciaviaz, Nicole Hood, Teke Beck, Jason, Pat, Joe Linton, Quick (Terry Williams), Grave Digger (Donnell), Billy Pen, Anthony Frisco, Tony and Olga Owens, Dana, Deon, Ronnie, Marcus, Thomas, Lisa, Mildred, Betty, Matthew, Bubba, Marshall Simmons, Rene Simmons, Tony, Daphane, Briana, Ebony, Belinda, Avante, Amaya, Audrey, Darlene, Jimmy, Keanna, Deandre, Jennae, Juwan, Gail, Rodney, Ivory, Sylvia, Uncle Jerry, Aunt Libby, Aunt Joyce, Cookie, Pam, Uncle Richard, Uncle Thomas, Uncle Billy, Aunt Fanny, Thad, Comfort, Big Cibon, Trisha, Anna, Gloria, the Smith Family, the Spellmon Family, the Williams Family, the Lacour Family, the Washington Family, the Small Family, the Luna Family, the Gafford Family, the Small Family, the Stephens Family, the Hearn Family, the James Family, the Bailey Family, the Sheffield Family, the Dawson Family, the Childs Family, the Huff Family, the Owens Family, the Shaheed Family, the Moorman Family, the Zumalt Family, the Hernandez Family, the Gordon Family, the Capprietta Family.

Those of you who I forgot to mention, it was not on purpose. Please forgive me. I owe so much to so many, and I sincerely thank you all for being there for me all of these years.

Chapter One

Jamaica had always been blessed: physically, emotionally, spiritually, financially, and mentally. From her beautiful, silky, copper-colored skin to her captivating emerald eyes. She was blessed with smooth almond-colored hair, which flowed steadily down her miraculously well-proportioned, sultry, sinewy figure. But most of all, she was blessed with a voice.

It was a voice that could deliver notes so high, that the bats which inhabited the cool dark Gotham night danced and rejoiced at each melodious rendition. It was a voice that could resound so low that walls shook, and a cannon's deep thunderous boom would fall silent in envy. It was a harmonious voice, a melodious voice, a multiplatinum, over one hundred and fifty million albums-sold worldwide voice. It was the voice of Jamaica Tiera Rochelle, who, to her tens of millions of fans worldwide, was simply known as Tiera.

"Cut! That's a wrap!" bellowed Tony Battles, the hottest young director in the entire music video industry.

Tony was young, black, gifted, and arrogant. His short-cut, wavy hair, and hip, urban fashions, which hung from his thin frame with just the right amount of cool baggyness, along with his quick devilish smile, made him feel that he was God's gift to women. *ALL WOMEN.*

Tony rose carefully from his director's chair, which had been custom made so that the word *DIRECTOR* loomed large on its front and back. He sauntered confidently across the set, stepping over cables and wires, dodging video cameras and lighting equipment, as well as personnel.

The video shoot had occurred outdoors at night. The weather was quite mild for New York this time of year, and everyone was taking advantage of it. Dancers, lighting equipment, cameras, spectators, fill-ins, gofers, makeup artists, pyrotechnic experts, models, choreographers, animal trainers and animals, along with the usual assortment of by-standers and hangers-on, filled the area.

Jamaica, tired and perspiring from the previous dance routine, as well as the intense heat of the lighting and the thick layers of commercial makeup, strode across the set to speak with her friend, publicist, and personal assistant, LaChina Anderson.

"Good job, Jai." LaChina clapped. She pulled several pieces of tissue from her pocket and handed them to her friend.

"Thanks," Jamaica told her. She took the tissue and wiped away her beads of perspiration. Along with them came thick globs of television makeup.

Jamaica exhaled a cool sigh of relief. "Ooooh, girl, I'm glad that's finally over." She smiled wearily at her friend. "No more videos?"

LaChina returned Jamaica's smile and nodded reassuringly. "No more videos…for now."

"I need a vacation," Jamaica told her. She rubbed her hand across her stomach, now realizing how little she was actually wearing, and how much she was actually exposing. Her black knit tights were almost see-through, while her white cotton half-shirt exposed her sexy, tight mid-section. Her well-proportioned figure was the product of natural endowment, as well as a dedicated and expensive personal trainer.

LaChina, on the other hand, was exquisitely dressed as usual. Chanel frames rested comfortably midway down her nose. They stylishly matched her DKNY pantsuit and Ferragamo shoes. And, of course, in her hand rested her ever-present, leather-covered, gold-embroidered Mont Blanc clipboard.

LaChina had been Jamaica's best friend since as far back as either could remember. They had grown up together in several of the wealthiest communities in New York state. Each of their futures had been decided by their mothers prior to their births.

Jamaica's mother designed a future for her daughter that included singing, acting, dancing, modeling, and a life of sheer glamour. Hundreds of talent shows, music lessons, voice coaches, personal trainers, and performance academies later, here she stood.

LaChina's university professor mother stressed education over all else, despite her daughter's natural beauty. Growing up, LaChina often tied, and sometimes even defeated, Jamaica in beauty contests. Her flawless skin, pearlescent smile, and long silky hair often caused men to stop in the street and stare. Nevertheless, many honor rolls, academic awards, certificates, scholarships, and class presidencies later, here she stood.

LaChina graduated magna cum laude from Spelman College in Atlanta, and returned home with a degree in management to New York, where she began working for her best friend.

"Jai, girl, Bev and I were just talking about how tired you've been looking," LaChina told her. "I think a vacation would be a pretty good idea."

LaChina lifted her index finger to her face and tapped lightly at the bottom of her chin. "How about a working vacation?" she asked Jamaica. "We want to shoot the next video in a sunny location, so…while we lounge around like tourists, we put on hats and sunglasses, and scout locations."

Jamaica clasped her friend's arms and shouted excitedly. "Yes! Yes! You know how I love the Caribbean. When do we leave?"

"Actually, we have to do the Sea World promotion first, and from there we can head to the Caribbean."

The thought of sea animals and slimy skin made Jamaica recoil. "The Sea World thing, yuck!" Jamaica's head fell to one side and she exhaled forcibly. "Do I have to?"

"Jai, it's for the kids," LaChina told her. "Plus, every time somebody kisses that damn fish, their popularity goes up, their record sales boom, and their bank accounts fatten."

Jamaica released LaChina's arm and shook her head emphatically. "I have to kiss that thing? Uh-un, hell no!" Jamaica turned and started to race away. "There is no way that I'm going to kiss a giant fish!"

LaChina quickly grabbed Jamaica by her arm stopping her. "It's a whale."

Jamaica turned and stared at her friend. "You called it a fish first, not me."

"We're going," LaChina told her.

Jamaica pouted. "It might eat me."

"Jai."

"It's slimy!"

"Jai."

Tony Battles, who had stopped to chat with Jamaica's label representatives, finally closed in. He had the gleam of money in his eyes. Lots of money.

"Hello, ladies," he greeted them.

Jamaica smiled and gave a slight wave. "Hello, Tony."

"Hi, Tony," LaChina replied.

Tony Battles' smile resembled the cat that bought the canary and had it tied up inside of its litter box. He focused in on Jamaica. "Tiera, with you we didn't even need lighting. Your beauty lit up the place."

When Jamaica turned to LaChina, she found that her friend was already staring at her. Their eyes locked for several seconds, before Jamaica spoke.

"Girl, I give that a one," she told LaChina.

LaChina nodded. "Yeah, that was kinda weak. I was gonna give it a two, but when I consider the fact that it came from a Morehouse man, who should have come a lot stronger, I'm inclined to agree with you. That's a one."

Together they turned and faced the young director.

"Good-bye, Tony," they said in unison.

Deflated, Tony's mouth remained open, as he watched them walk away.

Jamaica placed her arm inside of LaChina's, as they casually strolled toward the dressing room. In this case, the dressing room was a converted trailer, which had been lavishly outfitted.

"See what I have to put up with?" Jamaica asked her friend. She exhaled loudly and tossed her hair back over her shoulders as they walked. "From dancers, actors, professional athletes, and scores of other people. Either they want to screw me because of the money, or they want to fuck me because of the fame."

"I know, girl." LaChina nodded. "I get it all of the time, and from educated, professional brothers too."

Jamaica rested her head on her friend's shoulder and clasped her hand.

"I just want a good man. One without a line, without the number to the tabloids inside of his back pocket, and without dollar signs in his eyes. I want a man for Jamaica, not for Tiera, the Grammy Award-winning artist. Not for Tiera, the *Billboard* R&B and Pop Artist of the Year. Not for Tiera, the Soul Train Music Award-winning songstress…"

LaChina poked out her bottom lip and interrupted her friend. "Not for Tiera, the ga-zillion platinum-selling recording artist, and most sought-after actress in Hollywood?"

"You understand?" Jamaica asked.

LaChina smiled and leaned to the side, wrapping her arm tightly around Jamaica. "Oh, my sister! Looking for Prince Charming to come and rescue you from a life of wealth, stardom, and fame. Poor little rich girl."

"Don't tease me," Jamaica whined.

They stopped just outside of the trailer, where Jamaica reached for the door. She pulled it open while still laughing at her friend. Inside at the table sat Jamaica's mother, Beverly Rochelle. She saw them first.

"Oh, Jamaica darling, I'm glad that you are…"

Jamaica closed her eyes and rapidly shut the trailer door, cutting her mother off in mid-sentence. She turned to her friend and leaned her back against the trailer's door.

"China," Jamaica called out softly.

"What?"

"Girl, get me outta here."

Chapter Two

The Wheatley Courts were some of the most worn-down, trashed-out, poverty-stricken, housing projects in America. Located on the east side of the city of San Antonio, they were home to a variety of sorts. From drug dealers to gang members to teen mothers and drug addicts, its tenants' lives mirrored the worst of society's ills. One apartment in this massive, bullet-riddled, rat-infested, broken-windowed, trash-strewn brick complex, was currently bearing witness to a heated discussion concerning one of America's social ills which knows no boundaries.

"I'm tired of coming home and having to clean up after you every day! Stop drinking and throwing up everywhere, and leaving your empty beer bottles all over the place!" Tameer kicked several of the empty bottles across the floor. "You get drunk, and you find the nearest corner thinking it's a toilet, and you piss all over the place! I can't even bring any of my friends over to study!"

Eddie Lee's answer was a solid, bellowing belch. A large-framed man now of expanding girth, Eddie Lee stood swaying in the center of the room. His muscle shirt now several times too small, and his once white boxers completed his unshaven scruffiness. Scratching his small, peppered, uncombed, and rapidly graying afro, he expanded on his first reply.

"You get the hell out, if you don't like it!" Swaying, Eddie Lee waved his massive arm toward the front door, almost losing his balance in the process. "Leave! If you would have kept playing football, instead of writing that gay shit, you wouldn't be here to see it!"

Eddie Lee's first step sent him stumbling. The floor of the apartment was littered with clothing strewn to and fro, and numerous crushed beer cans and bottles rested on top of the clothing. The coffee table, which had never hosted a cup of coffee, was covered with stacks of old newspapers, many of which had yellowed with age. The end tables were no better off, for they were turned on their sides indicating that once again, Eddie Lee had trashed the place.

"And leave Savion here alone with you? You'd like that, wouldn't you?" Tameer shouted. "You'd like to beat up on him like you beat up on the apartment, and like you beat up on my mom!"

Eddie Lee came alive like a bear awakening from a long hibernation. His inebriation seemed to decline.

"Shut up!" Eddie Lee shouted. "Just shut the fuck up! You don't know what happened between me and your mom, so just shut the hell up!"

Eddie Lee turned, lifted a nearby beer bottle, and tossed it against the wall. Only the tip of it shattered.

"Besides, she's the one who left your ass!" Eddie Lee continued. "So why are you always mouthing off at me?"

Tameer planted his feet and stood erect. "If I had some place to go, and take Savion, I would leave you too, Dad! Look at you!" Tameer's voice crackled, so he swallowed hard to try to get rid of the crackling. It didn't work. "You hurt your back, you retire from work, and you become a drunk. You sit around all day and drink, and then you want to fight. She couldn't take your punches anymore, Dad! I'm glad she left. I'm glad she jumped ship and saved herself! Somebody had to survive!"

With that, Tameer turned and jogged up the creaking stairs and into his bedroom.

Tameer's room resembled that of a high school's athletic department. All District, All City, All State, and All American pennants, banners, trophies, certificates and letters were spread all throughout the room. Three Five A state championship football trophies shared a desk with two Five A state basketball trophies, and two for baseball. The dresser held the state championship trophies for track and field, and swimming. Ribbons and plaques adorned the walls, sharing space with posters of great athletes and literary notables.

Of the two paths Tameer had to choose from, he took the one most disappointing to all, but most fulfilling to himself. He chose to accept an academic scholarship at a local university, declining several athletic scholarships from numerous national ones. In fact, many of the major universities had pursued him with considerable vigor.

Born with a powerful frame, natural speed, and unnatural maneuverability, he quickly transformed his body into a muscular sports machine. His father drove him relentlessly, and starting with his freshman year in high school, Tameer had dominated the Texas sports scene. He was a college coach's wet dream.

The boosters had offered him jobs, cars, credit cards, daughters, and everything else under the sun. The Catholic schools offered him God, Heaven, absolution, redemption, and salvation. The California schools offered him movie roles, Hollywood, a life of wealth, fame, and fortune, along with his choice of sunny bunnies to share it all with. The Texas schools offered him oil, oil money, cattle, cattle money, and Houston, or a nice patch of land comparable to. He turned them all down.

The pain he felt came not from disappointing so many people, but from a conversation between his father and his uncle. He had overheard Eddie Lee saying that he thought his son would rather have been in a cheerleader's skirt, than wearing a football jersey. It hurt. It had hurt more than anything in this world, as Tameer had always done his best to please his father. His desire to please Eddie Lee had driven him to greatness. It's what made him elevate himself to legendary, record-shattering, football demi-god status. He became the greatest student athlete in the annals of Texas football history, in an effort to make Eddie Lee say something nice about him. He would have almost killed for a smile or a pat on the back from his father. It never came.

Once again, Tameer found himself alone in his bedroom after having another argument with his father. Once again, Tameer found himself removing his journal of poetry to make an entry. Finally, like all of the other times, he found himself falling asleep on his bed, haunted by memories of his mother.

San Antonio International Airport was a thoroughly modern facility. Large, comfortable, efficient, and like most others, found itself not holding a candle to New York's massive JFK International.

"China, what is this God-forsaken place? Where have you brought me to?" Jamaica strode through the airport wearing a sizzling red leather ensemble from North Beach Leather. It was a three-piece with jacket, skirt, and a matching oversized leather hat. She completed her *Vogue* look with a red Chanel purse, and matching red oversized Chanel frames.

"Jai, I'm not going to put up with your whining." LaChina strolled alongside her friend, dressed less ostentatiously. Her cream-colored, soft-cotton, pleated bell-bottom pantsuit, and reasonably-sized Fendi frames barely registered a second glance. "We're going to do the promo, then get the hell outta here and head for the Bahamas."

Jamaica waved her hand through the air, dramatically fanning her face. "I don't see how Savannah and Jemia tolerate this awful weather. I feel like I'm going to bake."

"You're the one who put on all of that leather," LaChina told her. "Girl, this is Texas, not New York."

"You said to dress incognito," Jamaica countered.

LaChina stopped, turned, and stared at her friend. "Jai, girl, that hat looks like something out of a Doctor Seuss book. That is not discreet, nor incognito."

"You bring me down here to take pictures of me kissing a big, slimy, black fish, and then you talk about me? If you weren't my sista, I would deck you."

"It's a *whale*, and you have to hug it, and then kiss it." LaChina smiled at Jamaica. "I hope it licks you in the face."

Jamaica slapped LaChina across her arm. "Yuck!"

The airport was semi-crowded today, with people returning from the Thanksgiving holiday, or departing for their Christmas one. Airport patrons were darting to and fro, left and right, conducting their business. Still, the difference in atmosphere, ambiance, and energy made Jamaica yawn. She was anxious to conduct her business and leave the place.

"Did you tell your cousin what time to pick us up?" Jamaica asked.

Tired of answering the same question for an undetermined number of times, LaChina's answer was brief. "Yep."

Frustrated, Jamaica exhaled loudly. "Do they have paved streets, or did she have to drive a mule cart?"

"Shut up, Jai."

"Do they at least have indoor plumbing?"

"Shut up, Jai."

"Well, what are we going to do about the luggage?" Jamaica inquired.

The question brought a smile to LaChina's face. She turned toward Jamaica, and upon visualizing her friend struggling through the terminal carrying her own bags, she laughed.

Jamaica didn't understand. "What?"

"What do you mean, what?" LaChina asked.

"The luggage. What are you laughing at?"

LaChina shook her head. "Nothing."

"Well, you know there's no limo, which means there is no chauffeur. There are no bodyguards, either, since we are going to sneak in, do the promo, and sneak out." Jamaica whipped her head around toward her friend. "So, who's going to carry it?"

"We are."

Jamaica shook her head emphatically. "No, no, no, no, no, no, no. Don't you started speaking French on me now, what do you mean, we?"

A voice from across the lobby called out excitedly, causing them to peer in that direction.

"China! China! Over here!"

A tall, slender young lady with caramel-colored skin and a short hair-cut approached waving. LaChina's face brightened instantly.

"Hey, girl!" LaChina shouted, as she rushed toward the oncoming young lady.

The young woman with the smart pixie cut outstretched her arms widely, welcoming LaChina's body. "Hey, cuz!"

They embraced tightly.

"Jemia!" Jamaica called out as she approached. She, too, outstretched her arms, and she and Jemia embraced.

After the hugs, Jemia stepped back from Jamaica and outstretched Jamaica's arms, examining her. "Oh, sister, you look so good! I saw you on the MTV Music Awards, strutting your thang!"

Jemia's hands flew up into the air, where she snapped them in a quick Z-type motion. "I said, you go, girl!"

Jemia leaned forward again, and embraced Jamaica tightly. "Congratulations."

"Congrats to me? No, congrats to you." This time it was Jamaica waving her hands through the air with fingers snapping. "Ms. Magna Cum Laude, future Berkeley Medical School Student!"

Again, they embraced.

"So, where is Kenya?" Jemia asked.

Kenya Roleisha Rochelle was the younger sister of mega star Jamaica Tiera Rochelle. Kenya was just as talented, and even more gorgeous, than her older sister. Fortunately, she was able to escape the grasp of their mother, who had been preoccupied with Jamaica. Kenya had been able to go her own way.

"She's coming down later," Jamaica explained. "She told me to give you all her love, and to tell you that she misses you."

Jemia smiled. "We had so much fun this summer, you wouldn't believe it! She told me that she was going to come back down this winter so that we could get some private time in, before the sorority sisters got here. We're all meeting here, and then heading for the beach on South Padre Island."

Jamaica tilted her head to the side. "Beach, islands, sand, sounds wonderful." She turned toward LaChina. "Christmas should be spent somewhere tropical."

"C'mon, let's get your luggage, I have a porter waiting," Jemia told them. She interlocked one of her arms inside of Jamaica's, and the other inside of LaChina's arm.

"I have so much to tell you, and we have so much to catch up on," Jemia told them, as she led them off in the direction of her waiting porter. "Jai, what was that you were wearing on stage at the awards? It was stunning..."

Chapter Three

Tameer darted left, and then reversed himself and twisted to the right. The basketball landed dead center inside of the rusted, aluminum, garbage can and rolled around noisily inside.

"Yeah, boy!" Tameer shouted. "I'ma take you to the hoop."

Tameer's smile was genuine, as was his brother Savion's. Savion jogged quickly to the brown spot on the lawn that played host to the garbage can, and retrieved the tattered leather ball. Bouncing it rapidly on the cracked, pebble-paved street, he dared his older brother to take it away.

"Come on with it," Savion taunted. "You want this, come and get it."

With that, a quick fake to the right, followed by a spin to his left, he was off. Savion's six-foot-eight-inch height, stretched over a lanky two hundred and twenty-pound frame, allowed him to outmaneuver his six-foot-five, two hundred and fifteen-pound brother. His shot landed dead center, knocking the badly beaten garbage can over onto its side.

"Yes!" Savion leaped into the air, pounding his fist.

"Shit!" Tameer's labored laugh flowed out between his heavy breaths. He placed his arm around his younger brother and smiled. "I taught you too good."

The brothers' laughter came to an abrupt end, leaving only their smiles, when a convertible Mustang GT pulled up. The car was magnificent.

The Mustang's burgundy paint glistened like wet marble, while the chrome twenty-two-inch wheels sticking out from beneath the wheel wells gleamed brilliantly in the beaming South Texas sun. The Mustang's ground effects kit included not only lowered side skirts and front and rear air dams, but a massive burgundy whale tail that added a dramatic flair to the vehicle. The car screamed money.

The two occupants were shirtless, revealing heavily illustrated torsos that were draped in gold jewelry. Their smiles sparkled brightly in the sunlight, revealing gold and diamond teeth that looked as though their teeth were worth a fortune. Raising his arms high into the air, the driver spoke first.

"What's up, Tameer?" Anthony asked. "What's up, Savion?"

Still breathing heavily, Tameer stepped forward. "What's up, homie?"

Savion, entranced by the massive chrome rims, patrolled the car's perimeter, examining every inch of its beauty. When finished, he peered up at the driver.

"Say, Anthony, your shit is cleaner than a mother fucker!" Savion told him.

The compliment caused Anthony to sit up a little high in his seat.

Tameer reached over into the snow-white interior of the car and shook hands with the passenger.

"Alonzo, where's your Five Point O at?" Tameer asked.

"Getting painted," Alonzo answered, motioning in the direction from where they had just turned the corner. "We're about to go and pick that bitch up right now."

Anthony and Alonzo were both members of the notorious Wheatley Courts Gangsters, or WCG's for short. It was a brutal drug gang that infested the local neighborhood. In fact, it was the most violent gang in one of the hardest areas in the entire state of Texas. Anthony and Alonzo were two of its most prominent members.

"Shit, T, why don't you get down for the hood and get your serve on," asked a smiling Anthony. "You could be rolling in a Five Point O, too."

"You know that you can get anything you need from any of us," Alonzo added. "We'll front you. Your credit's good."

It was an offer that had been made several times, and each time it had been refused. Tameer shook his head and smiled. His steps toward Savion were slow and deliberate, as was his arm's grip. Still smiling, Tameer pulled his brother close, and refused the offer for both of them.

"Thanks, homie, you know we down for the hood and all that, but we gotta try to do it another way," Tameer told them.

Alonzo smiled. "I ain't mad at cha. I know that y'all down, and y'all know that y'all got mad love coming from the hood."

"Shit, that reminds me," Anthony said, snapping his fingers. He pulled out his wallet and removed several hundred dollar bills. He handed the bills to Tameer. "Here you go, homie."

Tameer smiled and took the money. "Thanks."

Alonzo put away his wallet and shook his head. "Ain't nothing. You know you got that coming from me. Say, if you ever need anything, any snaps for school, or anything, just hit me on my cell."

Tameer and Anthony clasped hands.

"I know you ain't down for the dope game," Anthony continued. "But it's all good in the hood, homie."

"You know that y'all got much love coming from me too," Tameer replied with a wide grin. His affection for Anthony was deep, as was Anthony's affection for him. The two of them had been best friends since kindergarten, and had done everything together while growing up. Although they had chosen different paths after high school—Anthony the drug world; and Tameer, the academic one—their bond remained strong.

"Shit, we gonna be kicking it around the corner later on," Alonzo told Tameer. "Come on through and get you some of this bomb-ass boo-bonic."

Tameer and Savion laughed.

"Lonzo, I knew you were the devil," Tameer told him. He shifted his gaze toward Anthony. "I'll probably be through to kick it for a minute. Right now, me and Savion are gonna go to the mall."

Tameer shifted his gaze back toward Alonzo. "You want me to bring you back a few job applications?"

Alonzo threw his head back in laughter. The sun reflected brightly off his sparkling gold and diamond teeth.

"I got a job," Alonzo told him. "I make people happy."

"Did you file income tax last year?" Tameer asked.

"Am I still out on the street?" Alonzo replied.

"Then you ain't got no job!" Tameer told him.

The boys all broke into laughter for several moments, before Anthony turned up the volume on his car stereo. The throbbing bass notes resonating from his trunk-mounted sub-woofers were almost deafening. They had to shout to be heard.

"I'll get with you later, T," Anthony shouted. He raised his fist into the air.

Tameer returned the gesture, and then leaned inside of the vehicle and punched Alonzo lightly on his shoulder. "Y'all be cool."

The burgundy Mustang pulled away slowly, with its custom stereo blaring and rumbling the windows of each apartment that it passed. The stop at the corner allowed it to trigger the alarm systems of several nearby vehicles, before taking off again.

A baby-blue 1978 Oldsmobile Cutlass Supreme, traveling from the opposite direction, had a stereo system that matched Anthony's in volume, but its bass notes seemed to resonate somewhat louder. The Cutlass had a custom paint job, chrome twenty-six-inch wheels, and a custom dark-blue leather half-roof with chrome trimming all around it. This car, like Anthony's, was also a work of art.

As the Cutlass slowly passed Anthony's vehicle, its occupants opened fire.

Anthony Fernandez was twenty-one, and a father of two.

The park's aquatic stadium was the size of a large college football stadium. The main pool itself encompassed an area the size of a large suburban mall parking lot. It could best be described as a small ocean, or an extremely large lake. The seating was of the staggered-row, auditorium variety, except of substantially better quality. Anheuser-Busch owned the parks, and Anheuser-Busch had money—lots of money. For this even they had advertised well, and as a result, the stadium was packed to the rafters.

Jamaica stood waiting patiently in a shallow pool of water that was elevated to the point where it encompassed a shallow deck within the larger pool. She wore a snug black-and-yellow Gortex body suit, provided to her by the park. Her hair remained neatly tied in a long, flowing, pony-tail, and fell like strands of silk down her back. It was held in place by a matching yellow tie, which accented her body suit.

Next to Jamaica stood Mark and Amy, two of the park's highly trained, and extremely well-paid, marine biologists. They were also the Orca's primary trainers.

The stadium remained lit by a constant bursting of flash bulbs and camera lights from all of the reporters present. The spectators also con-tributed a considerable amount of camera flashes, as they took untold numbers of photographs of their idol, Tiera.

Along with LaChina for tonight's event, were her aunt, Savannah, and her cousin, Jemia. They stood watching the massive glass wall in front of them, which was actually a part of the main pool. They could see the massive size of the Orca each time it swam by.

"I hope that she does well," a nervous Savannah said, clutching LaChina's arm.

LaChina smiled and patted her aunt's hand reassuringly. "She will, Jai's a pro at this."

LaChina turned away from her aunt and uttered a quick, silent prayer.

"Are you ready?" Mark asked.

Nervous, but ready to get things over with, Jamaica nodded. To calm her jitters, she thought of the joyful revenge that she would wreak on her friend. Over and over she repeated silently to herself, *kill LaChina*. A smile slowly made its way across Jamaica's face as she thought of killing her best friend, bringing her back to life, and then killing her again.

Mark walked to the edge of the platform, where before him laid the main aquatic performance pool. He lifted his arm high into the air to ensure its visibility, and at the right moment, he gave his signal. From the water before him, a massive killer whale leaped into the air, and upon returning to the surface of the water, made a tremendous splash. Jamaica's heart fell to her bare feet.

The second signal Mark gave commanded the whale to leap onto the platform where he, Jamaica, and Amy stood. The Orca obeyed. Its massive size required that it slide some distance onto the platform, where it stopped just short of a terrified Jamaica. She continued to play her calm, cool, and collected superstar role brilliantly. Smiling for the cameras, she waded through the water, placed her arms around the head of the massive Orca, and then slowly leaned forward and kissed it on its mouth. The flashes erupted simultaneously, lighting up the stadium in such a way that it appeared as though an atomic detonation were taking place.

Holding her fingers crossed, LaChina silently begged Jamaica not to spit. On the platform, Jamaica prayed for the same.

Please don't vomit, she pleaded to herself. *Please, just hold it in. Please don't vomit, you can make it. Smile, Jai. Just smile, and everything will be okay. Remember, after this, you get to kill LaChina!*

Mark gave another signal and the killer whale slowly wiggled itself back into the main aquatic pool. The audience's applause had been deafening.

It's over! It's over! Caribbean, here I come! Jamaica turned and waved to the crowd of adoring fans. The applause grew louder. It made her turn back toward the whale.

"Good-bye, my friend!" Jamaica shouted. "Good-bye! I love you!" *Kill LaChina*, she thought. *I'm going to kill LaChina!*

Jamaica continued her smiles and friendly waves toward the crowd and the whale. She would have looked perfect on a float or in a beauty pageant. Her smile was as perfect as it was fake.

Yes, that's it. Wiggle your slimy butt back into the water, Jamaica thought, while staring at the whale. *I wish that I could push LaChina's butt into the water when no one's looking, and make her kiss you. You big, slimy, son of a ...*

"Well, how about that, ladies and gentlemen, boys and girls?" asked Amy. She waved her hand through the air like a circus ringmaster. "Tiera and Shamu!"

The crowd's applause grew once more to a thunderous level. Amy was a professional.

"Let's ask Shamu what he thinks about Tiera!" Amy told the crowd. She moved closer to the edge of the platform and waited as Mark gave a discreet signal.

Highly trained, the Orca stuck its head out of the water, obeying Mark's command. Lifting her large black-and-yellow, waterproof microphone, Amy stared directly at the whale and posed her question.

"Well, Shamu," she asked dramatically. "What did you think about Tiera?"

Mark again signaled the Orca, giving it a command. The massive whale immediately rolled over quickly and swam to the center of the pool, where it performed a gigantic leap out of the water, making a large splash upon returning to the surface. The kids loved it, and again the cameras went wild.

Amy turned toward Jamaica. "Boy, Tiera, he sure likes you!"

Jamaica lifted her waterproof microphone and smiled. "Well, I like him too!"

The whale quickly swam back to the edge of the platform where its trainers stood, and Mark rewarded it with several fish and a few rubs on its head. Amy took her cue.

"Shamu, Mark says that he like Tiera too," Amy told the whale. "What do you think about that?"

Another discreet signal from Mark made the Orca roll over on its back and flap its massive black fins. Water flowed all over the platform, most of it on Mark. The crowd loved it. Mark lifted another waterproof microphone and turned toward his fellow trainer. "Thanks a lot, Amy."

The crowd again broke into laughter.

Mark turned toward Jamaica. "Well, Tiera, I hear that you're going to do a show for us tonight?"

Jamaica smiled and spoke her lines. "You bet, Mark! And what a show it's going to be. Fireworks and all!"

Jamaica's lipstick was waterproof as well, and hadn't smudged a bit. The tie-in with Cover Girl had made sure of that.

Exhilarated at the thought of having just spoken her last line, Jamaica turned toward the exit.

"Boy, Tiera, Shamu must really like you, he doesn't want to leave the tier," Amy told her.

Jamaica froze. This wasn't part of the script; it was time for her to go.

But, she was a professional, and her smile remained in place. She turned and smiled even wider at Amy.

Of course he hasn't left, he's hungry, you idiot! How would you like to weigh a million tons and have somebody throw you a raw fish? Jamaica turned toward Shamu and blew him a dramatic kiss.

"Good-bye, my friend!" Jamaica told the Orca. "Tonight's show is for you!"

The crowd applauded wildly.

"Would you like to go for a ride?" Amy asked.

Again, Jamaica froze. This time she could feel the micro strands of hair rise on the back of her neck. Yet, the crowd's applause told her that she was trapped.

Jamaica turned back toward Amy and smiled. "Sure... I'd love to!" *You bitch! You prissy little freckle-faced bitch! If I thought that I could get away with it, I'd whip you and that slimy-ass fish!*

"Hop in!" Amy told her. She waved her hand toward the massive body of water before them.

He smiled, Jamaica thought. *The hungry bastard was smiling at me!* Jamaica turned and stared at LaChina. *I'm going to kill you, my friend.* Her glance back toward the waiting Orca startled her. Its mouth was open, and its teeth were visible to her now. Jamaica knew that it was smiling at her.

Mark was the first one into the water. He turned and helped a terrified Jamaica into the massive pool, and then helped her to mount the large black mammal.

"Yes! Yes!" LaChina shouted from the side of the pool. She performed a short moonwalk backward as Jamaica and Mark floated by on the back of the massive beast. She turned and hugged Jemia.

"Every time someone is seen with that damn whale, their record sales bloom!" LaChina declared. "SWV showed him jumping around, and zoom! Jacko kissed it, and boom! But, Jai, you rode it! Girl, you actually rode it! Number one, here we come!"

Unbridled, LaChina grabbed her cousin and spun her around. She began singing her own version of SWV's song: *Lately there seems to be, some financial security, about the way I feel, where I'm gonna be!*

Jemia broke away from her. "That's not the way that song goes!"

LaChina grabbed her again. "I don't care, that's the way I see it!"

LaChina spun Jemia around again. "What better way can you think of to prepare for the release of a new album? Just look!"

Jemia turned, and saw the same thing that her jumping, twisting, dancing cousin saw. Every camera in the stadium was exploding. All of the television cameras were zoomed in on the pool, where Jamaica was bestride a massive killer whale.

"Can you see the headlines?" LaChina asked her cousin. She spread her arms across the air. "*Tiera wins hearts of all mammals!* Or something corny like that. The tree huggers, whale savers, fur painters, bird watchers, animal activists, and goody-two-shoe green thumbs will all love her! She will be the poster girl for purity. Jemia, the only thing that could possibly top this, is a whole video with that thing!"

And that's when it hit her. A whale video!

LaChina's thought process would make Big Blue jealous. Her brain calculated business figures, demographics, sales charts, and the entire industry's activities with the speed of a lightning strike. *The next video is going to be shot in a tropical location, and definitely on a beach. They could turn it into a video shoot with Mr. Slimy Fish*, she told herself. *Hmmmm, how much would it cost to rent one of those things*, she wondered. *Who would care, with their budget. The label had made it clear a long time ago, that Tiera's videos had no expense caps.*

LaChina folded her arms, and her thoughts raced rapidly. *With the budget, they could buy a hundred whale thingys. I'll have to call Bev in New York, and then run the idea by Tony. But what if it ate her?* She wondered if the company had insurance for such things. *Was there insurance against being eaten by a big, hungry mammal?*

LaChina shook her head forcefully. She had to get those stupid thoughts out of her mind. *Business*, she told herself, *think business*.

LaChina knew that she would need a few days, perhaps even a week or more, to set things up. She would have to stay in town at least that long so that she could meet with the park's officials, and the whale's trainers. The question was, how could she keep Jamaica in town for a few days without arousing her suspicions. *Hmmmm, how can I keep Jamaica busy for a few days? Shopping! That's it!*

She knew that the city was filled with large shopping malls, and Jamaica couldn't resist a mall that she hadn't pillaged yet. It was perfect. Jamaica would get to shop until her heart was content, while she would get to set things up. *But... how would she break the news? How could she break the news?*

That's it, she thought. She would take Jamaica for a walk along the beach, and then point toward the water. *Jai, girl, what if that whale really does like you? What if he likes you so much that he's flying in first class to be in your next video?*

Police!

She would need lots of police to be around when she told her. And bodyguards! She would have plenty of bodyguards standing around so that they could break Jamaica's stranglehold when she tried to kill her.

LaChina tilted her head to one side and exhaled forcibly. She would have to think of a way to tell her friend. She thought of telling Jamaica that she loved her, and that she simply wanted her to stay on top and stay rich. But she knew that wouldn't work, either. *Jai would always be rich. Hell, Jai's great, great, great, great, great-grandkids would always be rich.* She could say, *Jai, it's my job. It's why you hired me.* But it still wouldn't keep Jamaica from trying to kill her. *Jai, I'm pregnant, so you can't kill me when I tell you this. Jai, you're pregnant. It's Shamu's baby and he's flying here for a paternity test.* She would still kill her.

LaChina knew that she would have to think of something later, perhaps on the plane. First things first. She turned to her cousin. "Jemia, how would you like to take me and Jai shopping? Everything's on me."

"Shopping?" Jemia asked, lifting an eyebrow. "And free shopping at that, are you kidding? When would you like to go?"

LaChina turned and watched as her friend slid off the whale, and climbed back onto the platform. The crowd's applause had been non-stop.

"Tomorrow," LaChina told her. "Tomorrow, we shop."

Chapter Four

The mall was large, modern, and clean. It was designed primarily for tourists traipsing through the city's pristine downtown area. The San Antonio River flowed through the shopping mall's three stories, giving it its name, the River Center Mall.

The ceramic-tile floor, along with plentiful amounts of chrome and glass, gave it a futuristic, funky, almost European feel. The massive crystal and glass lighting fixtures, and the gigantic water fountains spaced throughout, added to that look.

Sam Goody music store was on the second tier. Its music emanated into the general mall area, just enough to attract customers, yet not disturb the store's neighbors. It attracted Savion's attention.

"Hey, T, let's go in here and put in some applications," he told his brother. The brothers veered into the eclectic, flashy record store, where Savion approached the clerk for an application. Tameer walked straight to the rap section; he would listen to nothing else.

"Oh, China! Girl, this place is gorgeous!" Jamaica exclaimed. "The river flows right into the mall, and all of the little cafes, restaurants, and bars along the banks of the river are so cute! It's like being in Europe!"

Jamaica was like a kid in a candy store. Her doe-like eyes darted all over the establishment, and her giddiness was uncontrollable. It all made LaChina smile.

"See, and you didn't even want to come here!" LaChina told her.

"I didn't even know that there were places like this here." Jamaica whirled, and extended her arms into the air. "Three stories of shopping, all within walking distance of the hotel."

"And don't forget about the weather," LaChina added. "Virgin shopping centers that we haven't pillaged yet, and all of it being done while wearing comfortable sandals."

They were Fendi sandals, of course. The girls wore comfortable, plain, yet expensive Prada sack dresses, and disguised themselves using designer hats and sunglasses. Jamaica wore her gorgeous, silky hair in a long ponytail, which hung well below her shoulderblades. Her clunky, suede, Dutch clog sandals, along with the mall's ambiance, made her feel as though she were on a secret European shopping spree.

"Say, T, are you ready, top blaze?" Savion asked.

"Yeah, just let me pay for this CD real quick."

Savion and Tameer approached the counter together. When it was Tameer's turn to be waited on, he pulled a crisp twenty-dollar bill from his tattered, black billfold and handed it to the clerk. She took the CD, and using a special key, removed from it the bulky, white, plastic protector that was used for theft prevention. After adding up his purchase, and securing his receipt, she rubbed the CD case against a magnet so that it would not trigger the alarm in the metal detector that surrounded the exit door. Handing Tameer his receipt, she also handed him her telephone number and a smile.

"Thank you," was Tameer's only reply.

"I get off at nine," she told him.

Tameer nodded, turned, and walked out the store.

"Say, T, she was flirting with you like a mother!" Savion told his brother. "Why didn't you spit game at her?"

Tameer shook his head. "Man, I wasn't even paying attention."

Savion motioned back toward the store. "Shit, let's go back."

Tameer waved her off. "Naw, let's go over here to this clothing store."

Tameer took a deep breath, and then exhaled forcibly. He thought silently about his situation. He had been paying attention to the girl's gestures, but he knew that even if he did want to ask her out, she would laugh at his car. Besides, he couldn't afford to take her to much more than a movie, and he would never have been able to take her to his home. It had been for all these reasons why he had limited his dating to girls inside of the courts—girls, who were just as limited in their finances, and those who understood his situation. Savion thought his response was for another reason.

"You still tripping about Dawshanique, aren't you?" he asked.

Tameer shook his head, denying his brother's accusation.

"Naw, I'm not worried about her," he lied.

"Then what is it? Is it over Anthony getting killed?"

"Yeah, but more than just that," Tameer told him. "A lot of things. Sometimes I wish that I would have played football, that way I could have gone pro this year. You and Dad wouldn't have to be in the Courts living through stuff like that. Damn, Save, I don't want nothing to happen to you."

"T, quit tripping. Football wasn't what you wanted, you made the right choice. Pops rode you, like he's riding me right now. I don't even know if that's what I want to do. If he ever heard me say that, he would kill me. Let's just keep this between us."

Tameer nodded, and offered his brother a smile.

"Oh yeah, did I tell you?" Savion asked. "FSU offered me a full scholarship yesterday."

The news made Tameer laugh. He placed his arm around his younger brother and pulled him close. "How many does that make?"

"Fourteen full scholarship offers, and three partial ones," Savion answered.

Tameer shook his head and smiled. "You ain't gonna pass me."

"To hell I won't!" Savion laughed.

The brothers were still laughing when they entered into a clothing store. Tameer rushed to the men's section, where he started pricing casual polo shirts. FUBU, Nautica, Sean John, Polo, Rocawear, and Phat Farm were in this season, and Christmas was coming. Tameer knew that he would have to start buying things for Savion now, because there were only a few paydays left in the year.

Finished with his browsing, Tameer turned and began walking toward the counter, where Savion was filling out a job application. He didn't make it.

On the floor, there was a loose piece of carpeting sticking up, which caused him to stumble into a clothing rack and fall back onto his derrière. Embarrassed, he peered around the the store to see if anyone had been watching. Someone had.

"Are you okay?" a woman asked him.

Tameer peered up in the direction of the voice. She was gorgeous. Her finely manicured, mahogany-colored hand was extended toward him, offering him assistance. He was even more embarrassed.

"Yeah, I'm all right. I just wounded my pride."

Although there was no dust, as the flooring consisted of thick industrial carpeting, by habit, Tameer brushed off the rear of his pants.

"Thanks," he told her.

"For what?" she asked. "You didn't even allow me to pull you up, you rose on your own."

Tameer blushed.

"But thanking me was a nice gesture," she continued. "I guess chivalry lives on in Texas."

She smiled, and it caused Tameer to return a smile of his own.

She is beautiful, he thought. *Very beautiful indeed.*

Tameer's eyes blinked rapidly several times, partly to reassure his brain that he was not dreaming, and also to remind himself that it was impolite to stare. His eyes fell from hers.

"Thank you for asking me if I was all right."

His eyes returned to hers, only to see her eyes slowly walk down his body and examine him. He once again found himself blushing from embarrassment. He had never been checked out before, at least not this outright. Her boldness made him blush even more.

The weather was mild, like most days of the year, and as usual he wore shorts and a form-fitting muscle shirt. His comfortable, yet revealing outfit told the story of his almost zero-fat diet, and his constant running, weightlifting, and aerobic workout sessions. Tameer's muscles bulged from his arms, and his tight abdominal muscles rippled through the knit T-shirt.

She knew that she had stared too long, and upon realizing that he was observing her watch him, she too became embarrassed. Her petite hand flew to her flawless face and she covered her mouth, while letting out a girlish chuckle. He took her hand and shook it.

"Thanks again," Tameer told her.

Still laughing and covering her mouth, she quickly glanced over his body once more. "No, thank you."

Immersed in their exchanges of flirtatious smiles, laughter, and glances, neither noticed Savion's approach.

"Yo, T, let's roll," Savion told his brother.

Tameer nodded, and finally released her soft hand. "My name is Tameer, and this is my brother Savion. Savion, this is..."

"LaChina," she answered. "But everyone calls me China."

She smiled at them both.

"What's up, China?" Savion nodded.

"Hi," she said, offering him a slight wave. She turned back toward Tameer. "Well, it was nice meeting both of you. I hope that we bump into one another again."

"It was nice to meet you too," Tameer replied. "Next time, I hope that I'm not sitting on my butt."

Tameer and LaChina shared a laugh.

"Bye," LaChina said, waving again.

"Bye," Tameer told her, waving back.

He and Savion ventured into the mall area, on their way to other stores to fill out job applications. But LaChina's fragrance remained in the air, and her captivating looks remained on Tameer's mind. She was absolutely awesome.

Tameer cared little about his screwed-up car, or trashed-out apartment, at this point. He wanted to get to know her. She was gorgeous, outgoing, exotic, different, and most of all, she was actually interested in him. *Maybe,* he thought, *just maybe she really was interested. She certainly acted like she was.*

Tameer quickly made up his mind, he wanted her telephone number. This one wasn't going to get away, she looked way to good to allow that to happen. Tameer turned back to stare at his newfound friend, and not watching where he was going, slammed into someone else. They both came tumbling down.

"Watch where you're going!" shouted an angry, embarrassed Jamaica, who was lying on the ground. Her hat, sunglasses, and merchandise were scattered all around her.

Tameer was embarrassed again.

"Me?" he asked. "You're the one who needs to watch where you're going."

LaChina walked up and stood over him. "You love that position, don't you?"

Tameer looked down at the floor and blushed. Jamaica stood, and brushed off her clothing. Her strokes were rapid, and angry.

"China, you know this person?" Jamaica asked furiously.

LaChina peered down at Tameer and winked. "Yeah, Tameer is an old friend."

Tameer stood and brushed himself off. Jamaica lifted her hand into the air, holding two pieces of tinted plastic, and a thin, wispy, titanium frame.

"Well, your old friend just broke my Chanel sunglasses," Jamaica told LaChina.

"Look, I'll pay for your glasses, okay?" Tameer told a distraught Jamaica. "And you're right, I should have been watching where I was going. But you should have been watching too."

"I should have?" Jamaica stomped her foot down hard on the marble-tiled floor. "Do you know who you're talking to? I'll have you thrown out of this establishment! I'm..."

LaChina's hand quickly flew to Jamaica's mouth, covering it, and obscuring Jamaica's last words. Tameer and Savion shared a glance. They thought them both crazy.

"Her name is Jamaica," LaChina told them. "But everybody calls her Jai."

LaChina removed her hand from Jamaica's mouth.

"What the hell was that about?" Jamaica demanded.

"Please excuse us for one tiny little moment," LaChina said.

She pulled her fuming friend away from the group, leaving Tameer and Savion staring at a shrugging Jemia.

"Explain!" Jamaica shouted, once they were out of hearing range from the others. She shifted her weight and folded her arms in defiance.

"Jai, you trust me, don't you?" LaChina asked her.

"Yes, of course." Jamaica nodded.

"I have never made a bad decision, have I?"

Frustrated, Jamaica shifted her weight to her other leg. "No, girl, what are you getting at?"

The smile across LaChina's face at first appeared slowly, and then spread rapidly. She turned and nodded her head toward Tameer.

"That!" she told Jamaica. "That's what I'm getting at!"

Jamaica recoiled. "What?"

LaChina clasped Jamaica's arms. "Jai, he's cute, he's fine, and he's not some asshole pro athlete, or superstar actor or rapper. Best of all, he doesn't know who you are!"

"What?"

"Think about it!" LaChina told her. "Your hat and glasses are off."

Jamaica turned and stared at Tameer. "What am I going to do with him?"

"Attack, girl! Go get him!"

"China, have you flipped?" Jamaica asked. "I need a man, not a boy toy!"

"Jai, he's about the same age as you are, test him," LaChina told her. "If he fails the test, I won't say anything else about him."

Jamaica shook her head. "You're crazy."

"If I am, then you drove me to insanity. But anyway, just humor me." LaChina turned Jamaica in the direction of the group and shoved her toward Tameer. "Attack!"

Tameer laughed and nodded. "Yeah, I'll be walking across that stage in May," he told Jemia.

"I just graduated from Spelman," she replied. "Next fall I'll be heading to Berkeley to start my medical schooling."

"That's good!" Tameer told her. "So you went to Roosevelt High School too? I wonder why I never saw you there, even though you were a grade ahead?"

Jemia shrugged her shoulders. "I don't know. Did you play football or anything?"

Tameer laughed. "I played everything. I was their running back for four years, starting from my freshman year."

Jemia covered her mouth. "Wait a minute. You're not *the* Tameer Harris? All Star, All City, All Regional, All State, All Nation, All World, All Universe, Team USA, ALL Everything, are you?"

Tameer blushed. "Yep, that was me."

Jemia hugged him. "Boy, I used to go and watch you play!"

Jemia leaned back and examined Tameer for several seconds, and then slapped him across his arm. "I thought that you left and went to play for Notre Dame."

"Nope." Tameer shook his head. "I took an academic scholarship at Trinity instead."

"Why?" Jemia asked. "You were so good at football!"

This time, he shrugged his shoulders. "You know, I just wanted to do something else with my life. I didn't want to waste it playing sports."

Bingo! LaChina thought. She nudged Jamaica.

"Do you have a number so that I can call you?" Jamaica asked.

Tameer recoiled.

Jamaica was beautiful, but she was also mean, inconsiderate, and extremely full of herself. He wasn't interested in her. He wanted to talk to either LaChina or Jemia. Anyone, but the beautiful mean one.

"It's just so that I can know where to get in touch with you, and send you the bill for my glasses," Jamaica told him.

Tameer wrote his number down on the back of the receipt from the record store. He handed it to LaChina, who in turn, handed it to Jamaica.

"I'll be home about six," he assured them. *I hope Dad paid the telephone bill this month*, he didn't say out loud.

LaChina smiled and waved, as she, Jemia, and Jamaica turned and walked away.

God, Tameer said to himself. *Please let Dad have paid that bill!*

Chapter Five

LaChina pointed her finger accusingly at Jamaica. "Jai, you owe me!"

Jamaica nodded in agreement. "Ask me for another favor."

LaChina folded her arms in defiance and shifted her weight to one side. "Jai."

Jamaica folded her arms in defiance as well. "No. And besides, we're leaving tomorrow anyway."

LaChina shook her head. "No, we're not."

Jamaica sprang from the bed. "What do you mean, we're not?"

LaChina exhaled forcibly and turned away from her friend. She began pacing, as she prepared herself to give the explanation that she had rehearsed all morning. "Jai, the reservations at the hotel in the islands got all screwed up. Besides, the Sea World promo is going to take longer to wrap up than I originally thought."

Jamaica was furious.

"Wrap up?" Jamaica shouted. "What do you mean, 'wrap up'?"

Jamaica's arms flailed through the air as she became hysterical and stomped across the hotel-room floor. "I touched the fish, I hugged the fish, I kissed the fish, hell, I even rode the damn thing! They got their concert, what more do they want?"

"Jai, it's more that that. We're negotiating a big performance deal for the other Anheuser-Busch theme parks."

Jamaica wasn't convinced.

"Oh, no!" She shook her head, waved her hand through the air, and flew to the closet. "No more fish kissing for me. I am not the Little Mermaid!"

Jamaica quickly began emptying the closet, throwing all of her clothing onto the bed. LaChina grabbed her.

"It's not for Sea World. It's for Busch Gardens, and their other theme parks."

Jamaica froze. She stared coldly into her friend's eyes for several moments. "Why is it that I don't believe you?"

LaChina stuck out her bottom lip and began to pout. "You trust me, don't you...sister?"

Jamaica closed her eyes, she absolutely detested that expression. "Don't give me that look!"

LaChina persisted.

Frustrated, Jamaica quickly strode back to the bed and sat down. LaChina followed.

"Please...," LaChina whined.

"Uuuuuggggh!" Jamaica groaned loudly, and fell onto her side. She buried her head inside of the pillow. "You know how I hate it when you do that!"

Sensing victory, LaChina sat on the bed next to her friend. Her pouting face remained.

"Please...," she whimpered.

"Aaaargh!" Jamaica's tiny fist pounded the feathery pillow. "You got me! You know I hate it when you put on that ugly, sad-looking face."

Jamaica lifted her head and stared at LaChina. "Look, I'll do the damn concerts, but why do we have to stay here? You can conduct business from New York."

LaChina knew that Jamaica was right. She hadn't thought of covering that issue. She had to think fast.

"Sure, guess you're right. Beverly was just telling me today how she felt that a week in the islands was too much. In fact, she thinks that the few days we've been here, is long enough for your fatigue to have worn off. Well, I guess she was right."

LaChina rose from the bed and walked to the closet. She leaned inside and pulled out one of the large suitcases that they had brought with them from New York.

"Let's go back to New York," LaChina said sadly. "I'm sure Beverly has all sorts of interesting things for you to do."

Jamaica buried her head into the pillow again. "You don't play fair at all, do you?" she asked in a muffled voice.

After several moments of silence, Jamaica lifted her head from the pillow. "That's it! I just figured it out! You are the best friend from hell!"

Jamaica lifted her finger and pointed it accusingly at LaChina. "That's why you and my mother get along so well. That's why she loved it when I hired you. When she's not around to torture me, she knew that you would continue in her place." Jamaica's head rose, and she shifted her gaze toward the ceiling. "What is my sin?"

It was too good of an opportunity for LaChina to pass up. She quickly cleared her throat and mustered the deepest voice that she could. "Your sin is not getting any!"

Jamaica's mocha cheeks turned a coppery red. She grabbed a pillow from the bed and slung it at her friend, striking her in the head.

"I can't believe you said that!" Jamaica told her.

LaChina's laughter didn't stop. "Well, girl, it's true. You're gonna have to loosen up."

LaChina sat back down on the bed next to Jamaica. "Look, I'm going to call our friend, and you are going to go out with him. I have work, you do not. He is going to take you out, and you are going to enjoy it. You are going to shop, see the sights, and unwind. Just consider it a practice vacation, clear?"

Jamaica lifted her legs onto the bed. She curled up, wrapping her arms around her right leg. "I am not going out with him."

"You owe me."

"You go out with him!" Jamaica protested.

"I get mines every now and then."

Jamaica grabbed another pillow and flung it at her. This time LaChina ducked.

"Okay, okay." LaChina raised her hand signaling her surrender. "I'm teasing. Look, Jai, you don't have to sleep with the guy, just be a normal person for a while. Hell, get out of my hair while I'm trying to work!"

Jamaica tilted her head to the side and exhaled in defiance.

"Jai, I'm going to call him," LaChina told her. "But first, I'm going to call Jemia and have her bring you some clothes. Then, I'm going to have her take us to a motel. We are going to stay there, and I am going to work. You, on the other hand, are going to act like a normal person, and do normal things, like go out on a date with a man."

Jamaica licked her lips and held up both of her hands. "Okay, baby, you had me on everything until you said the 'M' word."

LaChina leaned back, moving away from Jamaica. "What 'M' word?" She peered at Jamaica strangely. "Man?"

Jamaica smacked her lips and rolled her eyes toward the ceiling. "Motel!"

LaChina leaned forward again and placed her hand on her chest. "Girl, you almost scared me for a moment."

Frowning, Jamaica tilted her head and shook it. "I'm not staying in anybody's motel."

"Jai, if he sees where we're staying, he may get suspicious and realize who you are," LaChina explained.

Jamaica's arms flew through the air. "So what, let him!"

It was LaChina's turn to smack her lips and look unimpressed. "That's not the plan, Jai. The plan is to be normal, to relax, and to be Jamaica. Not Tiera, Jamaica."

"It's not like I'm going to keep seeing the guy," Jamaica told her. "One or two dates, and that's it. Hell, dating me will work wonders for his ego!"

LaChina exhaled loudly.

Jamaica folded her arms defiantly. "I'm not staying in any motel, and that's final!"

"Jai, do you remember when we were sixteen and you wrecked Beverly's brand-new convertible Corniche? Do you remember me jumping behind the wheel and taking the blame?"

Jamaica leaned forward and hugged LaChina. "Yes, and I still love you for it."

"I'm going to tell her," LaChina said flatly.

Jamaica's eyes flew wide. "What?"

"I'm going to tell her everything," LaChina continued. She jabbed her finger into Jamaica's chest. "Every rotten thing that you ever did in your life, I will tell. From the time when we were eight, and you stuck the wet/dry vac into her ten thousand-gallon fish tank and sucked up all of her tropical fish, to last year when you got drunk on Chateau Lafite Rothschild and threw up all over Beaver Creek."

Jamaica shook her head. "You wouldn't."

"Motel, Jai."

"What?" Jamaica asked incredulously.

LaChina reached for the telephone. "I'm dialing."

Jamaica's eyes flew wide once again and she leapt for her friend's hand. "Okay, okay, motel! I'll even date your damn boy toy!"

"Incognito?" LaChina asked.

Jamaica nodded. "You drive a hard bargain. You know what?"

"What?" LaChina asked.

"I'm starting to think that you didn't go to Spelman," Jamaica told her. "I'm starting to think that you studied business at a fruit stand in Chinatown."

"Jai, it was either going to be the rough and tough, John Wayne style, or the pouting baby face. Since I used the pouting earlier, I didn't think that it would work again so soon. Besides," LaChina smiled, "I didn't want to seem redundant."

Jamaica folded her arms and pouted. "Bitch."

"Thank you."

They hugged.

"Hello?"

"Hi, this is China. Remember, the mall?"

Tameer quickly sat up on the couch and adjusted the phone. *How could he forget?* "Yeah, I remember the mall. How's your friend?"

"She'll live. As a matter of fact, since you asked, she would be doing a lot better if she had someone to show her around town."

"Hold on, I can get the Yellow Pages and give you the number to one of our local tour companies."

"Ha, ha, that's real funny. You know what I'm getting at."

"I know, and it scares me," Tameer answered. He decided to be frank. "Your friend's a snob. a mean snob."

"She's not, really. You just have to get to know her." *Damn, he already knew her*, LaChina thought.

"I guess," Tameer replied. *I hope that never happens*, was what he really wanted to say. "So, is this part of my punishment for breaking the sunglasses?"

"You could say that. But, I'd rather you thought of it as being a gentleman, and showing a nice, single, young lady around town."

"You, nice. Her, well...I'd rather pay for the sunglasses."

"I'm taken, and the glasses cost twelve hundred dollars."

"Twelve hundred-dollar sunglasses!" Tameer shouted into the telephone. "Are you crazy?" The last part slipped out.

"No, and she had just purchased them. We still have the receipt, you can see it if you like."

LaChina had played all of her cards, now she could only wait in silence to see if he would bite. He did.

"I'm sorry, I don't have twelve hundred dollars cash to pay for any sunglasses. I can make payments."

LaChina smiled. It was what she was hoping to hear.

"Well, we weren't going to be in town for very long," she told him. "Can you pay two hundred dollars a day, for the next six days?"

Of course, he couldn't. She knew it, she was banking on it.

"Two hundred dollars a day! I can't pay two hundred dollars a week!" Tameer exhaled into the receiver. "I was thinking something along the lines of a hundred bucks every payday."

LaChina smiled even wider. He was not doing anything illegal. He was perfect!

"Well, we really weren't planning on being in town that long." She breathed in heavily and counted to five. "I'll tell you what. I have a proposition for you."

"I'm listening."

"Well, you take my friend out, while I finish my business negotiations, and I'll pay for the glasses."

"You're willing to pay twelve hundred bucks just to get rid of her for a couple of days?" Tameer asked.

Together they laughed.

"She's not that bad," LaChina told him. "She's real sweet, you'll see."

"Well, I don't know if I can afford..."

"I'll pay for all of your dates," she interrupted. "I'll pay for the dates, your transportation cost, the glasses, everything. Please, take her out, show her the city, and let me conduct my business!"

"You're desperate, aren't you?" he asked. Her frustration was apparent.

"Yes, I am," she admitted.

"I've always been a sucker for a beautiful lady in distress," Tameer said. He exhaled loudly. "I'll do it."

"Oh, thank you, Tameer! Thank you! You are so sweet! I knew that chivalry wasn't completely dead. Listen, I'll give you our address so that you can pick her up..."

Chapter Six

It took only one knock to make LaChina bolt from her bed and answer the door. Staring out of the peephole, she confirmed his arrival.

"Girl, it's him!" she shouted to Jamaica.

"Whoopee!" Jamaica called out from the bathroom. She was dripping with sarcasm.

"I would do a flip, but it's a little crowded in here."

"Jai," LaChina called to her from the door.

"What?"

"Be nice." With that, LaChina opened the front door.

Staring at Tameer, LaChina's first thought was that she should have kept this one for herself. But, she had work to do, and he would keep Jai busy.

Tameer's dress was casual and neat. He had the good sense to dress appropriately, she observed. His attire would allow him into a nightclub, and at the same time it would allow him to feel comfortable inside of a movie theater or restaurant. His sports coat, white button-down dress shirt, and sharply starched trousers were an excellent choice. He had taste.

"Is she here?" Tameer asked with a ready smile, and a fabricated sense of exaggerated apprehension.

"Un-huh." LaChina nodded. "She's finishing up in the restroom." A smile spread across LaChina's face. "You know how ladies are."

LaChina placed her hand on Tameer's chest and slid it over the lapel of his coat, feeling the material. "Nice."

"Thank you," he replied. It came out with a flirtatious smile. "I'm glad you approve."

"Well," LaChina exhaled. "I guess I should take care of you real quick. You know, while she's not around."

LaChina produced an envelope of considerable girth from her back pocket. Just as she was handing the envelope to Tameer, the knob of the bathroom door squeaked and turned. LaChina hurriedly shoved the envelope into Tameer's hand.

"Take it and hide it!" she told him.

The bulging white envelope disappeared quickly inside of Tameer's breast pocket. When he looked up again, a smiling Jamaica was standing before him. She looked stunning.

Unconsciously, Tameer's mouth fell slightly open as he gaped at her. Tonight Jamaica was attired in a colorful red, white-and-blue hockey jersey, with a matching white turtleneck beneath it. Her blue jeans were loose-fitting and stylish, with just the right amount of fashionable fade. She wore a pair of bulky hiking boots, and large, round, gold earrings. She was dressed the part of an around-the-way girl.

Jamaica's flowing, silky, brown mane, was pulled tightly to the back, culminating in a lone, rope-like ponytail. Her hairstyle only served to accent her already flawless face. For makeup, Jamaica wore only a bright red lip gloss on her luscious, full lips. She needed nothing else. Speechless, Tameer stared.

"Hello?" Jamaica called to him, leaning slightly forward.

Tameer's eyes blinked rapidly for several moments, before he shook his head and released himself from her spell.

"I'm sorry, hello." He extended his hand quickly. "How are you tonight?"

Jamaica took his hand, smiled, and released a soft watery laugh that flowed disarmingly with her speech.

"I'm fine," she answered. "Are you all right?"

"Uh...yeah. You know, I'm not used to this. I'm real shy."

It was all Tameer could manage to say out loud. She was beautiful. In fact, she was more than beautiful. She was the most beautiful thing that he had ever laid eyes on!

"Well, I really don't do this much, either," she confided, offering another smile. "So, I guess we'll both just have to work our way through it."

Carefully, Jamaica examined Tameer. Her eyes cut across his figure several times, rapidly photographing him for her mind to dissect slowly. Good teeth, nice body, good hair, cute smile, and to top it all off, a sweet, innocent-looking baby face. Jamaica quickly concluded that the night may not be so bad after all. The best thing she liked about Tameer was his attitude. She was pleased that Tameer didn't act cocky, overly confident, or brash, and that he wasn't stuck on himself. The night showed promise indeed.

"Well, the car's over here," Tameer said. He waved his arm toward the parking lot in a grand sweeping gesture. Quietly, he led off, with Jamaica following close behind.

That's it, LaChina thought to herself. It couldn't be. There were no stupid things said, no twisting tongues, no utterly embarrassing moments! Watching them walk away quietly was too much for LaChina. She couldn't resist an opportunity to embarrass her friend. She called out to them.

"Hey, kids!" LaChina shouted across the parking lot.

Tameer and Jamaica turned to face her.

"Don't do anything that I wouldn't do!"

The color rapidly bled from Jamaica's cheeks, turning them pale vanilla. She rolled her eyes toward the sky, embarrassed that LaChina would shout such a thing across the parking lot. Tameer, on the other hand, found it funny. He laughed immensely.

Turning, Tameer and Jamaica continued through the parking lot of the motel. She watched with intensity as her date passed a sharp black BMW 750il. She smiled slightly and shook her head as they walked past the vehicle. It would have been too much to hope for.

Jamaica watched as Tameer also strolled past a burgundy entry-level Lexus. It was proletarian, but acceptable. Again, she nodded. *Okay, not the Lexus*, she thought. Then quickly, she began to pray as Tameer slowed near a massive, rusting, hulk of a Ford pickup truck, that should have long gone to that big junkyard in the sky. Her nerves calmed slightly as he continued past the old tool hauler, stopping on the other side of it.

Jamaica couldn't see the car over the bulk of the truck. That didn't stop her from smiling. Low roof line meant sports car. Super-low roof line meant super-duper sports car. *Not bad for a blind date*, she thought. Her smile faded as she passed the truck and spied Tameer's vehicle.

Tameer's Hyundai Elantra was primed in several different shades of gray, with the exception of the hood and the passenger-side door, which were both spray-painted in a dull, non-reflective black. Jamaica stood in horror as Tameer opened the clanging mismatched door for her.

Jamaica pointed toward Tameer's vehicle. "What is that?"

"What do you mean?"

Remembering her manners, Jamaica smiled. "I mean, what kind of car is this?"

"Oh, it's called a Hyundai, It's made in Korea."

"Or course." She smiled politely. *All of the best cars are made in Korea, everyone knows that.*

Jamaica's mind quickly ran through a quick things-to-do list. First on the list was to find a new best friend. Second, find a new assistant, and last, but certainly not least, she would call around for an assassin to *kill LaChina!*

Tameer had other thoughts. He quietly strolled around the rear of the car to the driver's side, silently thanking LaChina all the way. He would have to send her some flowers or something.

Upon entering into this vehicle, Tameer glanced at Jamaica, and they exchanged a pair of nervous smiles. His smile was genuine, while hers was to keep from crying. Quickly they both focused their thoughts elsewhere. Jamaica decided to preoccupy her mind with how to prevent herself from being seen inside of this Korean thingy, while Tameer's thoughts quickly advanced along a more religious line. He prayed silently that his car would start.

Still smiling, he casually stuck his key inside of the ignition. *Please, please, please! I'll go to church this Sunday, please just let the Gray Ghost start!* It did, and they were off.

"So, how was your date?" LaChina asked, without looking up from the table.

It was Jamaica's failure to respond that finally caused LaChina to stop writing and turn toward her friend.

"Jai, are you all right?"

Jamaica still provided no answer. Instead, she walked silently to the bed, sat down, and allowed her head to drop and face the floor. It was only after several moments of eerie silence that she finally spoke. Her glance remained locked onto the floor.

"His car wouldn't start after the movie," Jamaica said in a low, hollow, monotonous tone. "He said that it happens sometimes. He raised the hood, and then this lady passed by, and he got her to give us a jumper."

"You mean a jump," LaChina corrected.

Jamaica quickly lifted her hand toward LaChina, silencing her.

"Whatever!" Jamaica snapped fiercely. "I had to hold two greasy, grimy, oily, jumper connectors in my hands, while my date worked on his Korean thingy. He called it a Hi-un-day, or something. The doors were black, the hood was charcoal with streaks of orange, and the rest of the dented, coughing, dying thing was gray."

LaChina was unable to contain her laughter any longer. She chuckled heavily as she began to approach Jamaica, who again raised her hand sharply, staying her friend.

"Don't you touch me!" Jamaica shouted. Her voice made LaChina stop cold.

Unhurried, Jamaica continued. "After we left the theater, he said that everything was okay, so I let him take me out to eat."

LaChina nodded understandingly, but it only made matters worse. Jamaica exploded.

"He took me inside of a place where they used heat lamps to warm the food! There was a giant, plastic clown standing at the entrance..."

"McDonald's?" LaChina interrupted.

Jamaica leaped the bed and pointed at her friend. "Yes! He took me to McDonald's!"

Jamaica's head fell toward the floor and her tone quickly changed. "China, I hadn't been there since I was a kid. They had this big, giant menu on the wall, and he asked me what I wanted, and I didn't know."

Jamaica's eyes became watery, and she began sniffling. "They had names like Super Mac, Big Deluxe, Half-Pounders...I was so confused." Jamaica sat back down onto the bed and her head fell into her lap. "I ordered the happy one."

Jamaica's tears began to fall, and she began sobbing heavily. "It came in a box...and...and it had a toy... people were staring at me..." Jamaica reached into the pocket of her baggy blue jeans, and pulled out a pink, plastic toy, with frizzy, green, spiked hair.

LaChina Demitria Anderson used every bit of willpower that she could conjure from within, to keep from laughing. Her hands flew around her friend. "My sister! My dear, sweet, sister!"

Jamaica leaned her head against LaChina's shoulder and continued weeping. "I ate thin, greasy, potato sticks, and some ground-up meat, with domestic cheese, and it had round bread with tiny bird seeds on top." Jamaica sniffled. "And the little girl in the booth behind Tameer kept picking her nose and trying to get my toy."

Jamaica began crying heavily again.

"It's alright, Jai. It's okay," LaChina said, comforting her. "People eat those things all of the time. Those fried potato sticks were called French fries."

Jamaica sniffled, and slowly sat up. "French?"

"Yes." LaChina smiled and nodded.

"From France?" Jamaica asked weakly.

"*Oui.*"

"China."

"What?"

Jamaica's head fell back down upon her friend's shoulder. "I hate you."

Chapter Seven

"Hello?"

"Hi, T, this is China."

"Yeah, I recognized the voice." Tameer cleared his throat. "So, how are you?"

"I'm fine, thanks."

"So, how's Jamaica? Is she around?"

"As a matter of fact, she stepped out for a moment. Actually, she went to the mall to grab some clothes. I think she's buying something new to wear, in case you ask her out again." This time is was LaChina who cleared her throat. "She really enjoyed your date last night."

Tameer's voice perked up. "Really? Wow, she didn't seem like she was enjoying herself. She didn't really eat very much, either."

"Yeah, I heard. Well, Tameer, Jai is kind of special."

"You mean she's retarded?"

"No, no... She's different," LaChina explained. "Things that normal people enjoy, she is not really used to."

"Oh, I understand. You know, I grew up in kind of the same situation. Pops worked all the time, but we still didn't have much."

"Well, let me try it this way. Impress Jai by being different," she explained. "Be original, be natural!"

"Hmmm, natural." Tameer's thoughts began to race through his head. *Natural*, he thought to himself. *Impress Jamaica, by being natural.*

"Yeah, but something without a lot of people," LaChina told him. She did not want Jamaica to be recognized.

"Natural, without a lot of people." Tameer thought silently for several moments, and then snapped his fingers sharply. "I think I got it!"

"Great, great. So what time will you be getting her out of my hair?" LaChina asked.

Together they shared a laugh.

"How about two o'clock?" he asked.

"Two o'clock? That's kind of early."

"Yeah, but we'll be gone for a while"

"'A while'?" LaChina lifted an eyebrow.

"Yeah."

It was perfect, she thought. LaChina adjusted the telephone and shifted her position on the bed. It *was* perfect! She would be able to make a lot of calls, while people were still around the office. Two o'clock. Everyone would just be getting back from enjoying their nice fat lunches, and everyone knew how receptive people became after filling their bellies. She would get them to agree to a nice lucrative contract, and give her everything else that she wanted. It *was* perfect!

"You know what, Tameer, two o'clock is perfect," she told him.

"Okay, well, I guess I'll see you at two."

"See you," LaChina said.

"'Bye."

"'Bye."

"Hello?"

"Dawshanique?"

"Yeah?"

"Girl, this is Shamika! Guess who I saw at the movies last night."

Dawshanique stretched and yawned audibly over the telephone. She took the receiver and placed it on her other ear, lay back on the bed and got comfortable. She knew that she was in for a long, yet interesting, round of gossip.

"Who?" Dawshanique asked.

Shamika's excitement was obvious from the sound of her voice. The name burst from her lips like a firecracker on the Fourth of July.

"Tameer Harris! As a matter of fact, it was Tameer and another woman! Yo, man, and another woman!"

"Okay, I get the point!" Dawshanique exhaled forcibly and sat up in bed. "Girl, me and Tameer ain't together no more. I could care less..."

"Uh-un, girl, you don't understand," Shamika interrupted. "Tameer was looking good! And he had some Barbie doll on his arm."

"Tameer?" Dawshanique had to ask again. *Looking good?*

"Un-huh, girl! If he was yo man, then he wasn't last night!"

It was a different voice. It startled Dawshanique.

"Who is this?" Dawshanique asked, now sitting all the way up in bed. She was wide awake now.

"This is Shawntae," replied the second voice. "We're on three-way."

"Oh, well, like I said, Tameer don't faze me." Dawshanique's hand flew through the air and she snapped her fingers. "Girl, like Beyonce, I sent that nigga to the left, to the left."

"So you could move on to what?" Shamika asked. "Girl, Alonzo can't do nothing for you, just like Short Texas can't do nothing for me. All they good for is getting our hair done, getting our booty licked, and giving up some of that dope money."

"Un-huh, girl, she right," Shawntae agreed. "Tameer is getting up outta here."

Dawshanique smacked her lips. "Tameer ain't nothing, that's why I cut him loose. He turned down all of them football scholarships and lost his chance at the pros."

"Girl, you losing sight of the big picture," Shawntae told her. "Tameer is gonna finish college next year. Hell, Alonzo a be in the feds next year."

"Or dead," Shamika added.

"So, what are y'all trying to say?" Dawshanique asked, although she already knew where they were headed. They had a point: Tameer was about to finish school, and he would be getting out of the Courts. It would be nice to get him back just in time to reap those benefits, but she did cut him loose in the first place. She couldn't go back to him, it might look as though she were desperate. She had to let them suggest it. It would look better if it had been one of their ideas. They did her the favor.

"Duh! Girl, ain't it obvious?" Shamika told her. "Don't let some hussy steal your meal ticket! Girl, pro, or no pro, Tameer is getting up outta here."

"Get your man back... hold on..." They could hear Shawntae shouting in the background. "Baby Quinton, if you don't get outta that damn toilet, I'mma beat your ass! Just like your bad-ass daddy, always getting into shit! Okay, I'm back."

"Well, I did always kind of think of Tameer as my backup," Dawshanique told them. "I knew I could always go back to him."

"Not the way he was looking at Ms. Black Tails last night," Shamika said.

"Girl, I can always have Tameer back," Dawshanique boasted. "All I got to do is snap my fingers, and he'll come running."

"Not if Ms. Essence got him wrapped around hers," Shawntae declared.

"Who is this bitch y'all so worried about?" asked a frustrated Dawshanique.

"I don't know," Shamika told her. "I know she ain't from the Courts, or the Eastside, for that matter."

"And from the way Shamika described her, she ain't from the Westside, either," Shawntae declared. "Girl, this is a new bitch!"

The revelation made Dawshanique gasp. "New meat?"

"Yeah," Shamika said flatly.

"Then all of our men are in danger," Dawshanique observed. She leaned back onto her bed and contemplated the threat.

"Why do you think we calling?" Shamika told her.

"Girlfriend, you better take care of home," Shawntae added. "Hold on."

Although Shawntae made an effort to cover the receiver, Dawshanique and Shamika could still hear her loud and clear.

"Lil' Taurus, you better put that shit down, boy! You just like your bad-ass daddy!" Shawntae shouted. "Okay, I'm back, y'all. These kids are driving me crazy."

"Y'all find out who this bitch is for me, and where she's from," Dawshanique told them. "She's got to know somebody in town."

"She looks familiar," said Shamika. "I know her from somewhere. I know that I've seen her somewhere before! You know, she had her back to me for most of the movie, so I just got to get a quick glimpse at her when they first walked in. And even then, it was dark in the theater already."

"I'll bet she's one of them Northside Ms. Rich Bitches," Shawntae told them.

"Okay, start making phone calls," Dawshanique said. "I'mma start getting ready. I got to call Alonzo and give him some booty so I can get my hair done. Then I got to give him some more booty so I can get a couple a new outfits. Then give him some more booty so he can leave me alone. Then, I'mma go and see Mr. Tameer."

"Tears, girl!" Shawntae suggested. "Practice crying."

"I know how to handle Tameer," Dawshanique told her. "Y'all just find out who the enemy is."

"Girl, I live right across the street from Tameer," Shamika said. "You know I'm already on that!"

"Hold on," Shawntae said. "Little Quinton, leave Lil' Taurus alone! Lil' Anthony, put that down!"

"Oh, girl! You got too many kids for me!" Shamika advised. "I'm glad I only got three, and two of they daddies is still alive!"

"Hell, they both got life, so what does it matter!" Shawntae shot back.

"Y'all stop! Just stick to the plan," Dawshanique told them. "Now, listen up..."

"So where is this special place we're going tonight?" asked a smiling Jamaica.

Again, she was beautiful. Her hair had been pulled to the back and tied in a tight, neat, long brown ponytail. Tonight, she wore no makeup, except for some brilliant burgundy lip gloss, that contrasted beautifully with her walnut-colored skin and emerald eyes. Her beauty made him return her smile uneasily.

"I can't tell you where we're going, it's a surprise," Tameer replied. *She is going to love it*, he told himself. *It was quiet, it was natural, and it wouldn't be crowded at all. Best of all, she can't embarrass me by ordering "the happy one" again.* The thought made him smile. "Your friend China suggested a few things, so I'm sure you'll like it."

Jamaica shrugged her shoulders, and leaned forward, pressing the power button on the car stereo. It came alive instantly. The tune was the latest P. Diddy remix, which was a constant staple on radio stations all across the nation. The song was uptempo, and catchy.

"Wooooow, that's my boy!" Jamaica shouted. She bobbed her head frantically to the beat, and snapped her fingers to the rhythm. "I love P. Diddy!"

Her enthusiasm caused Tameer to glance at her strangely. "Oh really? I didn't have you being a rap music affectionado."

Jamaica shook her head. "I'm not really. I mean, I love rap, but it's just that me and Sean go way back. He did a remix for me."

"Excuse me?" Tameer turned and stared at her.

Jamaica knew that she had slipped. *Think fast, girl! Think fast!*

"I said, he did a remix for G," Jamaica told him. "G is my ex-boyfriend. He was a DJ."

"Oh, for a minute is sounded like you said that he did a remix for you!" Tameer shook his head and laughed.

It was her out.

Jamaica quickly produced a laugh, and slapped him gently across his shoulder. *He had bought it!*

Relieved, Jamaica turned and stared out of the window and watched several cars pass by on the other side of the road. *Be careful, Jai*, she told herself. *Do not slip again!*

Jamaica turned back toward Tameer. "So, where are we going?"

Tameer smiled at her. "Just relax. Besides, we're almost there."

Chapter Eight

Jamaica's hands flew up and she covered the lower half of her face. "Oh my God! Uh-un, are those what I think they are?"

Tameer smiled and nodded. "Yeah, they're fishing poles."

"But you brought two of them," Jamaica told him.

"Yeah, one for me, and one for you."

"But I don't fish," Jamaica said flatly.

"Why not?"

Jamaica turned and began pacing, as her hands flew through the air. "Because they have restaurants that kindly get out and retrieve them for you."

Tameer unloaded the fishing poles from the trunk, and placed them on the ground next to the white Styrofoam ice chest. "Well, we are going to retrieve some for ourselves."

Jamaica stopped pacing. "You speak French, I see."

"Huh?"

"You said 'oui,' so I assumed that you were speaking French. Unless of course, you are royalty, or, you have a hamster in you pocket." Jamaica turned and smiled at Tameer with a polite defiance. "Because if you meant 'we', as in you and me, then you are sadly mistaken."

Tameer continued unloading the trunk, ignoring her ravings. His ignoring her, only angered her more.

"Did you hear me?" Jamaica shouted. Her tiny fist pounded the air defiantly. "I do not fish!"

Tameer continued unloading the trunk in silence, until finally, he removed his last piece of equipment. He closed the trunk of his small car, and lifted several pieces of fishing equipment from the ground. With his hands full, he turned to her.

"Jamaica, could you grab that tray, and that tackle box for me?" he asked politely.

"Could I grab that for you?" she shouted.

Tameer nodded. "Yeah. Please?"

Jamaica's hand flew into the air, where she placed her palm in front of his face. "Wait a minute, Tameer, let me explain something to you. This is supposed to be a date. I am not supposed to carry things, I am not supposed to push cars, I am not supposed to hold greasy jumper thingys, and I am not supposed to eat food that comes from underneath a heat lamp!"

Before she completed her sentence, Tameer had turned away. He walked down a small, worn, dirt path which led to a grassy knoll just off the lake, leaving Jamaica all alone. Her loneliness caused her to scream.

"Tameer!"

Tameer ignored her calls as he continued walking along the banks of the lake. It infuriated her even more. Alone, the silence of the lake soon became eerie, causing her to examine her surroundings. Quickly, Jamaica lifted the plastic tray and tattered, gray, metal tackle box, and rushed along the path after her date. She continued to call to him along the way.

"Tameer!"

Soon, Jamaica reached the clearing at the end of the dirt path, which allowed Tameer to once again become visible. He had set up a pair of folding chairs on a mound next to the bank of the lake, and had quietly begun sorting his equipment.

"I suppose you think that this is funny?" Jamaica shouted furiously. "I suppose this is your idea of a joke!"

Tameer motioned toward a spot on the ground between the two folding chairs. "Set the worms down there."

"Worms? Aaaaaah!" Jamaica dropped the tray of worms and the old rusting tackle box, spilling the contents of both. Tameer laughed.

With the smile still on his face, Tameer knelled down and began gathering the long, brown, wriggling creatures back into their container.

"You pig! You uncivilized pig!" Jamaica shouted. She was beyond furious. "How dare you have me carry worms! How dare you!"

"They won't hurt you. Besides, they were all in a tray."

"What kind of person are you?" She wiped her hands on the top of her pants legs. "How dare you treat me like this! Carry this, carry that, put it here, set it there, and you walk off and leave me!"

"You were insulting me."

"You deserved to be insulted!" She spun and began pacing. "You do not take a woman on a fishing date! You just don't!"

He stared up at her from his knees. "Have you ever been fishing before?"

She was insulted. "Of course not!"

"Then how do you know you won't like it?" Tameer rose and dusted off his pants leg. "Look around you."

Tameer lifted his arms into the air and spun around slowly. "It's quiet, it's peaceful, it's natural, it's beautiful."

"Uuuuuugghh!" Jamaica screamed, and then pointed her finger in his face. "Look, nature boy, I don't fish! I hate fish, I hate trees, I hate squirrels, I hate the lake, I hate butterflies, and wildlife, and I'm really starting to not like you!"

Once again, Tameer picked up his fishing pole and walked away. "Fine, then you can stay here! I'll find a nice quiet spot somewhere else!"

"Tameer!" she shouted. "Tameer! Don't you dare ignore me!"

Tameer continued along the path.

"Nobody ignores me! How dare you! How dare you! You pig!" Jamaica lifted a rock and threw it at him, missing him by several yards. "You pig! You uncivilized pig!"

Tameer disappeared into the trees.

Jamaica was furious. She began pacing back and forth near the colorful fabric and metal folding chairs. She stomped forcefully with each of her steps.

How dare he, she fumed. *He is an ogre, an oaf, a viking! He is an absolute nobody! And nobodies can't treat somebodies like they are just anybodies! Especially if that somebody happens to be me, Jamaica Tiera Rochelle! Who in the hell did he think he is? Men fall all over themselves just to get an autograph! And this... this collegiate nature boy has the nerve to ignore the legendary Jamaica Tiera Rochelle!*

Jamaica kicked a rock into the lake, causing it to skip several times across the peaceful surface of the water, rippling it. *Had I ever been fishing,* she thought. *Fishing! The nerve of him! I...I...I...I... Shit!*

Tameer had found the perfect spot. He had set himself up on top of a large boulder next to the lake, where he was able to fish quietly and enjoy the coolness of the whistling breeze. It was the rustling and crunching of the dried fallen leaves that alerted him to her presence. He smiled when he saw the fishing rod in her hand.

"I overreacted," she said softly. "I'm sorry."

Without acknowledging her, Tameer turned his attention back toward the lake, where his red-and-white fishing bob had begun to dip below the surface of the water.

"I'm trying to apologize, could you at least talk to me?" Jamaica said softly.

Tameer turned to face her. "My dad used to tell me that if you can't say anything nice to a person, then don't say anything at all."

Jamaica let out a half-smile. "Sounds like some good advice."

"Yeah," Tameer sneered. "My old man was full of knowledge."

"You sound sarcastic," Jamaica told him. "Is that aimed at me, or at your old man?"

"Both."

"I know what I did, what did he do?" Jamaica eased herself onto the boulder, seating herself next to him.

Tameer turned and stared at her once again. "You're a real Jekyll and Hyde, aren't you?"

Jamaica laughed. "I'm sorry."

Tameer turned back toward the lake. "Apology accepted."

Jamaica extended her hand to him. "Friends?"

"Let's just say it's a truce."

Jamaica slapped Tameer across his shoulder. "That's not nice!"

Together they laughed.

"Oooooh, oooooh, I got a bite!" Tameer clasped his reel tight, and readied himself to wind in his catch. Jamaica's interest was piqued.

"Really? You caught one?" Jamaica's eyes watched intensely as the brightly colored bob dipped forcefully below the surface of the water.

"Yeah, c'mere." Tameer motioned for Jamaica to come closer. She did.

Tameer rose from the boulder, allowing her to slide over to the center of the massive rock, and then he sat back down behind her. He spread his legs so that she was now seated between them.

"Here, give me your hands," he told her.

Tameer took Jamaica's tiny hands and correctly placed them around the padded grip of the fishing pole. The butt of the pole was placed against her right inner thigh, while her right hand was placed on the reel. Looking over her shoulder, with his hands over hers, Tameer slowly began to reel in their catch.

"We got him, Jai. He's hooked real good."

Jamaica became excited. "Really?"

"Yeah." Tameer nodded. "He should be coming out of the water real soon."

Together they reeled.

"Here he comes!"

At first sight, Jamaica screamed. Then came a joyful whoop. "All right! My first fish!"

"You did real good!" Tameer told her in between their laughter.

She turned and stared at him over her shoulder. "How do we do it again? That was fun!"

"Well, first we have to take this one off, and put it inside of the ice chest. Then we'll have to bait the hook with another worm."

Tameer stood and removed the ten-inch bass from the hook. Displaying some of his athletic prowess, he leaped from the top of the boulder onto the ground, and placed the fish inside of their Styrofoam ice chest.

Jamaica waved the empty fishing line in front of him. "You do the worm for me."

Tameer nodded and smiled. "Yeah, this time. But next time, I'll show you how to do it. Deal?"

Jamaica hesitated for several moments, and then relented. "Deal."

Peering out over the lake, Tameer removed his T-shirt, revealing his chiseled upper body, and bulging muscles. Jamaica blushed.

"Tameer, I'm sorry," she told him. "You know, about how I acted."

He nodded. "It's okay."

"I just had a bad experience with fish." One big, black, slimy one in particular, she didn't say out loud.

"Yeah?" Tameer lifted an eyebrow. "I thought you hadn't been fishing before?"

"I hadn't," she answered, adjusting her position on the hard rock. She could feel the jaggedness of the boulder against her derriere. "Actually, it's sort of like a recurring nightmare. I have this dream where this big, shiny, black-and-white fish keeps licking me in the face."

Tameer laughed.

Jamaica folded her arms. "It's not funny! And you know what scares me? The more it licks me, the more I scream, and the more I scream, the more the crowd applauds."

"I thought that I had some weird dreams," Tameer told her. He leaped back onto the boulder and positioned himself just behind her. "Are you ready?"

"Yeah." Jamaica rose and maneuvered herself until once again she was seated between his legs. She leaned her head back against his muscular bare chest, as he wrapped his arms around her to grab the fishing pole.

"Okay, we're going to cast the line," he said.

Tameer carefully maneuvered the pole around his shoulder, and then sharply whipped it forward, sending the tightly wound line far into the blue-green waters of the lake.

"Wee, this is fun!" Jamaica shouted. She turned her head toward him. "So, who taught you how to fish?"

"My dad, when I was younger," Tameer told her.

"Yeah? Seems like you two are close."

"We were." Tameer nodded sadly. "But mostly we fight now."

"Why?" she asked.

"My mother left when I was a kid," Tameer explained. "My father turned to the bottle, and over the years, he's gotten deeper and deeper into it."

"That's awful," Jamaica told him. She turned and faced the lake again. "Me, I remember only a few things about my father. He went away when I was young, and even when he was with us, he was a workaholic."

"So, what happened to him?" Tameer asked.

Jamaica leaned her head back against his chest once again, and closed her eyes. "Well, I haven't told this to anyone before, and I can't believe that I'm even telling you."

She opened her eyes and exhaled. "He's in prison. He was an investor, and he supposedly laundered money, and sold a lot of bad bonds."

"Wow, that's heavy," Tameer said softly. "So, you haven't heard from him in a while?"

"All of the pictures that I have of him are old," Jamaica said sadly. "My mother tells everyone that he died in an airplane crash."

"Why?"

"She wants to protect us, and protect her good name."

"Do you know where he is?" Tameer asked.

Jamaica nodded. "Sure."

"You ever thought about going to see him"

Jamaica smiled again, and shook her head. "In my wildest dreams. I... I really wouldn't even know where to start, or what to say. Besides..."

"Besides, what?"

"Besides, he may tell my mother if I did." She turned toward him again. "Hey, let's talk about something else."

He nodded.

"So, you like rap music, huh?" she asked.

This brought out a smile. "Is there any other kind?"

This made Jamaica laugh. "Of course, silly! There's R&B, jazz, gospel, rock 'n' roll, pop, country, tejano, opera, and so many others."

"But they're not like rap," Tameer told her. "Rap is like poetry. Rap *is* poetry. It's urban poetry. You can hear the pain, and the cries of the inner city in the lyrics. Listen to the beats, the rhythm, the power. Rap is our purest form of expression now."

"So, you like poetry?" she asked.

"I love poetry."

"Do you write?"

"Of course!"

"Let me hear some."

"Sure, listen to this one..."

Chapter Nine

"He's bullheaded, he's arrogant, he treats me like... like... like I'm a buddy!" Jamaica griped as she paced the floor of the motel room, while LaChina remained sprawled across the bed, surrounded by her usual array of paperwork.

"But you had fun, didn't you?" LaChina asked.

"That's beside the point!" Jamaica shouted. Her hands flew through the air as she tried to find the right words. "He treats me... he treats me like... like... like I'm just..."

"An average person?" LaChina suggested.

Jamaica spun on her heels. "Yeah!"

Jamaica's frown made LaChina burst into laughter.

"That's good for him, and for you!" LaChina told her. "It's about time someone taught Her Royal Highness that her excrement does in fact exude malodorous."

Jamaica folded her arms and shifted her weight to one side. "Ha, ha, ha. You should try out for Def Comedy Jam."

"Look, Jai, he's not that bad. You waltzed in here yesterday bragging about how you caught eight fish! You, Jamaica Tiera Rochelle, caught fish!" LaChina sat up in bed, accidentally crinkling several sheets of her paperwork. "I'm sure that the angels in heaven stopped what they were doing and watched this miraculous event. I'm sure that it snowed it purgatory, and I'm sure that several of our snout-nosed, curly-tailed friends took to the sky. Jamaica, you fished, and you liked it!"

With her arms still folded, Jamaica closed her eyes and swayed back and forth as she reminisced about the previous day's events. Finally, a smile appeared.

"It was kind of fun," Jamaica conceded.

Jamaica unfolded her arms and sat down on the bed next to her friend.

"It was a lot of fun," Jamaica admitted. Motioning with her arms, she described her actions to her friend. "I cast my line, I reeled in my fish, and he even showed me how to take them off the hook. We sat and talked, and he even read me some of his poetry." Jamaica turned toward LaChina and smiled. "I sang for him."

"You sang for him?" LaChina shouted. "Jai, what were you thinking?"

"Don't worry, it was some of the new stuff that no one's heard yet. He wouldn't have recognized any of it, anyway. He only listens to rap music. He thinks of rap music as some type or urban poetry." Jamaica crossed her legs and leaned back onto the bed, closing her eyes and spreading her arms out. "It was beautiful out there. The breeze was blowing, and it was so peaceful that you could hear the wind blowing and rustling through the trees. Ummmmm."

The silence in the room caused Jamaica to open her right eye. She found LaChina staring at her. Jamaica quickly opened her other eye and sat up. "What?"

The frown of deep concentration left LaChina's face giving way to an expression of realization. Then, as quickly as her expression changed the first time, it changed again. LaChina's mouth fell open in astonishment, and she gasped.

Jamaica recoiled. "What?"

LaChina's arms flew forward and she embraced Jamaica tightly. "Oh, my sister! You are in love!"

LaChina rocked Jamaica back and forth while hugging her.

"I am not!" Jamaica protested.

"You are too! I can smell it!" LaChina released Jamaica, and lifted her arms high into the air. "It smells like... like fish, and trees, blowing wind, and poetry." LaChina's smile spread wide across her face. "You are in love!"

"I am not!" Jamaica stood. LaChina followed suit, grabbing her friend, and pushing her into the tiny motel bathroom. She positioned Jamaica in front of the mirror.

"Close your eyes, Jai," LaChina commanded.

Exhaling loudly, Jamaica folded her arms, shifted her weight to one side, and closed her eyes. "Now what?"

LaChina moved in closer and whispered into Jamaica's ear. "Think about the breeze, the rock, the trees. Think about Tameer with his shirt off, and you sitting between his legs. His arms are wrapped around yours. It's quiet, serene, peaceful. Your head is resting against his chest, and you can feel his breath against your neck."

LaChina stepped away from Jamaica, and examined her friend's reflection in the mirror for several seconds.

"Open your eyes, Jai," LaChina told her.

Jamaica opened her eyes to see herself smiling in the mirror.

LaChina stepped forward again, tongue in cheek, nodding. "You go, girl!"

Tameer walked from his bedroom, down the stairs, and into his father's room.

"Dad, my carburetor's acting... up..."

Tameer's father, Eddie Lee Harris, stood in the middle of the bedroom wearing only his boxers. His hand was extended to his face, where it held in place a broken piece of metal that had once been a car antenna. Inside of this antenna were stuffed pieces of torn-off Brillo pad to hold in place the small pieces of crack cocaine that co-inhabited that fashioned pipe.

Tameer could only close his eyes, and hope that when he opened them again, this nightmare would be over. That his worst fears would have vanished. They didn't.

"Don't you goddamn kids know how to knock?" Eddie Lee shouted. "What the hell do you want, any goddamned way?"

Tameer's head remained facing the floor. He couldn't bring himself to look up just yet.

"How long, Dad?" he asked. It was a whisper.

"How long what?" Eddie Lee asked.

The evasiveness of his father made Tameer look up. He stared at Eddie Lee with a penetrating gaze, though his tears would not let him see clearly. "How long have you been a crackhead?"

"What? Eddie Lee's arms raged through the air in a violent fury. His voice boomed with the rage of Armageddon. "How dare you talk to me like that! You get the hell outta my room! What I do is none of your god-damned business, anyway! I'm grown!"

"Bullshit, it ain't none of my business!" Tameer shouted back. "Now I know where your pension goes! Now I know why all of the bills are falling on me! Now I know why shit is getting cut off all of the time! Now I know why you stopped living and being a human being! Look at you! You've regressed into an animal!"

"Goddamit, boy! You don't talk to me like that! You get the hell outta my house!"

"I pay the bills here!" Tameer shouted. He breathed in slowly for several moments in order to regain his calm. When he finally spoke again, it was in a relaxed, serene tone. "Dad, look at what you're doing to us. Look at what you're doing to yourself."

Eddie Lee sat back down on his bed, crackpipe still in hand. Tameer stepped forward, and took several hard swallows before speaking.

"Who sold it to you, Dad? Was it one of my friends?"

Eddie Lee looked up at his son. "It doesn't matter."

"It does matter," Tameer told him.

"Goddamit, Tameer! Leave me alone!"

With his hands still shaking from his previous ingestion, Eddie Lee lifted the crackpipe back up to his lips, and using the cigarette lighter inside of his other hand, he quickly lit it.

Tameer leaped across the bed and swiped at the pipe with all of the fury and strength that he could muster. His blow sent it flying across the room.

Eddie Lee leaped to his feet. "My shit!"

At first Eddie Lee scrambled for the pipe, and then he turned toward his son. "You son-of-a-bitch!"

Eddie Lee threw a wild, frenzied punch towards his son, which Tameer was able to only partially dodge. Eddie Lee's fist landed across Tameer's ear, sending him back onto the bed. Eddie Lee quickly pressed on his attack.

"I paid twenty dollars for that, and you're gonna give me my money back!" Eddie Lee shouted.

Tameer quickly rolled off the bed and onto his feet, readying himself for his father's advance. Eddie Lee charged forcefully, and the two of them locked arms. Tameer, being younger, and in infinitely better shape, rapidly outmaneuvered his father and gained the advantage. Using Eddie Lee's momentum and weight against him, Tameer was able to send his father flying onto the bed.

Being of healthy size, with massive arms of his own, Eddie Lee's unrelenting grip allowed him to maintain a hold on Tameer, and bring his son crashing down onto the bed along with him. On the bed, Tameer's agility allowed him to quickly slip away, and finally gain the dominating position.

Blind with fury, Eddie Lee threw another punch, this one landing on his son's jaw. Instinctively, Tameer's left hand thrust forward violently, clasping Eddie Lee's throat. His grip was unrelenting.

Eddie Lee found himself clasping both of his hands around his son's wrist and forearm, in a vain effort to remove Tameer's hand from his closed airway. It was his father's gasping that gave Tameer pause.

In only seconds, the room had gone from a crashing, cursing cacophony of violence, to a horrific, screaming vacuum of eerie silence. It was in this sensory void that Tameer found himself looking around, and spying his hand in the air with his fist balled tightly, ready to strike his father. His breathing quickly became labored.

"Oh God... oh God." Tameer swallowed hard, and quickly climbed off his father, only to stumble backward.

"Oh God... Oh God..." He stared at his hands, and he hated them.

Stumbling and out of breath, he flew from the room, leaving Eddie Lee rubbing his throat and searching the floor for his lost pieces of crack.

The trip down the stairs was rapid. Tameer grabbed his work shirt from the arm of the couch, and bolted from the house with the speed of a greyhound, yet the grace of a drunken camel.

Inside of the car, the frustration of trying to get his key inside of the ignition switch was all it took. The floodgates opened.

"Fuck! Shit!" Tameer's fist struck the dashboard first, then followed with a blow to the windshield. His elbows joined in, by slamming themselves against his seat, and his feet took out some of his frustration on the floorboards.

Soon, the inside of the vehicle became a therapeutic cacophony of crashing, banging, pounding, stomping, kicking, elbowing, pulling, ripping, tearing, and cursing. The blood on his hands went unnoticed, as did the physical pain from his earlier fight with his father, and his current fight with his vehicle. The only pain that was felt, was that which he couldn't help. It was inside.

Chapter Ten

Jamaica and LaChina strolled into the store as Tameer was finishing up with a customer. Jamaica was all smiles. She clasped her hands together as if holding a fishing pole, and dramatically thrust them forward as if she were casting a line.

Tameer simply stared at her. His face remained passive, unsmiling, bitter. His bandaged hand rested visibly on the store's checkout counter, its brownish-red stain drawing Jamaica's attention.

"What happened?" she asked, placing her hand on top of his.

Tameer pulled his hand away, allowing it to fall out of sight behind the counter. "Nothing."

Jamaica pressed ahead. "Let me see that."

Tameer shook his head and stepped back. Jamaica shifted her gaze to his face. She now noticed the puffiness of his slightly swollen face.

"Tameer, you've been fighting!" Jamaica cried out.

Tameer turned away from her. "It's nothing."

Jamaica reached over the counter and clasped his face. "What happened?"

"Nothing." Tameer jerked his head away. "Don't worry about it, it doesn't concern you."

Tameer turned and walked away from the counter to the employee area in the rear of the store. Jamaica followed.

"So, it's like that, huh?" she asked.

"Like what?"

Jamaica stopped. "You know what. You're pathetic."

"I'm pathetic?" Tameer asked. "Why, because I don't have time to make goo-goo eyes and fall all over you?"

Jamaica shook her head. "I didn't ask you to do that. I just stopped by to see how you were doing."

"I'm fine," he said flatly.

"No, you're not, you're an asshole."

"I'm an asshole because I don't have time to be your damn shrink?" Tameer turned and faced her. "Look, I got problems of my own, all right? I'll listen to yours later."

He turned and was only able to walk several steps before his emotions came out.

"Goddamn it!" Tameer kicked a stack of boxes that were filled with shoes, sending them flying throughout the cramped storage area. "What does everybody want from me!"

"The only thing I wanted was a friend, but I see that I came to the wrong place!" With that, Jamaica turned and walked away and out of the store. LaChina stood silently in the doorway with her arms folded, leaning against the door jamb.

"What?" Tameer snapped at her. "I suppose you want me to take you out so you can tell me about your problems, too?"

"No, I want you to take your problems out on whoever caused them, and not on my friend," LaChina told him.

"Look, I'm sorry... I... I can't do what you asked me to do." Tameer shook his head and looked away. "Something came up. I'll give you your money back."

"I don't want the damn money, Tameer." LaChina stood and approached him, extending her finger into his face. "Let me tell you something. That girl was so happy when she came back to the room yesterday, she couldn't eat, she couldn't sleep, she couldn't do anything but talk about catching some damn fish. She remembered every word of every poem you recited for her. That little outing really meant something to her. Hell, you meant something to her. I hadn't seen Jamaica that happy in a long time. Men treat her like she's a Barbie doll, or like she's some damn trophy! But you..." LaChina shook her head. "You were different. At least I thought you were different. I thought that I saw something in you, something real, something pure. But I see that I was wrong. You're just like all the others. You're a boy trapped in a man's body. Well, here's a hint, boy! Real men don't run away from their problems, and they sure as hell don't take them out on innocent people. You hurt her, and you need to apologize."

Tameer's gaze fell toward the floor, and he let out a deep, hard breath. LaChina was right. He had treated Jamaica badly for no reason. Now ashamed, he held his head low, and walked past LaChina without saying a word.

The mall was not very crowded today, so he was able to spot Jamaica easily. She was seated on a bench a couple of stores down. Her hands were wiping tears away from her face, and the sight of her crying made him feel two inches tall.

Jamaica looked up, and upon seeing Tameer walking toward her, she quickly rose and headed in the opposite direction. He had to jog to catch up to her.

"Jamaica!" he called. "Jamaica!"

She ignored him and continued walking. Her steps advanced her along the mall's path quickly.

"Jamaica!" Tameer called to her again. She still did not answer. Quickly, he jogged past her, turned, and stopped in front of her. She continued her stride, causing him to walk backward in order to prevent himself from being trampled.

"Jamaica, I'm sorry," he told her. "I shouldn't have taken my problems out on you."

She continued walking in silence.

"Jamaica, please talk to me," Tameer begged. "I'm sorry!"

Jamaica continued in silence.

"Jamaica, would you please just stop and listen!" he shouted in frustration.

Jamaica stopped.

"You know what, Tameer, I'll stop, but I won't listen. The reason that I won't listen, is because now it's my turn to talk." Jamaica shook her head and smiled at him sadly. "You know, I didn't want to go out with you; it was China's idea. But I decided what the hell, I'll give it a try. The first date, we talked, but I kinda didn't know what to expect, so it was kinda awkward. But boy, the second date, the trip to the lake, that was original."

Jamaica closed her eyes and bit down upon her bottom lip, as she turned her face toward the ceiling. A smile wafted across her face as she reminisced.

"Right down to the poetry, you pulled one outta the hat on me that time. It took me by surprise. Guys usually don't do that. But you, oh, you did everything right. You were a gentleman on that boulder, you were charming, you were fun, I *had* fun. I actually got to relax, unwind, and be myself for an entire day. I got the chance to talk about my life, my past, and share my deepest secrets with a friend." She opened her eyes and turned toward him. "Tameer, I thank you for that. It was the first time I had ever been able to do that. It was the first time I had ever been fishing."

Jamaica turned away from Tameer, and closed her eyes once again, as she thought of another time, another place.

"When I was a little girl, I used to dream of one day going on an outing like that with my father. It would be perfect, like our day was." Jamaica turned back toward Tameer, and stared into his eyes. "Tameer, I will never forget that trip, or you. And that's how I want to remember things, that's how I want to remember you. I want to remember being between your legs, feeling safe in your arms, talking, laughing, singing, and catching fish together. Tameer, you don't owe me anything."

Jamaica shook her head slightly, and placed her hand gently upon his chest. "Not another date, not another trip, not an explanation, not an excuse, and not even for the glasses."

Jamaica leaned forward, closed her eyes, and kissed Tameer firmly on his lips for several moments. "Good-bye, Tameer, you take care of yourself."

Jamaica stepped to the side, walked around him, and disappeared into the mall. Tameer stood alone, still facing in the same direction, and listened as her footsteps faded.

"Why don't you just call her," Savion suggested, while sitting down on the edge of his brother's bed. "Just tell her that you was fucked up."

"I tried to tell her that at the mall," Tameer explained. "But she wouldn't listen."

Savion nodded his head in agreement. "Yeah, well, then in that case, I fully agree with you. You screwed up big time."

Tameer exhaled forcibly. "I sincerely thank you for your expert opinion."

Tameer bounced his basketball against the wall for the one-thousandth time since returning from work.

Savion slapped his brother across his knee. "Take my advice, big bro, beg! Call Jamaica and beg!"

"You think it's worth it?" Tameer asked.

"Do I think it's worth it?" Savion smiled, and tilted his head to the side. "Do you?"

Tameer nodded slowly. "Well, yeah... I mean, I guess. Of course!"

"Well, then, call her and beg," Savion told him again. "Tell her you're sorry, tell her you messed up, tell her you didn't mean it and that it'll never happen again."

Tameer lifted an eyebrow and smiled. "I take it you've done this before?"

Savion produced a small, black, vinyl-covered notebook. "I call this the Savion Harris book of apologies. I got a thousand of them in here."

Tameer laughed. It was his first time laughing since the previous day. "I guess you're right, I'll call."

"Good!" Savion rose from his brother's bed. "I'll see you tomorrow, bro."

"All right," Tameer told him, as they clasped hands. "Later."

"Later."

"He's an ogre, a barbarian, a...a...a pig!" Jamaica's steps were rapid, quick, determined. She paced the floor of the motel room with a vengeance. "I mean, whoever heard of a fishing date! Fish are slimy, oily, polluted, smelly creatures! The nerve of him!"

Lying across Jamaica's double bed, LaChina crossed her gorgeous mocha legs. "You're absolutely right, Jai. The nerve of him!"

"Can you believe him?" Jamaica asked. She took another long swig from her glass of Courvoisier.

"The nerve of him!" added Jemia, who had supplied the liquor for tonight's gathering. She raised her glass into the air. "All men are dogs!"

"Here, here!" concurred LaChina.

"Or frogs!" added Arianna, who was Jemia's cousin on her father's side.

All of them quickly broke into an alcohol-induced giggle.

"Frogs?" Jemia lifted an inquisitive eyebrow.

"Frogs!" LaChina nodded.

Jamaica sat her glass down on the nightstand and turned toward LaChina. "How can they be frogs?"

LaChina took another sip from her glass. "Girl, I don't know. Remember Chris?"

"Chris?" Jamaica asked.

"The stockbroker," LaChina slurred.

"Oh yeah, lil' hoppy!" Jamaica burst into an alcoholic laugh, this time covering her face.

Laughing, LaChina held up her pinkie and began wiggling it. "We should have nicknamed his ass Lil' Tadpole!"

All of the girls broke into uncontrollable laughter.

"Ooooh, girl!" Jemia shouted. "Not one of them!"

For the second time in twenty minutes, Tameer lifted his cordless phone to his ear. After listening to the dial tone for several seconds, he pressed the power button, turning his telephone off. Like before, he thought it useless. Slowly, the phone fell back down to his side, and again he found himself staring at the ceiling.

"I mean, I could have been in St. Moritz showing off my new Russian sable, or at Beaver Creek, skiing in my latest DKNY ski suit," Jamaica whined as she paced the floor of the motel room. "I...I could have been in Bora Bora where it's warm, drinking Chateau Margaux, or at the Vong in Hong Kong eating pastries. You know how Chin loves to fix crepes especially for me. I could have been in Paris, at the Hotel De Crillion, stuffing myself with canales from Bordeaux, or drinking Moet and Chandon at the Golden Door, while Romare gives me the best massage in the history of Western civilization.

"But no! I'm here in this God-forsaken place eating grease sticks and drinking hard liquor from a plastic cup! I'm here at this place, riding in multicolored, plastic, Korean death traps, and it's all because of you!" Jamaica spun and pointed at LaChina.

LaChina waved her hands in a calming motion. "Jai, it's okay."

"It's not okay!" Jamaica shouted. She began sobbing. "I have a Ferrari Enzo, a Bentley Continental GT, and an Aston Martin DB 9. I don't have to ride in a Hyundai, and hold jumper thingys, and wait outside of the car while my dates pop clutches!"

Jamaica's tiny hands rose, and she began walking toward LaChina. Her voice grew rough and deep. "I'm going to strangle you."

Tameer kicked his covers off, and tossed and turned in his bed for several minutes before finally sitting up. He knew why he could not fall asleep, as his first glance was toward the telephone. His fist pumped the air.

"Damn, I screwed up!" he said to no one in particular. "I had her, and I messed up! I had the most beautiful woman I had ever seen, and I treated her like crap. What the hell is wrong with me!"

He lay back down, knowing that sleep would not come easy.

"I hate you!" Jamaica screamed.

LaChina rubbed her throat. It was still sore from Jamaica's stranglehold. "Jai, murder is a felony!"

"I hate him!" Jamaica shouted. She stomped her foot hard against the floor.

"Then call him," LaChina suggested.

"Why? I hate him!"

"Then tell him," LaChina replied.

Jamaica sat down on the bed next to a snoring Arianna.

"I will not call him." Jamaica pouted. "He's a nobody. Besides, he knows where I am."

"Then go to sleep!" LaChina said forcefully.

Jamaica folded her arms and pouted. "I can't. I'm not sleepy."

"I am, and you're not keeping me up." LaChina rolled over to emphasize her point.

Jamaica nudged her. "It's your fault."

"Is not," LaChina told her.

"Is too."

"We'll discuss it tomorrow." LaChina yawned.

"We can't discuss it tomorrow, because tomorrow we'll be shopping," Jamaica retorted.

"I bet I can guess at which mall," LaChina taunted.

"Hah!" Jamaica said excitedly. "You're wrong! I'm not going anywhere near him, or that establishment."

"We'll see."

"What?" Jamaica asked. "You don't believe me?"

"I didn't say anything."

"It's the way you didn't say anything."

"Go to sleep, Jai."

"I can't."

"Good night, Jai."

Jamaica exhaled loudly, and lay back onto a narrow spot on the bed. "Good night, China," she said out loud. *Good night, Tameer,* she didn't.

Tameer pressed the power button on his cordless phone, again cutting it off. Slowly, he lay back in his bed with his thoughts on another part of the city.

"Good night, Jai," he said. It was a whisper.

Chapter Eleven

"I thought you said that we were not coming anywhere near this mall," LaChina said, while trying to keep pace with Jamaica's rapid stride.

"Tameer doesn't own this mall. He's just a lowly employee at one of the many and varied stores throughout this establishment," Jamaica replied. She raised her arms into the air and spun around freely, before stopping face-to-face with LaChina. "And, if he bothers me, I'll have him thrown out. Besides, I'm not going anywhere near his store."

LaChina folded her arms and exhaled forcibly.

Jamaica turned toward her friend. "What?"

LaChina shook her head. "I didn't say anything."

"I know, but it's the way you didn't say anything."

"Jai, girl, you are mental."

"Am not."

"Are too."

"I came to this mall to shop," Jamaica told her. "What's mental about that?"

LaChina extended her palm into Jamaica's face. "Girl, talk to the hand."

"I did!" Jamaica stomped. "I did come here to shop!"

"Okay, Jai, what do you want to buy from this mall that you couldn't have bought any number of times before?" LaChina asked.

"I saw some cute uh...uh..." Jamaica glanced over her shoulder and found a store out of the corner of her eye. "Shoes! Yeah, some cute little shoes."

LaChina folded her arms and shifted her weight to one side. "From where, Jai?"

Jamaica turned and pointed. "From there!"

LaChina turned in the direction in which Jamaica hand pointed. "Oh, yeah right, Jai! Since when have you ever been inside of a Payless?"

"I have." Jamaica nodded fervently. "They sell shoes, right?"

"Of course."

"Well, then, let's go," Jamaica said, as she led off.

LaChina followed close behind.

The store was of the mall variety, meaning of medium size, and staffed primarily by young freckled face teens. It was well traveled, and the carpet showed this clearly. The shoes were stacked on racks that created aisles throughout the store, and there were little benches spread throughout the establishment so that customers could try on their shoes prior to purchasing them. There were several customers throughout the store today, and it smelled of feet, and bubblegum.

"Oh...oh...oh my God!" Jamaica's hands flew to her chest, as she traveled through the aisles examining the shoes and their prices. "Cheap shoes, I'm... I'm... I'm hyper...ventilating. Get... me... out... of here."

LaChina folded her arms and glared at her friend. "I ought to leave your butt in here."

Jamaica continued her shallow breaths. "Don't play...get...me...out..."

LaChina grabbed Jamaica's arm, and headed for the store's exit. In the middle of the aisles leading to the mall, sat an extremely large woman, jamming her size-ten foot into a size-eight shoe. A child hovered near the fat woman, like a planet orbiting its sun. He popped his bubble gum loudly, and smiled at Jamaica revealing a missing tooth.

Jamaica leaned forward and smiled. "Somebody's going to get a visit from the Tooth Fairy."

Smiling back at Jamaica, the child of the fat woman stuck his short stubby finger inside of his once pink nose, turning it red, and then quickly jammed it into his mouth.

Jamaica's hands flustered about frantically. "Ooooh... oooh... China... air...air!"

It became a race for the exit.

"Miss, it's getting cold outside, and my children need shoes!" the woman at the counter reiterated. "I don't care what Check Rite says, my check is good. It has to be a mistake!"

The discussion caught LaChina's attention. She clasped Jamaica's arm and pulled her back into the store.

"Ma'am, I'm sorry, we can't take your check!" the manager intervened. He lifted his arms defiantly. "Now, I know you shop here, but thousands of others do as well. If I did business based on personal acquaintants, I'd be out of a job, and every housing project in the city would be full of people wearing new shoes!"

Jamaica stared at the children's feet. Their shoes were filled with holes, and were coming apart in several places. The little boy's shoes flapped when he walked, as the sole had completely come apart. LaChina nudged Jamaica.

"Did he just say what I think he said?" Jamaica whispered.

LaChina nodded and moved in closer.

"But, sir, my check is good," the woman continued. "Please..."

The store manager's hand rose into the air, stopping the woman in mid sentence. "If it's good, go to the ATM machine right down the hall, withdraw the money from your checking account, then come back and see me."

"Excuse me," Jamaica intervened.

The woman turned, and Jamaica reached into her gigantic Hermes Kelly Bag and pulled out her wallet. From it, she removed four crisp one hundred-dollar bills and handed them to the woman.

"Here, ma'am. There's a store just down the hall that sells high-quality athletic shoes." Jamaica glared at the manager. "I'm sure that you'll find the service much better."

The woman's thin wrinkled hand trembled as she took the money. "God bless you," came from her mouth, and tears from her eyes.

Jamaica hugged her. "It's okay."

Jamaica smiled at the little girl, and waved to the family as they left the store. It was the little girl who continued to wave.

"'Bye, Tiera!" the little girl shouted from the mall. Her mother peered down at her as they continued along their path.

"Who are you talking to?" the mother asked.

OFF.

Inside of the store, LaChina waited patiently until the family was out of earshot. Her steps toward the counter were cool, calm, collected. LaChina's demeanor made Jamaica cringe. She knew the look. It was LaChina's war face.

"Do you know what dignity is?" LaChina asked the manager.

He remained silent.

"I didn't think so." With that, LaChina turned and walked out of the store. Jamaica followed close behind.

"I thought that you were going to read him up one side, and down the other," Jamaica told her. She placed her arm around LaChina's shoulder.

"I wanted to, but I knew that I wouldn't be able to control it, once I let it out." LaChina smiled and pulled Jamaica close. "That was good, Jai. That was real good."

With their arms wrapped tightly around each other, LaChina and Jamaica shared a long, wide grin.

"I'm hungry," Jamaica said. "Let's get something to eat."

Their path to the mall's food court led them past a store that they had forgotten about.

"Jamaica! Jamaica!" Tameer bolted from the store calling to her.

Jamaica and LaChina stopped, turned, and stared at him. His words flowed out clumsily.

"I...I'm... I'm sorry," Tameer said softly.

Jamaica's expression remained stoic.

"It was my father. I... I caught him..." Tameer lowered his head, directing his gaze toward the ground. He couldn't decide whether to tell her and risk losing her, or not tell her, and lose her for sure. He decided to risk telling her.

"I caught him using drugs, Jai." His sniffle was unintentional. "I caught my father using drugs."

Jamaica's hands flew to her face and she covered her mouth. "Oh, my God!" Jamaica trembled at the thought, and quickly reached out and embraced Tameer. "Oh my God! I'm sorry, Tameer. I'm so sorry."

LaChina clasped Tameer's forearm and squeezed it reassuringly. "It'll be all right."

He nodded.

Jamaica leaned back from their embrace and smiled at him. "So, where are you going? Are you off work already?"

"No." He shook his head. "I'm taking a break."

Gently, Tameer took Jamaica's hand into his and led off. "So, where are you two going?"

"We were going to the food court to grab something to eat," Jamaica replied. She nudged him slightly with her shoulder. "Care to join us?"

"Yeah, sure." He smiled. "But first, I wanna stop by the record store and grab this new CD."

"A rap CD, I presume?" Jamaica smiled.

Tameer smiled sheepishly. "Is there any other kind?"

Together they shared a laugh.

"So, when are you taking me out again?" Jamaica asked.

"Well, my car is kinda on the fritz right now," Tameer told her.

"When is it not?"

"Well, actually, this time it's bad. It's kind of like... dead." Tameer shifted his gaze to the floor and exhaled loudly. "Yeah, the Gray Ghost is gone."

Jamaica tugged his shirt sleeve. "I'm sure that it's in that big junkyard in the sky."

"You know you didn't like my car," Tameer told her.

Jamaica smiled. "Actually, I thought that someone should have done a mercy killing on that thing a long time ago."

Jamaica and LaChina giggled.

"Hey, I loved that car." Tameer squeezed Jamaica's hand lightly. "I'm sure it's in Heaven."

"I'm sure it is," Jamaica told him. "So, what CD are you going to buy?"

"It's a new CD from this group called Southern Merchandise. I heard it on the radio last night during the mix show."

LaChina gasped. "The music store!"

LaChina leaned forward and peered around Tameer at Jamaica. "We're going to the music store?"

Tameer smiled and nodded. "Yeah, that's where one usually goes to buy music."

"Oh my God!" LaChina's hand flew to her chest and she started breathing heavily.

Jamaica stared at her strangely.

LaChina began nodding her head in the direction of the store. Jamaica caught on.

"Oooooh, ooooh!" Jamaica moaned, and her eyes flew open wide. "Oooooh girl, walk slow," LaChina told her.

Tameer shifted his gaze toward LaChina. "What?"

"I said, Swing Low," LaChina said, swallowing hard. "Swing low, sweet chariot. It's my favorite song."

LaChina began humming the tune and snapping her fingers. "As a matter of fact, I can't wait to get to it. I'll tell you what, I'm going to run ahead, and I'll see you two when you get there."

She was off.

After putting some distance between her and Jamaica and Tameer, LaChina turned back to her friend. "Jai, swing low, girl! Swing low!"

Jamaica nodded and grabbed Tameer's arm. She placed her arm inside of his, and stopped to stare into the nearest window display. It was a pet store window.

Jamaica put on her best entertainer's face and smiled, while pointing at the display. "Look at all of those cute little fishies! I just love fish. Ooooh, look at the little black-and-white one!"

Chapter Twelve

LaChina bolted into the record store, where she quickly located a salesperson to assist her. She was still breathing heavily from her all-out sprint to the store. "Uh...I...I...I'm looking for your...Tiera CDs."

The salesperson, a twenty-ish, freckle-faced female stared at LaChina as though she had just escaped from an asylum.

"Sure, ma'am." The salesgirl waved her hand toward a shelf on the far wall. "They're right over there."

The salesgirl led LaChina to a section on the wall which contained Jamaica's CDs. The store stocked a lot of them. Jamaica's face stretched for several feet, splashed across the front covers of each of her six CDs, which contained her numerous multiplatinum hits.

"Tiera is hot right now," the salesgirl gushed. "She's one of my favorites."

"Mine too." LaChina returned her smile. She folded her arms and stared at the wall of CDs. *I hope that they don't call the padded wagon on me,* she thought to herself. "In fact, I like her so much that I'll take them all."

The salesgirl removed one CD from each of Jamaica's previous albums, and then perkily glided to the counter. LaChina shook her head, exhaled loudly, and followed behind her. The salesgirl had not understood.

LaChina reached behind the counter and grabbed a large, blue, plastic bag. On her way back to the shelves containing Jamaica's CDs, LaChina shook the bag, filling it with air and opening it widely.

From the counter the salesgirl watched in astonishment as LaChina raked the entire collection of Tiera CDs into her bag, and then tossed the bag over her shoulders and staggered back to the counter. Her freckled face had turned pink, by the time LaChina reached the counter and tossed her black credit card onto it.

The store's silence made LaChina turn around. All eyes were on her.

LaChina smiled sheepishly and shrugged her shoulders. "I mean, I'm a really big fan."

When Jamaica and Tameer strolled into the store, they smiled at LaChina as they walked past her. She smiled stoically standing at the store's entrance, accompanied by two large plastic bags filled with merchandise. Neither Tameer nor Jamaica noticed the bags at her feet.

Upon reaching the rap section, Tameer again glanced at LaChina, who was still standing near the entrance, with a mannequin-like smile plastered across her face. LaChina waved at him.

"I'm sorry," Tameer said to Jamaica.

"What?" Jamaica asked, not understanding why Tameer was apologizing.

Tameer shifted his gaze from LaChina to Jamaica. "I'm sorry because I thought that you were the one who was crazy." He turned back to the display and continued to browse.

Jamaica ventured several feet from Tameer, and coughed loudly to attract LaChina's attention. When LaChina finally peered in Jamaica's direction, Jamaica waved for her to join them. LaChina vigorously shook her head.

Frowning, Jamaica again waved for her friend to join her, although this time even more vigorously. Her motioning was answered by a large exhale from LaChina. Again, Jamaica frowned, but this time it was a frown of confusion. LaChina answered by folding her arms, exhaling, and stepping to the side.

Behind the spot where LaChina once stood, was a life-sized, cardboard cut-out of Tiera, the award-winning songstress. The massive poster caused Jamaica's eyes to fly open wide. She quickly began motioning for LaChina to step back in front of the poster.

LaChina rolled her eyes at her friend. She knew what she was doing.

"Here it is!" Tameer proclaimed. He reached for the CD that he had come for.

"Are you ready?" Jamaica inquired nervously. She desperately wanted to grab Tameer's arm, and drag him from the store.

"Oh, yeah. Well, hold on," Tameer told her. "I'mma look around and see what else they have."

Jamaica put on her best entertainer's face and smiled nonchalantly. "No hurry. Take your time."

LaChina watched excitedly as a store clerk entered from the rear of the store. She knew deep down in her heart what was inside of the boxes he held inside of his hands. She watched in horror as he headed for the Tiera section, and once there, started to restock the shelves.

"Shit!" was what came out loud. Her outburst caused a few stares, but she no longer cared. Tameer was browsing along a path that would take him too near the R&B section, and she couldn't chance the fact that he may keep going into that section.

Leaping into action, LaChina quickly accosted the store clerk, removing several boxes of Tiera CDs from his hands. To his astonished silence, she hurriedly placed the CDs that he had stocked on the shelves, back inside of the box, and then raced to the checkout counter. Again her credit card flew onto the counter, this time stopping next to the hand of another speechless clerk. Again, LaChina could only shrug her shoulders and smile apologetically.

"I mean, I'm a really, really, big fan," she said sheepishly.

While Tameer ventured up to another checkout counter, Jamaica strolled up to her life-sized cardboard cut-out. She stood in front of it, placed her hand onto her hip, and examined the poster carefully. She didn't recall posing for this particular picture, but it didn't matter. Jamaica knew that thousands of pictures such as this one existed. The record company had thousands, her fans had thousands, and the magazines, newspapers, and tabloids all had thousands. It came with the territory.

Jamaica breathed heavily, and then turned toward the counter to see what Tameer was doing. Fortunately, he was pulling money out of his tattered billfold and not paying her any attention. The clerk helping him, however, was peering around the store in an effort to avoid staring into Tameer's wallet. His glance passed by Jamaica, and then by the poster of Jamaica, causing him to do a double-take. His mouth fell wide.

Nonchalantly, Jamaica turned back toward her effigy and examined it once more. Back at the counter the clerk began to stutter. He lifted his hand and pointed in Jamaica's direction, desperately trying to make his words flow coherently.

"Shhhhhhh!" was what he heard.

The clerk glanced in the direction of the sound, only to find an non-smiling LaChina leering at him, with one finger still posed over her lips. She looked as though she meant business. The clerk looked back at Jamaica, and then again at LaChina. LaChina balled her tiny fist tightly, and waved it in the air toward him. He got the message, and quickly shifted his gaze toward the counter.

Jamaica exhaled once again, and using her right hand, pushed the cardboard poster over onto its side, causing it to fall forward onto its face.

"I look fat!" she said to the fallen poster.

"You look beautiful," Tameer told her as he approached. "You ready to go?"

"Yeah, let's go," Jamaica told him. She placed her arm inside of his, and stepped over the fallen poster as they exited the store.

"Hey, was that…"

"Of course not," LaChina interrupted the querying clerk. She turned to her freckle-faced cashier and pointed to the bags of Tiera merchandise near the door. "Give that away to the kids that come in."

LaChina pushed the boxes of CDs that she had just purchased across the counter toward the clerk. "And these too."

LaChina turned, and haughtily strutted through the store's exit, stepping over the fallen poster as well.

Jamaica strolled out of the motel's tiny bathroom, tying her towel tightly around her. "China, I need a car."

"For what?" LaChina asked.

"To get around. Tameer's car is dead."

Jamaica made the sign of the cross and giggled. "And may it rest in pieces."

LaChina gobbled another hand full of popcorn and began crunching. "So, what do you want me to do about it?"

Jamaica reached into the bowl and grabbed a hand full of popcorn for herself.

"Duh!" She crossed her eyes and tossed the popcorn into her mouth. "How about buy one?" she said sarcastically.

"What kind?"

"I don't care," Jamaica answered. "No, wait. It has to be used."

Jamaica spun and braced herself on the cheap, rickety, motel table. "I can't believe I said that." She spun back toward her friend. "China, what's happening to me?"

"Something that should have happened a long time ago."

Jamaica frowned. "Funny."

"No, serious. Anyway, I'll call around and take care of it."

"I need one now," Jamaica whined.

"You'll have it first thing tomorrow. I'll have one delivered—dents, scraps, scratches, and everything."

Jamaica tilted her head to the side. "Not too bad."

"Of course too bad. Jai, the record store was a close call. We have to play this one through."

LaChina gathered her paperwork which was sprawled across the bed, and set it neatly to one side. "That reminds me, the little girl at the shoe store."

"Right." Jamaica nodded. "She recognized me."

"The hat's not good enough," LaChina told her. "Sunglasses, Jai, even inside. I would prefer it if you wore a ponytail and a bini hat. It's starting to get cold, so a bini or a hooded sweatshirt won't draw any stares."

Jamaica shrugged her shoulders. "Right. You're the boss."

Jamaica walked to the bed and sat down next to LaChina. She leaned over, placed her head against LaChina's head, and then gave her friend a great big bear hug.

"You always take good care of me," Jamaica told her.

"Whatever." LaChina was unfazed. "You'll be calling me a bitch tomorrow."

"It's only because I love you." Jamaica smiled.

"How sweet." LaChina gave her an obviously fake smile, and then sat up in bed. "So, where are you two going?"

Jamaica ran her fingers through her damp hair, sending it over her shoulders and down her back. "Well, we haven't been to the local amusement park, or to the Riverwalk yet. The pictures I saw in the magazine made them both look pretty fun."

"Yeah." LaChina nodded slowly. "And it won't be that many people at either of them because it's off-season. Great choice."

Jamaica rolled her eyes toward the ceiling. "Will you stop worrying and be young again!"

"Sure." LaChina nodded. "When we get back to New York, and you start being Tiera again. Until then, I'm going to do what I'm paid to do, which is worry."

Chapter Thirteen

"Oh my God, it's so beautiful out here." Jamaica clasped Tameer's hand, as they slowly strolled along the banks of San Antonio's famed Riverwalk. It was a constant flowing, never-ending bank of clubs, restaurants, cafes, lights, music, dancing, and good-natured reverie. Jamaica glowed in the lighting. It danced across her face, offering only tantalizing glimpses of her beauty, one section at a time. "Do they have these lights all year around?"

"Well, they keep them strung, but they only put them on after Thanksgiving, and they'll stay on until sometime after New Year's."

Jamaica turned, and again marveled at the millions of sparkling lights draped over the trees that stood majestically along the banks of the crystal blue river. The lights danced across the reflecting river, like children dancing across an elementary school stage. They were beautiful in their clumsiness, genius in their impreciseness.

The lights were strung along the banks of the river, as well as over the bridges that transversed it. Against the crystallized blackness of the crisp, South Texas skies, the colorful lighting gave the bridges the appearances of eerily magical floating structures. It was fantastical.

"Look at the way the lights reflect off of the river!" Jamaica pointed giddily. "Oh, this is so beautiful!"

Trying to be cool, Tameer simply nodded. "Yeah, it is."

The lighted barges floating by with a crowd of tourists made Jamaica even more excited. She tapped at Tameer's arm frantically. "I want to ride. Can we ride?"

"Of course," he told her. "We'll have to walk a little further down the river to get to where the riverboat tours start."

"Okay." Jamaica nodded. She rubbed her stomach. "But, I'm still hungry and I wanna grab something to eat. We'll ride after dinner."

Tameer nodded in agreement. Tonight, Jamaica was the boss.

They continued strolling leisurely along the banks of the river, taking in the sights and sounds, as well as its wonderful smells. It was almost like touring the world by nose. There was sauerkraut, weinersnitzel, polish sausage, and exotic French cuisine. There was gumbo, crabs, shrimp, and lobster. Fried egg rolls, and sweet and sour chicken. And of course, pizza, hamburgers, and hot dogs. The restaurants along the banks of the river constituted their own virtual United Nations. Almost every culture or country in the world was represented. The combinations of the various cuisines made them even hungrier.

"There!" Jamaica pointed. "Let's eat there."

It was a large Mexican restaurant, nestled along a set of rocks which jutted out into the leisurely flowing river. It was the screaming red lights, as well as the shouts from the Mariachi band, that had attracted her attention.

Together, Jamaica and Tameer sat down to an abundant meal of sizzling beef, flaming chicken, Spanish rice, beans, fresh guacamole, fresh, hand-made tortillas, Spanish salsa, Spanish canales, and salted margaritas.

The margaritas had been made with an expensive imported liquor, a famous brand of Mexican tequila, freshly squeezed lime juice, sugar, salt, and an imported rum. They were exceptional.

Jamaica downed drink after drink of the lime-flavored concoctions, barely tasting their alcoholic content. After a while, she became giggly.

The mariachi band, making its rounds, soon arrived at their table. The band's serenade lasted only a brief moment, as Jamaica, emboldened by her lightheaded state, stood and interrupted. She removed one of the mariachis' large sombreros, motioned for them to continue their ballad, and then extended her hand toward a slightly inebriated Tameer. Also emboldened by his liquid courage, he took her hand and stood. Jamaica wrapped her arms around Tameer's shoulders, pulling him close. She wanted to slow-dance to the Spanish ballad. The mariachis had something different in mind. They broke into a series of party yelps and screams, and switched the tempo of their music. The restaurant once again came alive. Jamaica came alive.

She twirled, with a continuous stream of laughter pouring out of her, and broke out into her best senorita dance, making Tameer struggle to keep pace with her. She was contagious.

The restaurant soon erupted into a lively fiesta of food, laughter, and dancing, as others, emboldened by their inebriated state, began taking to the floor. One of the mariachis' hats was soon tossed onto the floor, and a circle quickly formed around it. Together the patrons laughed and performed a lively, but highly distorted, variation of a Mexican hat dance.

The crowd loved Jamaica's partnership with an elderly Hispanic gentleman, and broke into a wild frenzy of hand clapping and foot stomping with each of her twirls. Smiling and laughing, she spun and dipped, turned and whirled, tapped and stomped. She was radiating, intoxicating, utterly addictive. Tameer stood back inside of the crowd, and watched her perform.

Clearly, she was the most beautiful woman in the restaurant, yet she didn't lord her beauty over anyone. In fact, she shared it. From older Hispanic man, to older Anglo man, to older African American man, she twirled and danced, enlivening all, and sharing her beauty with them. She took an elderly Hispanic woman by the hand, and danced slowly around the sombrero with her. The crowd truly loved her.

There was something about her, Tameer thought, as he watched her twirl. The way she was so relaxed performing, dancing, and mingling with the crowd. She had a relaxed beauty about her, an inner comfort, a quiet confidence with people. She was definitely at home performing.

It was the little girl in the wheelchair who did it. Jamaica's laughter, hugs, and dancing with her had been genuine. Not sympathetic, not out of pity, or a demeaning sort of compassion, but a genuine sharing of life, of love, of laughter.

It was Jamaica's flying parka, her bouncing ponytail, and the way her earrings clinked against her soft caramel cheeks as she danced. It was her baggy jeans, it was the way her hiking boots moved when she spun. The easy smile, the flying sombrero tied around her neck, that slapped against her back whenever she suddenly changed directions. He watched it all. Tameer folded him arms and watched as this star twinkled brighter than the millions of sparkling lights providing her backdrop. Tameer watched, and slowly, he fell in love.

"C'mon, Tameer!" Jamaica called. She clasped his hand and forcefully pulled him into the clapping, dancing, whooping crowd. Together they danced, laughed, and partied for several hours, before Jamaica remembered the boat.

The riverboat was not very crowded because of the chill in air, and the time of the evening. It was late.

Jamaica wrapped herself up inside of her coat, and Tameer wrapped himself around her. The cool breeze radiating from the river made it necessary.

"You're getting protective, aren't you?" Jamaica asked, with a teasing smile. She was glad to have his warmth. It felt comfortable, cozy, trusting.

"Yeah, I am," he answered matter-of-factly. "Are you cold?"

"Yes, a little." Jamaica nodded. "Why, are you going to give me your jacket?"

"No." Tameer shook his head. "But I'm going to wrap my arms around you and hold you close."

"Mmmmm, even better." Jamaica rubbed her head against his chest.

"Jamaica," Tameer said softly.

"What?" His answer was barely audible.

Tameer didn't reply, and that caused Jamaica to look up. He peered down at her, and their eyes met. She now knew what he wanted, and it made her smile.

My God, she thought. *He looked like a cute, little, lost puppy.*

Jamaica knew that Tameer wanted to kiss her, but she also knew that he was afraid to. She decided to make it easy on him. She closed her eyes and slowly leaned forward.

Tameer wanted to jump for joy, and shout hallelujah, but that would have definitely ruined the moment. So instead, he also slowly leaned forward. Their lips met, for the second time since they'd met. But instead of saying good-bye, this kiss was about forever. Their tongues touched, slightly at first, then more so after they became comfortable. The warmth of each other contrasted greatly with the chill of the night air, which whistled crisply across their faces. They warmed each other, and both imagined how wonderful it would be to warm the other totally.

The river barge moved gently to the banks of the walk, to pick up more passengers. Jamaica rose.

"Wait!" Tameer held up his hand. "They'll take us back down the river." He wanted to kiss some more.

"C'mon." Jamaica reached into the boat, and grabbed Tameer by his jacket collar. She had other things on her mind.

Puzzled, Tameer followed Jamaica as she strode confidently into the nearest building. It was as if she knew where she was, and exactly where she was going. Tameer wondered whether he had done something wrong, whether he had been too forward, or whether he had come on too strong. *But then again*, he told himself, *she did kiss back. Maybe it was the cold. Maybe Jamaica wanted to get out of the cold for a minute, and enjoy the warmth of a building*. Suddenly, she stopped and turned toward him.

"Wait here," Jamaica commanded.

Tameer nodded obediently, and then watched as she rounded a nearby corner. *That's it*, he thought, *she just wanted to use the restroom*. Tameer stood for several moments, rubbing his cold hands together, before spying a comfortable place to sit down. He started towards it, just as Jamaica rounded the corner again.

"C'mon." She nodded for him to follow, as she strode past him.

Tameer raced to keep up. "Where are we going?"

Jamaica turned and placed her finger over his lips to silence him, as they entered into the elevator. The elderly couple on the elevator smiled at them politely, and Tameer returned the gesture. The remainder of the trip in the elevator was spent watching the numbers above the door.

On the thirtieth floor, Jamaica exited, and waved her finger at Tameer, motioning for him to follow. She strutted down the wide, posh hallways with a fierce determination. It was as if she were on a special mission, and nothing was going to stop her.

"Where are we going?" Tameer asked again.

Jamaica stopped at a room, and inserted her card into the slot next to the door handle, causing the door to pop open. She turned to Tameer.

"I'm going to teach you not to start something you can't finish." Jamaica turned and strutted into her still-rented suite at the Marriott on the Riverwalk.

Still standing in the doorway, Tameer swallowed hard, and thought about how wonderful God was, and how he would have to go to church for an entire year to pay this back. Tameer also knew that he had to ask.

"Jamaica, are you sure that you want to do this? I mean... it isn't the alcohol, is it?"

Jamaica began undressing as she approached him. "Oh, yeah, it's the alcohol. But I'm not drunk. I feel good, mellow, but most of all, extremely horny."

Jamaica's threw her blouse across the room, and allowed her jeans to drop to her ankles. "It's been a long, long, long time. Boy, you are in trouble."

She could hear LaChina's voice shouting into her ear. *You go, girl!* It made Jamaica smile.

Although she was moist when Tameer tried to enter into her, he couldn't. When finally, after much patience, she worked him inside, they both nearly screamed—she because of the girth, length, and depth to which he plunged; and he because of the soft vise which he found clamped around him. They both gave each other a tremendous amount of pleasure. All told, that night they coupled three times, she came twelve. He exhausted, she relieved, and they finally entered into a deep, relaxing, all-consuming sleep.

Chapter Fourteen

Tameer marveled at Jamaica's beat-up convertible Volkswagen Golf. "I can't believe you had the nerve to talk about the Gray Ghost!"

Tameer ran his hand across the door, feeling some of the extra dents and scratches that Jamaica and LaChina made prior to Jamaica picking him up from work the previous night. "The Ghost would tear this Barbie Mobile up, from stoplight to stoplight."

"I don't think so!" Jamaica protested as she unlocked his door. *Besides*, she thought, *I know my Murcielago would run rings around your little Korean thingy, if this one couldn't.*

Tameer plunged inside of the car and smiled at her. "You're lucky the Gray Ghost is in retirement."

"Tameer, the Gray Ghost wouldn't even start! That car has been in retirement." She smiled coyly. "You just kept driving it."

Tameer threw his head back in laughter. "So what is this thing's name?"

"Name?" She turned to him. "What do you mean, name? It doesn't have one."

"It doesn't have one!" Tameer said, feigning shock. "That's bad luck, you have to give it a name. You have to give it a name and talk to it, and it'll take care of you when you need it."

"Okay, how about Betsy?" Jamaica asked.

He shook his head emphatically. "Something original. Hey, turn left at the light."

"How about Lucy?" Jamaica asked.

"Lucy? Why Lucy?"

Jamaica shrugged her shoulders. "I don't know. Kind of like, *I Love Lucy*. She is red, and Lucille Ball was a redhead."

Tameer nodded and smiled. He slapped the car's dashboard. "Okay, Lucy! I like it!" He turned toward Jamaica. "Now your car officially has a name, she officially has a soul, and now you have to treat her like it."

Tameer shook his finger at Jamaica. "Watch, she'll take care of you."

Jamaica smiled. "You're crazy."

"No watch. She'll get you through snow, rainstorms, floods, traffic jams, and hot summer days. She won't ever break down in the middle of the freeway, and she won't ever run out of gas on you, on a deserted stretch of highway. You'll always make it to a safe place, I guarantee it."

"And if you're wrong, I'm going to call you and you're going to come and get me."

"Yeah, in what?" Tameer asked. "Hey, turn left here."

"So how are you getting to work and school and stuff?"

"VIA and Nike," Tamer told her.

She stared at him puzzled. "What's that?"

"The bus and my tennis shoes," Tameer answered.

"Public transportation?" She felt nauseated.

Tameer nodded. "Yeah. You seem a little put off by that."

Jamaica shook her head. "No, I'm familiar with public transportation." *Air France, Swiss Air, Lufthansa, British Airways.*

"Well then, how about this?" Tameer turned slightly in his seat and faced her. "We'll catch the bus downtown and ride the horse-drawn carriage and see the sights around town."

Like hell I will! Jamaica put on her entertainer's smile. "Sounds like fun."

"Okay, then." Tameer nodded. "We'll do it right before you leave."

"Can't wait." Jamaica smiled.

"Turn right here, and stop," Tameer told her.

Jamaica turned right, pulled to the side of the road, and stopped. The question was bouncing around inside of her head and so she had to ask him.

"Why here?" Secretly she thought of the possibility that Tameer was living with someone. *A woman! He has a woman!*

"I live just a few blocks over, this is cool," he answered uneasily.

"But I can take you all the way home."

Tameer shifted in his seat, and slowly shook his head. "No, you can't."

You bastard! It *was* another woman! Jamaica's face contorted, but she managed to maintain her composure.

"Why not?" she asked dryly.

"Well…" Again he squirmed. "I don't think I ever told you about where I live."

Jamaica's eyes caught his, and he looked down. That was when it dawned on her. It wasn't another woman, it was his pride.

Jamaica caressed Tameer's hand softly. "Tameer, I don't care about where you live."

"I do." He leaned over and kissed her on her cheek. "I'll see you later."

Tameer climbed out of the vehicle, and Jamaica watched in silence as he jogged through an alley, scaled a fence, and then disappeared.

Before Jamaica could stick her key inside of the motel room's lock, the door flew open and LaChina yanked her inside.

"Stayed out all night, huh?" LaChina asked, tapping her feet rapidly on the worn motel carpeting.

The question caused Jamaica to blush. "Yeah."

LaChina, tongue in cheek, folded her arms and peered around the room. She was trying to be nonchalant. "Where'd you stay last night?"

Jamaica knew what LaChina wanted to hear, but she was determined to make her wait. Jamaica strode to the table and set her keys down.

"At the hotel," Jamaica replied matter-of-factly.

LaChina's foot tapped even more frantically against the floor. "Hmmm, at the hotel, huh? Any guest?"

Jamaica smiled. "Maybe."

Jamaica's coolness frustrated LaChina. She knew the game that her friend was playing, so she decided to play a little also. LaChina approached Jamaica, and leaned forward and began sniffing. Jamaica recoiled.

"What do you think you're doing?" Jamaica asked.

LaChina continued her sniffing. "I'm sniffing for sex."

"Oh my God!" Jamaica's hands covered the lower half of her face. "And just what, may I ask, does sex smell like?"

LaChina was really enjoying herself now. She knew how to embarrass her friend. She leaned forward and sniffed again.

"It smells like that," LaChina said, pointing toward Jamaica's neck. "Like... like hotel soap. And it has this certain look to it also."

LaChina turned and took several steps away from Jamaica. "It looks like... like a person without lip gloss. Like a person who didn't take any combs or hair care products, and just hastily tied their hair into a ponytail. It... it looks like the glow of a new moon."

LaChina spun rapidly and faced Jamaica. "You got you some last night! You go, girl!"

LaChina began leaping up and down like a teenager after passing a driver's test. "Jamaica gave up the booty! Jamaica gave up the booty!"

Jamaica screamed, ran to the bed, and grabbed a pillow, and then threw it at her friend. "You're crass!"

"Uh-un, girl! Tell me how it was! How was Mr. Tameer!" LaChina waved her hand snapping her fingers through the air. "Mr. All State, All Star, All Nation, Mr. put a smile on my sister's face, a strut in her step, and a glow in her cheeks!"

"China!" Jamaica turned even redder.

LaChina rushed to Jamaica, clasped her arms, and hugged her. Using all of her strength she pulled Jamaica down onto the bed. "I want every detail, don't leave out anything! Right down to where he pulled your panties off with his teeth!"

Jamaica shook her head. "He didn't do that!"

"Lie to me, Jai! Embellish, exaggerate! It's been a long time for me, and I need to hear some good stuff!"

Jamaica lifted her hands into the air and spread them apart, indicating length. "And that's not an embellishment."

LaChina's hands flew to her face and she gasped. "Oh my!"

After several moments of contemplation, LaChina sheepishly leaned forward. "How old did he say his brother was?"

Jamaica recounted the previous night's events, and then headed for the shower. From the bathroom, she called out to her friend.

"China, what's the deal with the local radio stations? Do we have any strings to pull?"

"Yeah, with a couple," LaChina answered. "The label can twist arms with most of the others, why?"

"I need a one-man contest."

"Jai, what are you talking about?"

"Tameer needs to win," Jamaica said, as the shower came alive.

"Girl, I thought he won last night!"

Jamaica's head appeared from around the door sill. "Ha, ha, very funny. Anyway, I was talking about a car."

"A car!" LaChina sat up in bed.

"He needs a car, China. He goes to school and work, and he rides the bus. Besides, he came up with some crazy idea about me catching the bus! Baby, he needs a car."

LaChina tilted her head to the side. "A car, Jai?"

"China, how much money do I have?"

LaChina exhaled. "A lot." She knew where Jamaica was going with this.

"Over one hundred million?"

"Of course, Jai."

"Over two hundred million?"

LaChina folded her arms. "Yes."

"Over three hundred million?"

"Okay, Jai, I get your point."

"Good." Jamaica disappeared back into the bathroom.

LaChina shook her head. "He was that good?"

"China!" A bar of soap flew from the bathroom toward LaChina, missing her by several feet.

"Okay, okay." LaChina held up her hands. "What kind?"

"I don't know, you figure it out."

LaChina already knew the answer to her next question, she just wanted to get a rise out of Jamaica. "A Mercedes, Jai?"

"It don't get that good!" Jamaica shouted from the shower.

LaChina laughed. "Let me see..." LaChina's finger tapped at her chin for several moments, before she snapped it. "I've got it! I have the perfect car for him!"

"Under thirty thousand!" Jamaica shouted from the shower. "Something not too ostentatious!"

"Then it's perfect," LaChina told her. "I'll call the radio station and set things up."

"Do it now, China!" Jamaica told her.

"Jamaica, the myth is that after you get laid, you're supposed to be mellow," LaChina replied. "Take a cold shower, and stop trying to give orders. It'll get done!"

LaChina lay back down on the bed and lifted the bulky, cheap, motel phone. She stared at the telephone for several moments before rolling over and staring at the motel's stained ceiling. "Twelve times?"

"China!"

Chapter Fifteen

Jamaica waved from the mall area in front of the shoe store. "Hey, T!"

Upon seeing her, Tameer quickly walked from behind the counter and greeted her. "Hi, Jai!"

They met in the middle of the store and kissed passionately for several moments. When finished, Tameer stared at Jamaica with a broad smile.

"You're not gonna believe what happened to me today!" Tameer said excitedly.

"What happened?" Jamaica asked, not sure if it was because of her and LaChina's scheme.

"Well, I got a call from a radio station saying that I won a car, and that I can pick it up from the dealership any time after two o'clock today."

Jamaica bounced up and down excitedly and hugged him. "That's wonderful!"

Tameer scratched his head and shifted his gaze to the floor. "Funny thing is, I don't remember entering into any contest."

"Well, don't worry about that," Jamaica said, hugging him tightly. "If they say you won, you won. Just be happy, Tameer."

Tameer nodded. "Yeah, I guess you're right."

"So, what kind of car did you win?" Jamaica asked. She was truly anxious to find out.

"Well, the person on the phone said…" Tameer cleared his throat and prepared his voice to do his best impression of a game-show host. "Congratulations, you're the winner of a brand-new 2008 Shelby GT 500 Convertible Mustang!"

The title sounded impressive. A little *too* impressive.

"Wow, what does one of those cost?" Jamaica asked. She managed to keep her expression neutral.

"Hell, about forty-seven K," Tameer told her.

Jamaica reeled slightly, but managed her best entertainer's smile. *China, you bitch! I'm going to kill you!* "Well, I bet you're happy."

Tameer shrugged his shoulders. "It really doesn't make a difference to me. I'm going to sell the thing."

Tameer nodded his head, motioning for Jamaica to follow. "C'mon, let's walk to the food court before I stand here and use up all of my lunch break."

Jamaica locked her arm into his, as they started off for the food court. "So, why are you going to sell the car?"

"Well, Savion has scholarships, but he'll need some cash for other expenses," Tameer explained.

"Tameer, you're a nice person, you deserve nice things," Jamaica told him. "You've worked hard, you've put yourself through school, you've made sure that your brother stayed out of trouble and stayed in school. Tameer, you deserve it."

"I guess. But Savion is gonna need..."

"Tameer..." She interrupted him, stopped, turned, and faced him. "I'm sure Savion will be okay. Something will come through for him, just like it came through for you." Jamaica shook her head. "Don't sell your car."

Again, he shrugged. "I'll see. Hell, I can always sell it later, if things get tough for Savion."

Jamaica leaned her head against his shoulder as they continued their stroll through the mall. "You're so sweet."

"Say, cuz," a voice called out from behind. "What's up with that bullshit?"

Unaware that they were being spoken to, Tameer and Jamaica continued along their path to the food court. The shove from behind caused Tameer to stumble forward. It got their attention.

"I said, what's up with that bullshit you're wearing?" the voice asked again.

Tameer and Jamaica turned. Now standing in front of them were four young men wearing royal-blue T-shirts, black Dickies pants, and blue Converse tennis shoes. Tameer quickly shoved Jamaica behind him.

"It ain't nothing," Tameer told them. He waved his hand at the boy, signaling his unwillingness to engage them. Deep down, he knew that it was not going to be that easy.

"Naw, man, it is something," one of the blue-clad boys told him, as he made his approach.

The boy extended his hand, and tugged forcefully at Tameer's burgundy down-filled parka. "You don't slob in this mall and think that you can get away with it."

"Yeah, that's awfully disrespectful, cuz," another boy chimed in.

Tameer shook his head. "I'm not in a gang."

"Did I ask you that?" the first boy asked.

Tameer raised his hands again, indicating that he wanted no quarrel. "I'm not in a gang, and I don't want any trouble. I'm just walking through the mall, minding my own business."

Tameer reached behind himself and clasped Jamaica's badly shaking hand. He rubbed it gently to calm her nerves, and then turned and began to walk away from the boys.

He was shoved again, and this time he fell.

"Tameer!" Jamaica shouted. She rushed forward and began to kneel, but Tameer was already getting up.

Tameer squeezed her hand. "Go to the car," he told her. He knew that he had to get her away from there.

Jamaica shook her head. She wasn't going to leave his side.

"Jamaica go!" Tameer said forcefully.

"No!" she said emphatically.

"Your little bitch ain't going nowhere," the first boy told them. He lifted his shirt, and rested his hand on a semi-automatic handgun.

Jamaica's hands flew to her mouth. "Oh my God!"

Stunt props she had seen; a real gun, she had not.

"What do you want?" asked a frustrated and angry Tameer.

"We don't want no fucking undercover slobs walking around disrespecting us," the leader told him.

Another boy, this one with long curly hair tied into sections with blue rubber bands, stepped forward. He too flashed a weapon. "Come out the jacket, cuz."

It is simple, Tameer thought. He would give them what they wanted, be rid of them to ensure Jamaica's safety.

Tameer unzipped his jacket, pulled it off, and tossed it onto the ground in front of the leader's feet. Inside he was boiling with anger. He wanted to punch him. He wanted to whip them all.

Several of the boys broke into laughter. "What a ho!"

One of the boys turned to Jamaica. "Say, Lil' Mamma, you need to get you a real man!"

Another one of the boys grabbed himself. "One with some nuts!"

The leader of the group stepped on Tameer's jacket and ground it into the floor of the mall. The curly-haired boy stepped on the jacket also, while giving Tameer a haughty smirk. Satisfied, they all turned and walked away laughing.

It is over, Tameer thought. *It is finally over*. He exhaled loudly, and bent slowly, lifting his jacket from the mall floor. He held it into the air and examined it. Fortunately, the mall's floors were kept clean, so the jacket was relatively unsoiled. Tameer brushed his hands across it several times, clearing away loose particles, and then slowly, he put it back on.

Jamaica turned in the direction in which the boys had gone, and pumped her tiny fist in the air. "Ooooh, I'd like to catch each one of them..."

"Why? What for?" Tameer asked. Again he brushed off the front of his jacket. "Then they would have to come back and catch you, and then you would have to catch them again, and it would never end."

Tameer stared down the corridor in the direction in which they had left. "Then, you'd become just like them."

Jamaica shook her fist again. "But still! I mean, we weren't even bothering them!"

"That's why," he told her. "Because we weren't bothering anyone."

Tameer clasped Jamaica's still trembling hand, and started off again. "I had a cousin, his name was Paul. Paul was real cool, but he was a little bit of a trip though. At first Paul was just like me; he loved poetry, and he wanted something better out of life than the hood. In fact, he turned me on to poetry when we were younger. Of course, back then it was to impress girls."

Tameer smiled. His smile made Jamaica smile.

"But anyway, my cousin was smart. He could have been anything that he wanted to have been. Doctor, lawyer, scientist, engineer, anything. But, he snapped." Tameer snapped his fingers loudly to emphasize his point. "Paul was born with a hyperpigmentation deficiency. He was what you would call an albino. But, he was also mixed. He had long, sandy hair, and pale ice-blue eyes like his dad. But inside, he was black. The guys didn't like him because of his pale, white skin, and growing up, he got it from directions, Jamaica. Some say he just snapped. He dropped out of school, started hanging with the wrong crowd, doing drugs, selling drugs, robbing, and all kinds of things. When I say 'all kinds of things,' Jamaica, I mean all kinds of things. Drive-bys, murders, everything."

Tameer swallowed hard before continuing. "What I'm trying to say, Jamaica, is that some people survive by becoming monsters. They become worse than their nightmares, worse than their tormentors, so they can stop being tormented. They survive by becoming the worst of the worst. The most feared, the most dangerous, the king of the jungle. They survive by becoming the nightmare."

Tameer peered off into the distance, and shook his head slowly. "I don't want to be like that, Jamaica, I can't be like that. So I decided a long time ago, that I was going to survive by not playing the game. I refuse to play the game."

Jamaica leaned her head on Tameer's shoulder as they approached the counter to place their orders. Tameer was brave, but in a different way. He was a good brave.

"So what happened to Paul?" she asked softly.

"Paul became somebody else, somebody that no one knew. He became a monster named Lil' Fade."

Jamaica lifted her head and stared into Tameer's eyes. "So where is he now?"

Deep down, she already knew the answer to her question, but she had to hear it from him. It had to be said out loud.

"He's dead," Tameer said softly. "He killed himself."

Jamaica squeezed Tameer's hand, and her entire body shivered as she tried to provide a comforting smile. Her smile failed.

Tameer looked down at the floor, and repeated to himself softly. "He's dead." It was almost a whisper. "Lil' Fade is dead."

Chapter Sixteen

Tameer's tongue, cold because of the ice cubes inside of his mouth, slowly parted Jamaica's steamy paradise. The cool, sensual wetness caused her to moan and move slightly to her left. Her movement made Tameer grip her silky, smooth, caramel legs, and spread them open even farther. Again, his tongue parted her deeply, and again, she moaned. Consistently, his lashing strokes built in their frequency, with each of Jamaica's watery moans.

After several long, pleasurable moments, Jamaica gripped the back of his head tightly, and soon found herself built up to a climactic release. His bold, deep, rapid strokes continued relentlessly until...

"Ooooh, T...T...Tameer!"

Slowly, the tension bled from her body, and Jamaica spread herself wide. Gently, she pulled him up toward her, where she kissed him passionately, and began rubbing his sweating, bulging muscles. Jamaica was ready. Carefully, she maneuvered herself until he was pressing forcefully against her.

Tameer kissed Jamaica's neck wildly. His tongue lashed at her continuously, while his mouth consumed her sweaty juices. It was then when he took his hand, and rubbed himself against her until parting her, and finding her paradise. Unintentionally, Tameer burst inside of her too quickly, causing Jamaica to arch her back and cry out.

"Ooooo, Tameer." It was a watery whisper.

"Oooooo, Jamaica."

Carefully, he plunged into her in depth, causing her to grip his back tightly, and exhale in watery moans. Jamaica's tight warmth gripped him, pulled at him, massaged him. The captivating pleasure of her warmth would not allow him to speak coherently. Tameer could only grunt in guttural cries of immeasurable pleasure.

Jamaica spread herself even farther, trying to widen herself to ease the pleasurable pain. It only made him slide into her even farther, causing them both to cry out. Slowly, they began to counter rotate against each other, and with each rotation, Tameer's girth and depth made her inhale, squeeze him, and exude a soft cry of pleasure. With each rotation, Jamaica's warmth and tightness made him release a low guttural grunt of pleasure. Slowly, their grinding built in speed and force. Lips and tongues touched, then glided soothingly over necks, faces, and shoulders. Their motion built, until their hands became uncontrollable, as did the sounds of their carnal bliss. Their speed built, until their rhythmic thrusting culminated into an all-consuming, back-arching, shoulder-biting, teeth-clenching, back-scratching, hair-pulling, toe-curling, pulsating, screaming, bursting release.

Jamaica lifted the remote and turned down the television. Lying next to Tameer, she turned and placed her arm across his stomach and rubbed.

"So, how is it that you came to be single?" she asked him.

Tameer managed to conjure up a half-smile to hide the hurt. "Well, it's a long story."

Jamaica sat up. She lifted her arm to her forehead and moved the hair out of her face and smiled. "We have all night."

Her smile widened as she peered at the covers near Tameer's waist. "Or at least until he wakes up again."

Jamaica lifted the covers and tried to peek underneath. "Is he awake?"

It made Tameer laugh. He pressed down on the covers blocking her view. "My God, you're trying to kill me!"

Just as quickly as his laughter had begun, it faded. Still smiling, he turned toward her. "So how is it that *you're* single?"

Jamaica shook her head slightly, sending hair everywhere. "I asked you first."

Tameer exhaled forcibly and gathered his thoughts for several moments, before he began speaking. He didn't want to tell the story again, but since he had to, he wanted to tell it right. Finally, he turned toward her again.

"She wanted something different," he said, trying to sum up his previous relationship.

Jamaica wanted to know more. "Like what?"

"Like a life that I couldn't give her. Well, in all honesty, I could have given it to her. It would have made her happy, Pops happy, and everyone else happy...except me."

Jamaica sat up even further in bed. He had her attention. He knew that she wanted to know more.

"She wanted me to play sports," Tameer continued. "She said that she wanted to marry a professional athlete."

The thought made Jamaica snicker. "Child, if she only knew."

"Well, she broke up with me after I finished my freshman year in college, and showed her that I was determined to leave my sports playing at the high school level."

"She left you for that?" Jamaica's tiny nose crinkled, as she tried to contemplate the idea of leaving someone for such a reason.

Tameer nodded. "Uh-huh."

"Sounds like she was mental." Jamaica carefully adjusted the sheets around her body, and sat up even further. "So who came after her?"

Tameer smiled, and allowed his eyes to meet Jamaica's. "You."

"Me?" It took her by surprise. "But you broke up with her almost two years ago."

"Yeah." He nodded. "But I had been with her since middle school."

Tameer's glance fell to the bed. "Honestly, Jamaica, I hadn't thought of a life without her. It never occurred to me that we might not make it."

He lifted his head and again their eyes met. "I mean, don't get me wrong,

I dated after that, but it was always a four or five date thing. No rela-
tionships. I... I loved her." The words slipped out softly.

Jamaica closed her eyes and bit down softly on her bottom lip. Although
his words had been spoken softly, they had hit hard. She was afraid to
ask, what she knew that she had to ask. She was afraid of his answer.

"Do you still love her?" Her words slipped out as softly as his.

"Honestly?" Tameer asked, staring into her eyes.

The question made her turn her head away. Internally she braced herself. "Yeah, Tameer, honestly."

"The way it all went down still hurts a little, but...no."

Jamaica couldn't help the smile that crept across her face. Inside, she
was shouting and jumping for joy.

Tameer leaned forward and kissed her.

"I... I..." He tried to speak, but Jamaica placed her finger over his lips.

"Please don't say that," she pleaded. "Don't tell me that yet."

It made him swallow hard. "Why?" He had thought that she felt the same.

"Because I'm scared." It was a whisper.

"Why?" Tameer asked.

"Tameer, I don't know what's going to happen tomorrow. I don't know
what's going to happen next week."

"I'll be there," he told her.

"I... I..."

It was his turn to place his finger over her lips.

"It's only hard, if you make it hard." He stared into Jamaica's eyes.
"Jamaica, I'll be there."

She looked down. "How could she ever leave you? How could she have
ever let you go?"

"Trust me, it was easy." His smile lightened the mood. "All of those
gossiping, cackling, loudmouth friends that she worships, could convince
her to jump off a bridge."

Jamaica laughed. "So, where is she now?"

"Oh, she's in the Courts. Probably in somebody's business, as we speak."

"Tameer, what are Courts?" She felt more unknowledgeable than stupid.
She simply did not know.

"Um...projects. But only like two or three stories," Tameer explained. "More like flats, I guess."

Jamaica knew that if she asked what projects were, it would have only made her look stupid, or suspicious, or both. She accepted his answer.

"Oh, is that where you live?" she asked.

"Yeah." Tameer nodded.

"I wanna see."

"Why?"

"Because, I wanna see where you live," Jamaica pleaded. "Is it a sin?"

"I guess not, but I have to tell you about Pops first."

Jamaica nodded. "I remember, you caught him using drugs."

Tameer nodded, confirming what she'd remembered. "He's been going to treatment since we fought. It's a residential treatment program, so he's not at the apartment often, but he may show up while you're there. He's rough around the edges. A big, burly, union type of guy. Don't let him scare you."

Jamaica laughed. "If it's one thing I've learned, a big man, means a big heart. The bigger they are, the more gentle and fragile they are on the inside."

"Ha, not this guy! He's as hard as nails. My whole life I've been afraid of him. He's always driven me." Tameer tightened his fist and pounded the air. "Be the best, run faster, lift more, throw farther, run harder, catch better!"

Tameer lifted his head, and stared into Jamaica's eyes. "Have you ever been pushed? I mean, constantly pushed?"

Jamaica's face turned pale and became contorted as she thought of her childhood, as she thought of her mother. She, more than anyone else, understood what it meant to be pushed. She understood better than most, about having to follow someone else's dreams. Her half-smile that she pulled deep from within, hid her pain.

"Sounds like he had high hopes for you," she said softly.

"Yeah, he had high expectations of everybody, except himself. He drove my mother away."

Jamaica caressed Tameer's hand. "Maybe it wasn't his fault. Maybe she wanted to leave."

It was Tameer's turn to smile and hide his pain.

"I thought about that. But growing up, I convinced myself differently. I convinced myself that he made her go, because mothers just don't leave their children." Tameer's fist grew tight. "I hated him for that."

Jamaica caressed his chest. "Don't hate your father, Tameer. And don't give up on him, either. Good or bad, he's your father. Good or bad, he put a roof over your head, and food on the table. Good or bad, he made you into a nice, caring, kind, responsible, young man."

He turned toward her. "And you, Jamaica? Where is your knight in shining armor? C'mon, tell me what your story is?"

"I don't have one. I've dated, but the guys never saw past what was on the outside. They, well, most of them, would have been content to leave me inside of their cars. That way they would be able to hop in, ride around the block, and show us both off at the same time. You know, sometimes I felt like that. Like I was just another prized possession because of the way that I looked. I've never lain in anyone's arms and talked about family, or problems, or life in general."

"So I'm different?" Tameer smiled.

His smile made her smile.

"Yeah." Jamaica nodded. "You're different."

"Good different, or bad different."

"I like different. You wanna be my knight inside of a shiny new Mustang?"

"Yeah, I'll take you away from a life of bad dates," Tameer told her.

"And I'll rescue you from a gold digger, and her merry band of gossiping friends."

Together they laughed. After several moments, Tameer pulled his arm away.

"Hold on, Jai, I've got to go use the restroom real quick."

Tameer rose from the bed, and Jamaica quickly leaned over and pinched him on his derriere. Her pinch made him jump.

"Hey!" Tameer shouted. "I'm gonna pay you back for that when I get back."

Jamaica smiled. "Ummm, I like the sound of that! Any more ice?"

"I'll check," Tameer answered, as he left the room.

Jamaica waited for several seconds to make sure that he was gone, and then reached for the telephone. She punched the number to the motel with lightning speed, and waited impatiently for LaChina to pick up.

There was no answer.

Frustrated, Jamaica dialed the number to her friend's voice mail. "China, this is Jai. I need a scholarship... no change that. I need cash for Savion. I need it to get to him by tomorrow! Tameer's going to sell the car to get Savion some cash to go to school. Take care of it for me. Love ya, Jai."

Jamaica quickly hung up the telephone, frightened that she may have taken too long. Tameer walked into the room seconds later, with his hands hidden behind his back, and a devilish grin plastered across his face.

"What do you have?" Jamaica asked suspiciously.

Tameer's smile grew wider, and he shook the object that he had hidden behind his back. It clinked.

Jamaica smile, and threw open her arms welcoming him. "Ice cubes! My baby!"

She waved her hands at him seductively, motioning for him to join her. "Come to Mommy!"

Tameer leaped onto the bed with the glass, the ice cubes, and a big, wide grin.

Chapter Seventeen

Tameer pulled to his apartment, driving his straight-off-the-show-room-floor, bright-red, 2008 Shelby GT 500 Convertible Mustang.

The temperature outside was close to freezing, so the car's white convertible top was up. However, the resounding bass notes from the car's MACH stereo system could be heard clearly outside of the vehicle. Smiling broadly, Tameer honked his car's horn several times.

Savion opened the front door to the apartment, and looked outside in time to see the car's power window sliding down slowly.

"Tameer! You got down?" Savion knew that his brother had started selling drugs. It was the only obvious answer.

Shaking his head and smiling, Tameer exited his brand-new car. "You know better than that. I won this."

Savion smiled suspiciously. "You won it?"

"Yeah." Tameer nodded. "Trust me, everything is on the level."

"Well, bro, I guess luck runs in the family," Savion told him, as he shook his head in disbelief. "I just won a twenty thousand-dollar cash scholarship from some grocery store."

"What?"

Savion nodded again. "Yep, this morning."

This time it was Tameer who shook his head. "This can't be real."

Savion turned toward the Mustang, and waved his hand over it. "Bro, this is real."

Tameer scratched his head. "I guess you're right."

Tameer frowned as he thought of the oddness of it all. His family had never been this lucky. Heck, his family had never really had any luck at all. Jai was right, things did work out. He would be able to keep the car after all. He shifted his gaze to Savion. "Well, Save, you need to put the money in the bank and use it while you're in school."

"I know." Savion smiled. He turned and faced the car. "And now I see that I have a way to get to the bank." Savion held out his palm for keys.

Tameer laughed and placed his arm around his brother. Together, they walked happily back inside of the apartment.

Across the street, Shamika bolted from the window to her bed, and grabbed her telephone. Her hands dialed at the speed of a Formula One race car.

"Hello?"

"Girl, put Dawshanique on the phone!" It was a shout.

"Hold on," replied Joniece, Dawshanique's younger sister. Her shouting could be heard over the phone line.

It took only a few moments for Dawshanique to pick up.

"Hello?"

"Yeah, girl, this is Shamika! I got some news for you!"

"What?"

"Girl, Mr. Tameer Harris just pulled up in a brand-new, bright-red convertible!"

"You lying!" Dawshanique quickly lost all pretense of disinterest.

"My right hand, girl! A brand-new one," Shamika replied.

"Hold on, girl, I'mma grab my Blue Book." Dawshanique set her phone down for several moments, while she retrieved her book on automobile values.

"Okay, I'm back," she finally told Shamika. "So what page are you on?" she asked, knowing that Shamika had already appraised the vehicle's worth.

"Girl, it's on page eighty-nine, Shelby GT 500 Convertible."

Together they flipped pages.

"Okay, I've found it," Dawshanique told her. "Convertible, huh? Forty-seven thousand."

"If fully loaded, sports package, performance package, and everything else, fifty-two thousand. And, Dawshanique... It looks fully loaded."

"Goddamn, is he in the game?" Dawshanique asked.

"Uh-un, no change in clothes, no expensive jewelry, and besides, you know Tameer is a goody-two shoes."

Dawshanique exhaled loudly. She knew that Shamika was right. But where on Earth had Tameer gotten the money for a car like that? It was puzzling. Worse than that, it was frustrating.

"Right, so what about a league?" Dawshanique asked. "League Football?"

"Ain't happening," Shamika answered. She had detailed files on those types of things. "Not right now, anyway."

"So where did the money come from?"

"That's a good question," Shamika answered. She thought hard for several moments, before coming to a conclusion. "Hell, it doesn't matter, anyway, you just get your ass in gear. And you better hurry before all these hoes in the hood find out." Shamika smacked her lips. "A man with a new car, girl... friendship is nice but..."

"I know, I know. I'm getting dressed as we speak," Dawshanique replied. She knew the rules of the jungle. She could already see several of her home girls circling the vehicle like sharks. But it didn't make sense.

"Mr. Tameer," Dawshanique wondered out loud. "New car, new bitch, but no new job. What's going on?"

Flashbulbs went off inside of Shamika's head. "Uh-un, it couldn't be!"

"What?" Dawshanique asked.

"Just what you said. New car, new bitch," Shamika explained. "You think this ho bought the car?"

"Not unless she's confused." Dawshanique laughed. "It's the niggaz who buy the cars, we just drive 'em."

"Well, do you think it's hers, and maybe he's just driving it?" Shamika suggested.

Dawshanique liked the sound of it. Instantly, she became more animated. "That may be it! Tameer's taking her to the cleaners!"

"Well, that means one of two things," Shamika explained. "One, he's got this Barbie doll who's paying out of her ass and letting him drive her new car. This could mean that you don't stand a chance. Two, it could be your win, if you can get him to cough up everything she gives him. Hell, get him back, let him keep her, he gets the car, and brings it home to us... I mean, you."

"Ooooh, girl, I didn't think about it like that, good idea!"

"Uh-oooh!"

"What?" Dawshanique asked.

"Shawntae just walked her big butt ass by the apartment, and was eyeballing out man's... I mean, your man's car. Girl, you better move something!"

"I'm on my way out the door, I'll call you later!"

"Bye!"

"Bye!"

"LaChina!" Jamaica shouted from the motel's bedroom.

"Hold on, girl, I'm coming," LaChina shouted from the bathroom.

Jamaica placed her hand on her hip as the bathroom toilet flushed. Soon, LaChina emerged from the bathroom.

Jamaica smiled. "China, I just moved some of your papers off the bed, and well, I glanced at a few lines..."

LaChina quickly rushed to the bed and gathered her assortment of loose papers. "You've always been nosy, Jai. Always. You have no right to rumble through my things!"

"China, I didn't rumble," Jamaica replied. "I was going to lie down, so I was trying to move them. My eye glanced across the papers and I saw Sea World, location, and some other key words."

Suddenly, Jamaica stopped explaining. A frown appeared, and she extended the palm of her hand toward LaChina's face. "Wait a minute. You think you're a smart bitch, don't you? You get me on the defensive, you make me feel guilty, and then I can't ask you what I want to ask. And you know what I'm going to ask you, but you don't want to answer."

LaChina gathered her papers, and then pretended to be in deep concentration as she organized them.

Jamaica placed her hand on her hip again, this time shifting her weight to one side. "Why don't you want to answer questions about Sea World, China?"

LaChina looked up quickly, causing her hair to fall down over her face. She shook her head and tossed her hair back over her shoulder, then outstretched her hands, palms skyward.

"I don't know what you're talking about, Jai," she replied nervously. Her eyes darted back and forth across the room, in an effort to avoid eye contact with Jamaica.

"Yes, you do." Jamaica was calm, serene. Her mood and tone scared LaChina even more.

"Jai, you haven't asked me any questions!"

Jamaica folded her arms and again shifted her weight. "What's the deal with Sea World?"

"It's... It's a theme park. An aquatic theme park that showcases various..."

"That's not what I mean!" Jamaica stomped her foot on the ground hard. "You're trying to set up another promo, right?"

Jamaica pointed her tiny finger accusingly at LaChina. "You are, aren't you? Where, San Diego? Orlando?"

LaChina shook her head from side to side. "No, Jai, I'm not."

Jamaica wasn't buying it.

"You're lying!" Jamaica declared flatly. She turned, and slowly walked away from her friend. After several paces, Jamaica quickly wheeled and faced LaChina again. "Put it on sisterhood!"

LaChina raised her hand. "Sisterhood, Jai."

It had been said quickly. A little too quickly for Jamaica's comfort.

Jamaica pointed her finger at LaChina again. "Say the clubhouse pledge!"

"Jai!"

"Say it!"

LaChina turned away. "Jai, I'm not going to recite some pledge we made up when we were six years old!"

"Ah-hah!" Jamaica shouted while pointing at her friend. "You're lying!" After a brief moment of thought, Jamaica shook her head. "No, you're telling the truth technically, but you're lying in spirit, because you won't say the pledge."

Jamaica frowned, arched her back, and balled her fist. She began to speak in the lowest, deepest voice that she could conjure. "You're a disgrace to the Sisterhood or The Treehouse Chipmunks."

LaChina began bouncing up and down frantically, and flapping her hands near her sides. "Jai, don't say that!"

"I'm calling Tammy, I'm calling Erika, I'm calling Portia, Tamara, Naivasha, Germany, and all of the other clubhouse chipmunks, and we're going to initiate..."

LaChina quickly covered her ears and began to shout. "Don't say it! Don't say it! Alright, alright, I'll tell you. Just don't take away my nose. I had to kiss Piggy Parker for my Chipmunk nose!"

"Alright, then answer!" Jamaica pointed toward the bed. "Sit!"

LaChina sat instantly.

"Am I going to have to do another Sea World promo?" Jamaica asked.

LaChina looked down. "No."

"China?"

"Noooo," LaChina whined. "It's...it's a whale video," she whispered.

Jamaica leaned forward and cupped her hand around her ear. "It's a what?"

LaChina pouted, sticking out her bottom lip as she stared at the floor. "A whale video."

"A whale video!" Jamaica's hands quickly flew toward LaChina's neck. "But, Jai, sisterhoo..."

"Who is it?" Tameer shouted through the door.

"It's Dawshanique," the voice on the other side of the door declared.

Tameer wasn't quite sure that he had heard the name correctly. It sounded like someone had said "Dawshanique," which to him was impossible. He had to ask again.

"Who?"

"It's me, Dawshanique."

Slowly, Tameer opened the front door, and standing before him was his first true love. Dawshanique had managed to make herself look rather presentable, in the short period of time that she had to get ready. Tameer was much taken aback at how wonderful she looked. He had to try very hard to suppress his smile.

Dawshanique presented to him her best sad and sincere look. She had been practicing it in the mirror for days.

"Tameer, I need to talk to you," she said softly.

Tameer's eyes blinked rapidly at the sound of her voice. He hadn't heard it in a long time. It sounded good.

So, she wanted to talk, huh? Tameer turned and quickly examined the state of the apartment. It was decent, okay for company, but still, he chose to step outside. Closing the door behind himself, he offered Dawshanique a nervous half-smile.

"What's up?" he asked, his voice cracking.

Dawshanique stepped forward. She was now standing intimately close to Tameer. "Well, I didn't have this in mind." She turned and stared at his car. "I mean, I know that you have guests."

He saw what she was staring at, and shook his head. "Oh no, it's mines."

Dawshanique exhaled loudly. *Good*, she told herself, *now that that's confirmed, down to business*. She lifted her arms slowly and hugged him, breaking into tears at the same time.

"Tameer, I'm sorry. I never meant to hurt you, or to...to... Tameer, I miss you so much." She began sobbing heavily. "I wanted the best for you, for us, but now I see how much your education meant to you. Tameer, I want to make things right. I need you, I need to hold you. Oh, Tameer!"

Dawshanique laid her head against his chest and continued her sobbing. Tameer looked down at her, and rubbed his hand gently across her micro braids.

"It's okay. It's okay," Tameer whispered. He leaned down and kissed Dawshanique on her forehead. He could taste her sweetness on his lips, he could smell her familiarity. It felt good having her in his arms again.

"Oh, Tameer...," she cried out again.

Tameer swallowed hard, and cleared his throat. "Dawshanique, hold on for a minute." He sniffled. "I need to get something."

Slowly, she pulled away from him and nodded. Dawshanique lifted her hands to her face, and wiped away her tears. *Bring the keys with you, sucker*, she didn't say out loud. She sniffled several times.

Tameer stepped back inside of the apartment, locked the door, and placed the chain across it. Slowly, he sauntered across the floor of the apartment, and sat back down on his living room couch, where he lifted the remote for the television. He was tired. His fatigue made him yawn.

Propping his feet up onto the coffee table, he channel-surfed leisurely, until finding something of interest to watch.

Outside, Dawshanique, who had heard the lock and the chain, began knocking.

"Tameer. Tameer. Tameer!" She began pounding on the door forcefully. "Tameer! Tameer, open up the door! It's not funny! Tameer, it's cold out here! Tameer! Tameer! Tameeeeeer!"

Chapter Eighteen

"Jai, I can't believe you wanted to come here," Tameer told her, as he climbed inside of the roller coaster.

"It's off season, it's not crowded, and it's fun!" Jamaica replied.

"Fun?"

"You're scared, admit it."

"I'm not scared. This is like any other roller coaster, except that it's wooden which means that it's susceptible to termites...and rot...and it could collapse on us."

Jamaica pointed at Tameer and laughed. "I knew it! You're scared."

"I don't like heights."

Jamaica slapped Tameer across his shoulder. "You big baby!" She buckled her restraints, and then turned back toward him "Don't worry, I'll protect you."

Tameer could only smile as the roller coaster lurched forward. "You'll protect me as we both plunge to our deaths. Wonderful!"

"So did you enjoy yourself at the amusement park?" Jamaica asked. She snatched the car keys from Tameer's hand.

"Of course I did!" he lied.

Jamaica pressed the button on Tameer's key fob, disarming the car's alarm system. "Are you sure? You looked a little sick after we got off the roller coaster."

Tameer smiled through clenched teeth. "Oh yeah, which time?"

Jamaica laughed. "All of them."

When they approached Tameer's vehicle, Jamaica raced to the driver's side.

"You know that I'm driving, don't you?" Jamaica asked. She lifted her gloved hands, and tucked a fallen strand of hair back beneath her thick, multi-colored bini.

Tameer smiled. He wrapped his arms around Jamaica and pressed his body against hers. He leaned forward and kissed her on her cheek.

Jamaica smiled and rested her head gently upon his chest. "What did I tell you about that?"

"About what?"

"Don't start anything that you can't finish," she said softly.

Tameer engulfed her earlobe, and slowly made his way down her neck. The warmth of his tongue made her close her eyes and moan. Tameer stepped away from Jamaica and laughed.

"Okay." Jamaica nodded. "Okay, so you want to play?"

Tameer stepped forward again, and placed his arms on her shoulders. "You know I'm just messing with you."

Jamaica extended her palm to his face. "I'm not trying to hear it."

Jamaica turned away from Tameer and opened the driver's side door. Still smiling, Tameer quickly made his way to the other side of the vehicle and opened the door. Jamaica called to him over the top of the vehicle.

"Tameer, have you heard that song by Bobby Womack?"

"What song?"

Jamaica began singing. *If you think you're lonely now, wait until tonight, baby.* Jamaica threw her head back in laughter, and slid into the driver's seat.

Tameer slid into the passenger seat and clasped her hand. "Relax, baby, it was just jokes."

Jamaica continued singing the song, while buckling her seatbelt and starting up the vehicle. She turned to Tameer and smiled. "Babe, you better buckle up."

The tires screeched.

"So why do you insist on seeing where I live?" Tameer asked for the fifth time in ten minutes.

Jamaica turned another corner and exhaled forcibly. She was clearly growing more and more frustrated with Tameer's obstinacy. "Tameer, you may as well tell me which apartment is yours, or we'll be circling this place all night."

Jamaica was determined.

Tameer understood Jamaica's determination. In fact, he had come to appreciate it. The worst was now over, he had convinced himself. And the fact that she was already in the neighborhood, alleviated some of his concern. He finally relented.

"Stop right here," he told her.

Jamaica slammed her foot onto the brake pedal, sending the car into a screeching halt. Tameer shook his head and smiled at her.

"Not right here." He pointed. "I meant up there. The next building."

Jamaica parked the car in front of Tameer's building, and together they exited the vehicle. Tameer uttered several quick, silent prayers under his breath, hoping that his father would not be home. He didn't need the drama, especially in front of Jamaica. Tameer's second prayer was that even if his father wasn't home right now, he hoped that he'd not been there earlier and trashed the place. Broken beer bottles and piss in the corner of the living room, would not make a good first impression. He sighed, and hesitantly searched his key ring for the proper key.

Jamaica clapped her hands together under the guise of warming them from the evening cold, although it really had been done out of nervous anticipation. She wanted to know more about Tameer. She wanted to know everything about Tameer. Jamaica turned away from the front door and examined her surrounding. She wanted to take it all in, but the darkness that cloaked the housing project of that starless evening revealed little.

The air was cold, crisp. It caused their breaths to crystallize in the moist night air and mimic the puffiness of cigar smoke. Finally, Tameer opened the door to his apartment, to his world. Jamaica could feel the warmth oozing from the apartment past her, and into the night air. She closed her eyes, counted to three, and then slowly turned around.

Tameer's father had not been home. The apartment was fairly decent, with the exception of the mess made by Savion and his basketball buddies who were gathered inside of the living room. Their presence made Jamaica adjust her bini, pulling it down almost to her eyes. She wrapped the scarf around her neck twice more, covering the lower half of her face. She wasn't taking any chances. Savion spoke first.

"What's up, T?" Savion asked, greeting his brother.

Tameer pulled off his jacket. "Hey, what's up, y'all?"

"What's up, Jai?" Savion asked.

Jamaica waved. "Hey, what's up?"

Jamaica turned, and began to examine her surroundings. She had never been inside of a place such as this. She wanted to take it all in. Surprisingly, it didn't look that bad to her. In fact, she thought, it only needed a little straightening, perhaps some new furnishings, but overall, it was habitable.

Jamaica casually strolled across the room to the far wall, the one farthest away from the door, and examined the photographs that hung haphazardly on it. They had not been attended to for some time, and were crooked, old, abandoned, almost as if they had been of another family. Tameer was younger, when they were taken. His large, out-of-style afro told her that much. The photo of him sporting a large Jheri Curl made her snicker. She knew that the older woman in the picture had to be his mother, and the man in the picture, his father. He resembled them both. Again, she laughed, because initially, it had not been a good mixture. Tameer had been homely as a child.

The bounce of the basketball startled her.

"Vonnie, don't you go anywhere without that basketball?" Tameer asked.

"Nope," Vonnie answered matter-of-factly. "I'm trying to get as good as you."

Vonnie was tall, thin, young. He sat on the couch lost inside of a large down-filled parka, with his face buried beneath his monstrous afro. A large, black, plastic hair pick hung defiantly out of his hair, seemingly determined not to get lost.

"Never!" Tameer replied. He held out his hands, waiting for Vonnie to toss him the basketball.

Vonnie tossed it. "As a matter of fact, I think I can out-hoop you now," Vonnie told him. It was a challenge made with a smile.

Tameer caught the speeding ball. "Not in your wildest dreams, kid!" Tameer bounced the ball and passed it between his legs several times, displaying his skills.

Vonnie waved him off. "Tameer, you're a fossil already!"

Vonnie stretched out his long, spindly legs, placing them on the coffee table. "Me, I'm in my prime."

Tameer turned to Jamaica. "That's Lil' Fade," he said, startling her.

Jamaica wasn't aware that anyone had been paying attention to her. She had become entranced by the picture.

Lil' Fade's eyes were like sparkling blue diamonds, and his skin was grotesquely pale. His hair was long and curly, almost feminine, as were his facial features. But his eyes, his eyes were frightening. His eyes were cold, penetrating, unrelenting. His eyes made her shiver.

"The one on the left, that's my mom," Tameer told her.

Jamaica nodded, examined the picture for several moments, and then turned to him. "She's beautiful."

Tameer nodded. "I know."

Jamaica turned and walked toward the kitchen. She wanted desperately to finish her examination of the house. She wanted to see, to discover, and deep down, to uncover. She wanted all of Tameer's secrets. Her mission was interrupted.

Jamaica screamed when Tameer sneaked up from behind and grabbed her. Easily, he lifted her from the ground, high into the air, and twirled her around.

"Ahhh! Tameer, stop!" Jamaica gripped his arms tightly. "Put me down!" she shouted in between her bursts of laughter.

Tameer laughed as well. He turned her through the air twice more, and then gently placed her back onto the ground. She instantly sat down on one of the metal folding chairs inside of the dining room. She refused to be lifted into the air again.

Jamaica kicked Tameer softly when he came close. "Boy, you better not do that again!"

"I won't."

Tameer extended his hand to her and she took it. Gently, he lifted her from the chair and pulled her close. He wrapped his arms around Jamaica, stared into her eyes, and leaned forward to kiss her. Jamaica closed her eyes and leaned forward. Tameer quickly lifted her into the air again.

"Tameer!"

He twirled Jamaica again, and then sat her down on the cheap, metal, folding table and maneuvered himself in between her thighs. She slapped him on his shoulder.

"Okay, you're going to pay for that one." She nodded. "The first one was free, but the second one, uh-un."

Tameer placed his hands on Jamaica's tiny waist and kissed her neck. "Are you ready to go?"

Jamaica shook her head. "No, I'm staying here tonight."

Tameer smacked his lips and rolled his eyes around the room. "Man, Jamaica, what are you trying to prove?"

Jamaica knew how to handle this one. She was learning how to work Tameer. She folded her arms and pouted.

"I want to stay with you."

Tameer's hands flew to his face and he rubbed his eyes. His mind raced, as he thought about the current situation in the Courts. Who were these guys into it with, and would there be any gunfire tonight? Drive-bys had been on the decline lately, and he really couldn't think of any group in particular that the Courts was at war with.

Tameer knew that he couldn't allow Jamaica to get hurt, he knew that he had to protect her. For the first time in a long time, he had someone who trusted him, someone who really believed in him. He wasn't going to let her down. She would be safe here with him tonight.

Tameer opened his eyes and nodded. "Okay, Jamaica, you can stay."

"Yes!" Her arms flew around his neck and she hugged him.

Chapter Nineteen

J amaica awoke to the sound of a clanging, whining, screeching, rattling garbage truck, inhaling refuse from one of the neighborhood dumpsters. She yawned, stretched, and examined her surroundings.

Tameer's room was fairly neat, if one was to discount the scattered, crumpled pieces of paper which orbited the cheap, plastic, white trash can that occupied the corner. The brick walls were painted in a thick, industrial white, while the floor was covered with a thin, cheap grade of commercial carpeting. It was not unlike the kind one would find inside of a bank branch, a school, or a hospital corridor. It was a far cry from the plush, almost cotton-like materials that graced the inner sanctums of where Jamaica had grown up and played. Nevertheless, it did its job, she thought, as she emerged from the comfort of the bed and ventured onto the floor.

Jamaica flounced her long, silky, but now disorderly, tresses over her shoulder, and stretched once again. It was with this stretch that the realization of her nakedness came. A quick turn of her head reassured her that Tameer was in fact gone, and that she was alone.

Again relaxing, she strode over to the full-length mirror on the wall opposite the bed, and smiling, she examined her flawlessness.

Jamaica's stomach was flat and tight, her breasts were round and perky, and her teeth were as pearly as ever. Clearly, she liked what she saw. Her frame was chiseled, yet petite and feminine. She had lost some weight in the preceding months, as a result of her hectic schedule. In fact, she had lost enough weight for her to be concerned about her shapely figure.

Quickly, she turned to the side and glanced down. Yes! She still had plenty back there, she told herself.

Her personal trainer, the balanced diets, and the years of strict, self-willed discipline had paid off. She was perfect. Or rather yet, still perfect, she corrected. Jamaica rubbed her silky-smooth, caramel skin, and again turned to her side. Thirty-six, twenty-four, thirty-eight. Perfect! Perfect! Perfect! Perfect!

A childlike smile appeared, followed by another rapid glance around the room to reassure herself that she was in fact alone. After this quick confirmation, she began a dance routine. Flouncing, jumping, spinning, and singing, Jamaica unwound. She jumped onto Tameer's bed and continued her unbridled, liberating performance, until finally, she was startled by a knock at the door. Jamaica's eyes flew wide, and she dove beneath the covers. A second knock came.

"Jamaica?" the voice on the other side of the door called out to her. It was Savion.

Now even more embarrassed, Jamaica cleared her throat and peered out from beneath the bed linen. "Yes?"

Savion slowly pushed open the door to the bedroom. "T said to tell you that he had to go in early, but he left some money for you to get something to eat."

"Tameer's gone?" she asked in disbelief.

Savion nodded. "Yeah."

"How am I supposed to get back to my room?"

Savion smiled. "He left some bus money for you in case you had to leave. But, he told me to tell you that he would like for you to wait for him here."

Jamaica's hands flew through the air. "Just where am I supposed to get something to eat, and how am I supposed to get there?"

Another smile. "I'm going to walk with you."

Jamaica's mouth fell slightly open. "Walk?" *I have a Lamborghini, two Ferraris, a Bentley, an Aston Martin, a Rolls, and a Porsche, and I'm supposed to walk? The boy was crazy!*

Savion could see that Jamaica was growing upset. "It's not far."

Jamaica placed her hand on her forehead and exhaled forcibly. "Savion, I'll be downstairs in a minute. I'm going to shower first."

Savion nodded, and began to close the door.

"Hey!" Jamaica shouted. She pointed to a garment lying on a chair next to the door. "Toss me that shirt before you go, please."

The smile on Savion's face slowly disappeared, as he grabbed the shirt and tossed it to her. He had been hoping to see her dance around the room naked again. Disappointed, he closed the door, and settled for watching Jamaica get dressed through a peephole next to the door.

When Jamaica finally appeared downstairs, Savion was still cleaning up the residuals from the previous night's excesses. The festive gatherings had become a nightly ritual, since he and his friends had been out of school for the Christmas holiday break.

Jamaica was dressed mostly in Tameer's clothing, as she had not brought along a change of clothing for herself. She exhaled and plopped down forcefully upon the tattered, brown, living room couch.

"So, what's up, Jai?" Savion asked while picking up pieces of popcorn from off the floor.

"Nothing, just bored." She blew loose strands of hair from her face.

After several moments of watching Savion work, Jamaica rose from the couch, dropped to one knee, and began gathering fallen popcorn kernels. Savion moved in close and nudged her.

"How can you be bored?" he asked. "You're with the Save-ster!"

Jamaica laughed. "Ohhh, really? And is the Save-ster going to entertain me with one of his rap performances from last night?"

"I may." Savion smiled. *Especially if you get naked and dance for me again*, he didn't say out loud.

"Do you have one of those straw brush thingys?" Jamaica asked. "You know, this would go a lot faster if you could brush this stuff away."

"Good idea!" Savion disappeared momentarily, and returned with a broom. Triumphantly, he held it up in the air. "I have found the straw brush thingy to sweep with."

Jamaica turned and looked for something to sweep the popcorn onto. Spying a folder on the end of the coffee table, she lifted it, accidentally spilling its contents.

"Dang!" she cursed, kneeling down and gathering the fallen papers. "I'm making a bigger mess than the one we're trying to clean."

While kneeling and gathering the papers, Jamaica glanced at the contents of several of the loose sheets of paper. Reading them, she rose slowly.

"This...this is good." She turned toward Savion. "Your brother's?"

Savion nodded. "Yeah, that's probably some of his older stuff. He keeps the new stuff in his room."

"Why hasn't he published this?" she asked, raking her hand through her hair, sending it back over her shoulder. "I mean...it's really good."

Savion shrugged. "You know how T is."

Jamaica nodded and continued to read.

Savion swept the popcorn into a pile, and then swept the pile toward the door. Jamaica extended her arm and waved her hand around to get Savion's attention.

"Savion, go and get me the rest of Tameer's poetry." She peered up at him. "Is there a copying machine around here?"

Savion nodded. "Yeah, it's on the way to where I'm going to take you to eat."

"And where is that?" Jamaica inquired.

"Slim's Smokehouse. The best barbecue in the entire world."

"Well, I guess we'll be eating barbecue and reading poetry today," she told him with a smile.

"Jai, what's on your mind?" Savion asked. He shifted his weight to one side and waited for her answer. Savion loved to be part of a plot. Any plot.

Jamaica tapped the pages of poetry that she held in her hand. "I'm going to send your brother's poetry to a friend of mine. There's this big poetry contest in New York every year, and the winner gets twenty thousand dollars and a publishing contract." She peered up at Savion. "Your brother can win."

Savion shrugged. "Good. I'll get his poetry journal, you finish sweeping."

"Savion!"

Savion extended his arm, handing her the broom. The two of them stood staring silently at each other for several moments before Jamaica finally snatched the broom from him and frowned.

"I see stubbornness runs in the family!" Jamaica fumed.

Savion smiled, winked, and then bounded up the stairs to retrieve the poetry journal. Jamaica set the pages of poetry down upon a nearby table, and then began using the straw brush thingy. Using one hand she raked and struggled with the broom until she was finally able to gather all of the popcorn by the door. She cursed the entire time.

Opening the door, Jamaica was surprised by the presence of a stranger about to knock. It was Dawshanique.

"Yes, I'm looking for Savion," Dawshanique announced, while placing her hand on her hip. "Well, actually, I'm looking for Tameer, but I see that his car is gone, so, is Savion here?"

Jamaica nodded. "Yes, he ran upstairs to grab something."

Jamaica turned toward the stairs, as Savion was coming back down. "Savion..."

Jamaica was interrupted by Dawshanique.

"Savion, you got a cute little girlfriend here," Dawshanique shouted. "She even cleans up for you and everything. So, where is my baby at?"

Savion's mouth fell open in silence. Jamaica quickly spun back toward Dawshanique.

"I'm not Savion's girlfriend," Jamaica told her.

Dawshanique waved Jamaica off. "Ooooh, girl, I'm sorry. I should have known you was a little too old. But, you never can tell these days."

Dawshanique slung her micro braids over her shoulders. "My man sure has come up. New car, and now he's getting maid service!" Dawshanique snapped her fingers in the air. "You go, boy!"

Jamaica released the broom that she held in her hand, allowing it to fall to the ground. Her hand flew to her hip as she recoiled. "Baby, I'm not Tameer, nor anyone else's maid!"

Savion quickly maneuvered himself in between them. "Uh, Dawshanique, Tameer's at work right now. He'll be back later."

Dawshanique veered around Savion, and came face-to-face with Jamaica. "Oh, you must be..." Dawshanique smacked her lips. "You must be Tameer's little temporary play thing!"

Dawshanique's palm flew into the air, stopping just in front of Jamaica's face. "Well, Little Ms. Flavor of the Month, December's almost over, so you can start packing your shit. Momma's home!"

Jamaica shoved Savion to the side, and then knocked Dawshanique's hand away. She extended her finger into Dawshanique's face, while placing her other hand on her hip. "Well, momma, first off, I'm nobody's play thing. Second, you're standing on the outside looking in, and asking me where your supposed-to-be man is at! Third, I know where he is, and I damn sure knew where he was last night!"

Jamaica popped the collar on Tameer's oversized, button-down dress shirt. "Check the clothes, and smell the scent, because this is about the closest you'll ever get to Tameer again!"

"Bitch!" Dawshanique shouted, as she reached for Jamaica.

Savion jumped in the way.

"Bitch?" Jamaica shook her head. "Uh-un, let her go, Savion! Let her go!"

Dawshanique struggled to break free from Savion's grasp. "Bitch, if I catch you, you can give your heart to God, and your ass to me!"

Jamaica quickly exited the apartment. "Let her go, Savion!"

Jamaica tried to maneuver around Savion's imposing frame. Jamal, one of Savion's friends from last night's gathering, quickly raced from next door and grabbed Jamaica. Jamaica kicked and screamed.

"Uh-un, let me go! That bitch wants to fight me, and well... I got to give the people what they want!"

Vonnie quickly ran up into the yard. Together, he and Jamal were able to push Jamaica back inside of the apartment.

"You fake bitch!" Dawshanique shouted from the street. "You better stay away from my man!"

Jamaica clawed at the door sill, not wanting to enter all the way into the apartment. She was ready to fight. "Fake? Fake? Somebody please tell this heifer that synthetic braids and fake gold beads been out of style!"

The apartment door was closed.

Chapter Twenty

Jamaica shivered slightly, though not from the cold. She folded her arms as she walked through the streets of the Courts toward the neighborhood store. Another glance around at the desolation caused a second shiver. She turned toward Savion.

"So how long have you lived in this neighborhood?"

"As far as I can remember," Savion answered. His large, oversized, suede hiking boots kicked a rock in front of them, sending it skipping over the roughly paved, cracked, trash-strewn street.

"I grew up in the Courts," he added. It was said without pride, yet at the same time, there existed no shame in his declaration.

Jamaica stepped over a huge, jagged pothole filled with muddy water, and glanced down a nearby street. *They are all the same*, she thought. *The buildings are all the same. The streets are no different, either.*

The cheap, brown, industrial paint that covered the cement block buildings did little to hide the desolation. The broken-out windows, the disrepaired, pebble-paved streets, and numerous broken-down vehicles scattered throughout, all revealed to Jamaica a different world. A world which she knew nothing about. A world in which she felt lost, and even small. She was ashamed that she had never been to a place like this, and even more ashamed at the previous amount of thought which she had given its tenants.

"There's the hood park." Savion pointed. "That's where I sky over all them fools when I'm hooping, including your boyfriend." Savion smiled.

Jamaica returned Savion's smile. She nudged him slightly with her shoulder. "You haven't met Air Jamaica yet, have you?"

"Air Jamaica?" Savion waved her off. "Girl, you can't ball!"

Jamaica grabbed his arm and pulled him close. "I can out-ball you," she declared. "I played a little hoops in high school."

Laughing, Savion balled his fist and covered his mouth. "Yeah, right! You hooping, I'd like to see that!"

Jamaica extended her hand. "Deal?"

Savion shook it. "Deal!"

Together they entered inside of the neighborhood store. It was a small mom-and-pop shop, with a barbecue stand attached to the side of it. Moms ran the store, while Pops handled the barbecue. The smell of burning mesquite wood and sweet barbecue sauce hung thick in the air. It made Jamaica's mouth water. Inhaling dramatically, she extended her arms toward the ceiling.

"Mmmm, smells like Heaven," she declared.

"Tastes like it too," the stranger behind the counter told her.

He was a rotund, chubby-jowled, freckle-faced, elderly man, with a shiny bald head. His smile was disarming, easy, and ever ready, yet his voice was deep, booming, fatherly. He wiped his hands on his white apron, further smearing it with sauce, and smiled again.

"How can I help you kids?" His eyes twinkled and disappeared when he smiled.

"Hey, Slim," Savion greeted. "Where's your glasses?"

"Oh, Savion, that you?" Slim asked. "I just broke 'em a little while ago, and I can't see a damn thing without 'em. What do you need today, Poppa?"

"The usual, but make it two," Savion answered.

"You got it!" Slim's massive hand slapped the counter and he disappeared.

Jamaica smiled, leaned forward, and tugged Savion's shirt. "I see you come here often."

Savion nodded. "Best barbecue in the world."

"I'll see."

Slim returned to the counter with two folded paper sacks, and handed them to Savion. In turn, Savion handed Slim a ten-dollar bill.

"Keep the change, Slim," Savion told him.

Slim's smile made his twinkling eyes disappear again. "That's why I like you."

Jamaica and Savion laughed.

"Y'all enjoy and come back soon!" Slim told them, slapping the counter once again. He quickly disappeared into the rear of the store.

"Alright, Slim, thanks." Savion waved, and then turned and gazed around the smoky establishment, searching for a table. He found one in the rear of the dining area and headed over to it.

Jamaica took in her surrounding. She quickly deduced that Slim wasn't much for accoutrement. In fact, the word *minimal* would have been an understatement. Savion turned toward her and stated the obvious.

"We'll eat here."

Jamaica shrugged. "Okay." She'd try anything once. For now.

Jamaica rubbed her stomach and turned toward Savion. "That was absolutely the best barbecue that I have ever tasted. And I've tasted barbecue all over the world!"

Jamaica outstretched her arms and spun around. "I'm full!" She shouted to no on in particular.

It made Savion smile. They turned onto a side street that ran parallel to the neighborhood playground. It was the swings that attracted Jamaica's attention. She tugged at the sleeves of Savion's hooded black FUBU sweatshirt and nodded her head toward the playground.

"C'mon," she told him.

Before he could reply, Jamaica was off.

"I thought you said that you were full?" Savion called out to her.

Jamaica nodded. "I am, that's why I need to sit down!"

Jamaica plopped onto a swing and Savion walked around the swing and stood behind her. He examined her butt, which hung slightly off the small swing seat, and then grabbed the chains that held the seat. He pulled her back as far as he could, and then pushed her forward, propelling her high into the air. Jamaica outstretched her legs and leaned back, as the swing thrust her forward.

"You're going to get sick," Savion told her. "You better not throw up on me!"

"Yuck!" Jamaica turned toward him. "I can't believe you said that!"

"Just don't do it!"

"So, where's your little girlfriend at?" she asked, propelling herself forward.

"Which one?"

Her head swung around toward him. "Oh, it's like that, is it?"

Savion smiled. "Well, it would be very selfish not to share the Save-ster."

Jamaica shook her head and rolled her eyes. "Oh brother, not another wannabe player!"

Savion gave her a forceful shove, propelling her high into the air.

"Aaaaaah!" Jamaica screamed. "Stop that!"

"I'm not a wannabe anything!" Savion proclaimed, and then shoved her again, sending her even higher into the air.

"Okay, okay! I take it back!" Jamaica shouted.

Savion let her swing high into the air twice more, before grabbing the chain and slowing the swing down.

Jamaica dragged her feet along the ground, helping to slow the swing down further. "Boy, if I was your sister, I would kick your butt!"

Savion laughed and raised his fist into the air. "I don't think you could handle these."

"Oh, yeah?" Jamaica asked. She hopped off the swing and grabbed Savion, placing him in a head lock. "Did I tell you that I learned to wrestle in Europe?"

Savion placed his arms behind Jamaica's thighs, and scooped her high into the air. "Did I tell you I learned to wrestle watching Stone Cold Steve Austin?" He spun Jamaica around rapidly.

She screamed and clasped him tightly. "Put me down, boy!"

After a couple of turns, Savion sat her down on solid ground.

"You're alright, Jamaica." He nodded. "I think I like you."

"Well, I guess that's a compliment. So I guess that I like you too." Jamaica brushed her hands along her pants leg, and then her sweatshirt, straightening them both out.

"I've never had a big sis." Savion lifted an eyebrow toward her. "I guess a big sister-in-law would be cool."

Jamaica continued brushing her sweatshirt. "Well, I don't know about all that."

Savion stretched, popping his back. "My brother needs you. He loves you."

Jamaica smiled. She also became very curious. "Why do you say that?"

Savion placed his hand against the supporting bar for the swing and leaned against it. "I've noticed the change in him. He's happier."

"Really?" Jamaica's smile grew wider. She wanted to pick Savion for information, so she feigned surprise. The acting made her feel as though she were in grammar school again.

Savion shrugged his shoulders. "Yeah, and besides...he told me."

Jamaica waved Savion off. "Get out of here."

"I'm serious," Savion replied. "So, tell me this..."

"What?" she asked, still gushing.

Savion stood straight, and approached her slowly. "When are you leaving, and are you going to stay in touch with T?"

Jamaica turned away and folded her arms. She knew that one day she would have to answer that question from Tameer, and still, she had not thought of an answer. She knew that one day soon, she would, in fact, be asking herself that very same question. Would she stay in touch? Why would she? Why wouldn't she? What was she doing?

"I want to stay in touch with him," she answered, not knowing if it were true. She turned back toward Savion and met his eyes. "I'm going to try."

It was Savion's eyes that gave him away, even before his question.

"But it will be hard on the road?" he added to her sentence.

"What?" It still took her by surprise, even though she now suspected that he knew.

Savion nodded his head toward the street and started off. "C'mon."

Quietly, Jamaica folded her arms and followed.

Savion was the first one through the apartment door. He stuffed his keys inside of the front pocket of his baggy blue jeans, and headed straight for the DVD player. Jamaica stood behind him, arms folded, and watched as he stuck a disc inside of the machine. Savion lifted the remote and turned toward her.

"Tameer loves rap music, that's all he listens to. To him, it's like poetry. The rhyming, the anger, the message. But me, I listen to all types of music." Savion smiled and turned toward the television, pressing fast forward on the remote. When he finally stopped the disc, Jamaica Tiera Rochelle's latest music video was playing on the television.

"How long have you known?" Jamaica asked, her voice a crackling whisper.

Savion didn't turn. He responded while still watching the video. "Since the first day in the mall. I wasn't one hundred percent sure, until Tameer won the car right after his other one broke down. Then, the cash scholarship thing from the supermarket gave everything up."

Savion turned toward Jamaica and smiled. "Awards aren't given out in December, they aren't given out in cash, and you usually have to apply for them."

Jamaica laughed. Her laughter was infectious, as Savion soon joined in. Finally, after several moments, she stared at him.

Jamaica was relieved that her deception was over, and that she could now be herself. No more hiding, no more sneaking, no more lying. She could be Jamaica the singer. She wanted to be able to tell Tameer herself, that way she could explain things to him. She wanted Savion to give her the chance to straighten things out, and maybe smooth things over before he told his brother.

"Are you..."

"No." Savion shook his head. He knew what she was going to ask. He knew what she needed to ask. "Why should I? Besides, he doesn't need to know right now, anyway. You're good together. My brother is happy, and so are you."

Jamaica outstretched her arms. "Come here."

Savion stepped closer, and they embraced.

Chapter Twenty-One

"Okay, that's it!" Dawshanique declared. "I've called everywhere, talked to everybody I know, and nobody knows her."

"Well then, girl, that settles it," said Shamika. "She is some outta-town hoochie mama."

LaShay popped her bubble gum loudly over the telephone. It angered an already frustrated Dawshanique.

"Uh, LaShay, honey do you mind?" asked Dawshanique.

"Dawshanique, I'm not that bitch!" LaShay replied. "I ain't stole your man."

"Hold on, both a y'all," Shamika interrupted. "Y'all don't need to go there, 'cause we gots bigger fish to fry. Besides, Shay, that damn smacking is getting on my nerves too."

Dawshanique exhaled loudly over the receiver. "Back to Ms. Thang."

"What?" Shamika asked.

"I want her," Dawshanique told them. "I wanna pull some of that hair outta her head."

"Whew!" LaShay shrilled. "Now ya talking! That's the Daw I know!"

"So what are you saying... I mean, what's the plan?" asked Shamika.

"There ain't no plan!" Dawshanique told them. "You just keep a lookout for Ms. Thang, and let me know when she's outside."

"So what are you gonna do, run up and box her?" LaShay asked.

"Hell yeah!" Dawshanique answered.

"Oooooh, hold on," Shamika shouted. "That sounds like Tameer's car!"

"Damn, bitch, you know what it sounds like already?" Dawshanique said angrily.

"Daw, don't go there," Shamika warned. She peered outside of her apartment window. "Yeah, that's him. Ms. Thang just ran outside... and she's wearing his FUBU hoody!"

LaShay smacked again. "Damn, Daw, you didn't even sport his clothes like that!"

"Oooooh, bitch, you wrong," Shamika told LaShay. "Stop being messy."

Shamika and LaShay shared a laugh at Dawshanique's expense, before Shamika continued her window-seat reporting.

"Well, she's gotten inside of the car, yep, they kissing... exchanging slobber. Yeah, Daw, I think it's safe to say they sexin'," declared Shamika. "Hold on... oh, she's getting out. Now he's getting out... uh-un, girl, that ho is getting behind the wheel! He's letting her drive his car!"

"Ooooh, girl, she's got your man, your man's clothes, and your man's car!" LaShay wailed.

"Damn, Shay, I can hear her, you don't have to repeat it!" Dawshanique shouted. "You like this shit!"

"No, I don't," LaShay told her. "I'm glad it ain't me, though!"

Dawshanique was beyond angry. "It couldn't be you, all your babies' daddies are dead, you jinxy bitch!"

"Fuck you!" LaShay shouted.

"Hold on, both of you!" Shamika shouted. "We got to stick together. Remember, a new hoochie is a threat to all of us. We've got to get her out of the Courts, off the East side, and hopefully out of town!"

"Just let me know the next time she's around," Dawshanique told her. "I'll make damn sure she doesn't show her face in public again!"

"Good!" said Shamika. "Now, you two make peace."

"Peace," LaShay said dryly.

"Peace," Dawshanique agreed.

"Good, now let's concentrate on getting this bitch," Shamika told them.

❖❖❖

Jamaica pulled away from Tameer. She wiped the lipstick from his lips and smiled.

"I had fun last night," she told him.

Tameer nodded. "Me too."

"Are you gonna pick me up tonight?" Jamaica asked. She knew that he would.

Tameer nodded and smiled. It made her smile again. She tilted her head and stared at him curiously. His smile was a bit too mischievous.

"What?" she asked.

Tameer stepped back and shook his head. "Nothing."

Jamaica could tell that he was hiding something. She stepped forward and wrapped her arms around his waist.

"I can tell when you have something up your sleeve." Her hands moved slowly up his side, and she began tickling him with her nails. "I can get you to tell me."

Tameer laughed and wrapped his arms around her, pulling her close.

"It's a surprise. Can't I surprise you?"

"That last time you surprised me, we had a big fight." Her face contorted slightly.

He rocked her gently from side to side. "It's nothing like that."

Jamaica leaned back and stared into his eyes. "Are you sure?" She smiled. "So what's it going to be this time, ice fishing? No, don't tell me, mountain climbing? Survival school? Or how about a terrorist training camp?"

Tameer laughed and kissed her on her forehead. "You look good in that shirt. You look good in all my clothes."

"Yeah, well, you look good without any clothes," Jamaica told him. Her hand slid down to his derriere, where she pinched him. Her pinch made him jump.

"Hey!" Tameer grabbed Jamaica's hand. "It seems like you're trying to get into my pants, Jamaica."

She pulled away and winked at him. "Tonight." She smiled.

Jamaica reached behind herself and turned the knob on the door of her motel room. "Tonight," she repeated, this time more softly. "Tonight." It was almost a whisper. She then disappeared inside.

"Well, this is getting to be a regular habit," a familiar voice called out from behind.

Jamaica turned, and spied her friend in her usual position, sprawled out across the bed. This time, however, she was under the covers.

"China, you really need to lighten up." She sauntered across the floor of the motel room and sat down upon the edge of the bed. Smiling, Jamaica lay back, sprawling out her arms and legs until she covered the entire lower half of the bed.

LaChina knocked Jamaica's arms away. "Hey, watch my legs, Nature Girl."

Jamaica shook her head. "Ha, ha, real funny. You really need to unwind, relax, get a little."

The toilet flushed, and Jamaica bolted upright. She turned toward LaChina as the bathroom door swung open.

LaChina waved her hand. "Troy, I'd like you to meet Jamaica. Jai, this is Troy."

Jamaica covered her open mouth, and Troy, who was wrapped inside of a wet towel, quickly stepped back into the bathroom.

"Sorry, I didn't know you had company," Troy said, smiling sheepishly. His gaze shifted from LaChina to Jamaica. "Nice to meet you." He quickly closed the bathroom door.

"Oh my God," declared Jamaica. She turned toward LaChina, who shrugged her shoulders.

"I got bored, so I went to the club," LaChina explained.

"China, you didn't!"

"You did!" LaChina retorted. "I needed to unwind."

Jamaica slapped her friend across her shoulder. "I can't believe you!" She waved her hand toward the bathroom door. "You just met him!"

"It was a reward." LaChina leaned back and crossed her legs.

"A reward?"

LaChina wrapped the covers around her body and stood. "Yes, a reward.

I've wrapped up all of the loose ends and successfully closed the Sea World video shoot." She turned toward Jamaica and frowned. "You won't believe how protective they are of those damn things."

Jamaica fell back onto the bed. "Yippie. Now I've got to kiss a big, slimy whale on video for several minutes, for all the world to see. Tiera, the fish kisser."

LaChina knelt next to her friend. "Think of it like this, we don't have to stay here any longer. No more boy toys, no more cold, just fun in the sun, surrounded by half-naked island men, catering to our every wish."

Jamaica turned and rolled over on her stomach, so that she could come face-to-face with her friend. "Well, I was thinking about... you know... maybe hanging around until Christmas."

LaChina bolted up from her position on the floor.

"What?" It was a shout. "Hang around until Christmas!"

Jamaica nodded. "Yeah."

LaChina adjusted the blanket around her body and began pacing. "Uh-un, no way." She shook her head. "Jai, it's going to snow."

"So? Christmas should be spent in the snow. How else can you make snowmen?"

LaChina stopped her pacing and frowned at Jamaica. "You know what, I've just noticed something. One, your vocabulary has gone to hell, and two, you've gone crazy."

Jamaica smacked her lips. "China, what are you talking about?"

"You're crazy," LaChina told her, as she resumed her frenzied pacing. "Weren't you the one, who only last year... and a few weeks ago, said... and I quote, 'China darling, Christmas should be spent somewhere warm, somewhere tropical.' That was you, wasn't it?"

Jamaica extended her hands in a calming motion. "Okay, okay. So we did the tropical thing, now let's do the winter thing."

LaChina stopped once again, and stared at Jamaica. "We can do the winter thing in New York."

Jamaica shook her head. "I'm not going."

"What? What do you mean you're 'not going'?"

"I'm not going," Jamaica repeated.

LaChina sat down on the bed next to her friend. "Jai, I was kidding when I said that you were in love." She tapped Jamaica's shoulder, causing her to look up at her. "You haven't really fallen for this boy, have you?"

"Of course not. I mean, how could I? What does he possibly have to offer me?" Jamaica asked.

LaChina stared at her. The silence combined with LaChina's steady gaze caused Jamaica to shift nervously and shake her head.

"Nothing. He had nothing!" Jamaica said forcefully. "I mean, I'm a superstar, right?" Her eyes met LaChina's for a brief moment, before she cut them away.

LaChina shook her head. She knew her friend.

"What has this boy done to you?" she asked with an exhale.

Jamaica rolled over onto her back and gazed at the ceiling. "The same thing Tyrone did to you."

"Troy, his name is Troy."

"Whatever."

LaChina stared at Jamaica for several moments. Jamaica continued to avoid eye contact. LaChina shook her head.

"Like I said a minute ago, Jai, when I said that you were in love, I was only kidding before. But now..." LaChina shook her head. "Jai, what are you going to do with him? Girl, you're from two different worlds."

Jamaica exhaled forcibly and shook her head. "I don't know, China." Her fist rose to her mouth, where she bit down upon her knuckle and stared off into space.

"I don't know," she repeated softly.

Chapter Twenty-Two

The lighting was dim. The darkness of the room allowed the flourescent blue lighting which rounded the stage, and the massive mirrored columns throughout the room to show brightly. Its blue radiance reflected off the numerous chrome fixtures scattered throughout the room, creating a cool, modern ambiance.

The atmosphere inside of the room was expectant, restless, festive. Jamaica leaned back inside of her thick, overstuffed, blue leather chair, and sipped patiently on her gin and tonic. She watched as the first act appeared.

He was a young comedian. Slick, hip, urban. He dressed well for a comedian, Armani, she noticed. It spoke volumes about his talent. This guy was in demand, and he got paid.

"Welcome to the Comedy Club on The River Walk, my name is B, and I'll be your worst nightmare for the next ten minutes," he told them. "Like I said, my name is B, but all of my friends call me BB. I want y'all to know, that it has absolutely nothing to do with my hair, though. Hell, if that was the case, it would be a whole lot of people in here named 'Nappy'!"

The crowd laughed.

"And quite a few named 'Ugly,'" the comedian continued. He pointed. "And this one over here would be named 'Fat Ass'!"

The audience laughed hysterically.

"Damn, I'll bet your momma and daddy were fat too, 'cause that shit you got has got to be generational!"

The crowd responded with laughter, whistles, and cheers.

"Oh, so y'all like fat jokes, huh?" the comedian asked.

The crowd clapped wildly.

"Okay, well try this one," he told them. "Your momma is so fat, when her beeper goes off, people think she's backing up!"

The crowd went wild.

"Your momma is so fat, when she wears her yellow raincoat, people run after her yelling TAXI! Your momma is so fat, she left home with high heels, and came back with flip-flops! She is so fat, she has to iron her pants in the driveway! Your momma is so fat, she puts on lipstick with a paint roller!"

The crowd was laughing out of control. The young comedian nodded, laughed, and continued.

"Your momma is so fat, she sat on a quarter and got two dimes and a nickel! She is so fat, she sat on a dollar bill, and blood came outta George Washington's nose! Your momma's so fat, her senior picture had to be an aerial view! She is so fat, that she qualifies for group insurance! Your momma is so fat, I swerved to avoid her on the road, and I ran outta gas! Your momma's so fat, she sells shade in the summer! Your momma's so fat, her nickname is DANG! Your momma's so fat, she's got tan lines from the refrigerator light!"

By the time the young comedian finished, the crowd was laughing hysterically. He bowed politely.

"Ladies and gentlemen, my name is B. Brown. I hope that you enjoy the show. Good night, and God bless!"

"Yeah! Yeah!" Jamaica stood laughing and clapping wildly. She even ventured a few whistles. It felt good to applaud someone else's talent. "He's good, huh, T?"

No one answered her.

Jamaica turned toward Tameer's seat, only to find herself alone. Curious, she remained standing, and gazed around the club in a vain effort to find him. She could not.

Where in the devil did that boy go now, she wondered.

Soon, the clapping subsided, and Jamaica had to take her seat.

In all probability, he went to the restroom, she told herself. *Well, he sure did miss a good act.*

Tameer's voice was what drew her attention to the stage.

"I... I had written a poem to read, but I don't want to read it anymore," he told the audience. "Upon coming here, I realized that it didn't really say everything that I wanted to say. So, I guess I'll wing it instead."

Silence engulfed the audience, and all eyes in the room were now trained upon him. Nervous, and visibly showing it, Tameer cleared his throat, took a deep breath, and pressed on.

"My life had some unexpected turns, and I found myself lost. I found myself having my dreams shattered, and not being able to pick up the pieces and move on. You know how when you know, or always have known, how things in your life would be? Well, that was how I was. I had a plan, and it was a pretty good plan. But you know what? I didn't have a backup. I was devastated, reeling."

Tameer walked down the steps leading from the stage, and into the audience. Jamaica's hands were covering the lower half of her tear-filled face, wiping away the moisture. It hurt her to hear him say those things. Tameer continued, as he slowly walked toward her.

"I went on with the motions of life, but not on with life. I could see the colors, but I didn't understand them. I could smell the fragrances, but I didn't recognize them. Then... then one morning God sent me an angel. One morning he gave me two beautiful sunrises. One in the sky, and another in the form of a gift named Jamaica."

Tameer stopped in front of a balling Jamaica and stared into her eyes. "I... there... there's not one night that goes by, that I don't fall down on my knees and thank Almighty God for her. She... she gave me my dream back. She gave me life, she gave me breath, and now I feel as if I can't breathe without her."

Tameer held the wireless microphone in his fidgety left hand, as he slowly knelt down in front of Jamaica.

"Jai, I love you. I don't want you to leave. I... I know that I don't have anything to offer you right now. I have no money, I can't give you diamonds, or expensive furs. I can't give you exotic cars, or a big, fancy house. But, Jamaica, I promise you this. I will love you for all time. I will love you when my last breath leaves my body. I will love you on Earth, and I will love you in Heaven. I will love you while you're young, and I will love you when the years have gone by. I will love you deeper than the furthest depths of the mightiest oceans, and more infinite than the stars in God's Heaven. For in you, I have found my Heaven. Don't ever leave me, Jamaica. Don't ever take my Heaven away."

"I hate you, Tameer!" Jamaica screamed.

Tameer closed his car door and engaged his alarm system. "What are you talking about?"

Jamaica wiped another tear from her face. "Because you... I just hate you!"

Tameer walked around the car and wrapped his arms around Jamaica. "That's not what you said at the comedy club." He smiled and pulled her close.

Jamaica placed her hand in between their bodies and pushed away.

"That's why I hate you! You... I've never met anybody like you!"

Jamaica broke away from Tameer's rapture and walked into the street. It was cold, and with each of her breaths, puffs of smoke appeared in the air.

"Before I met you, my life was simple," Jamaica continued. "I knew everything I wanted to do, I had everything I wanted. I was happy."

"And now you're not?"

She stomped the ground hard. "Damn you, Tameer! That's not what I meant! You know what I'm trying to say. I... I ... I don't know anymore." She folded her arms and frowned in frustration.

Tameer smiled and closed in on her.

"Well, my life is clear. I don't know why yours is so confused."

"Because, Tameer, I already had a life before I met you. And now I have this life with you, and it's just as good."

Tameer laughed. "Jamaica, you don't have to choose! Just make me a part of the life you already have."

Jamaica unfolded her arms, and walked to Tameer. She lifted her hand and caressed his face.

"Baby, I wish it were that simple." She turned away from him, and again folded her arms. "I wish life were that simple."

Tameer walked up behind her, and pulled her close.

"Life is what you make it. If you make it complex, it will be complex." Gently he rocked her from side to side. "Feel how warm it is in my arms?"

Jamaica closed her eyes, and leaned her head back against Tameer's chest. It did feel good in his arms. She wished they could stand there, with him holding her all night long.

"Tameer, I love you. I... I don't want to leave you."

"Then don't."

Jamaica turned and faced him. "Christmas. ... After Christmas, I'll tell you something about me, and then we'll decide."

"Tell me now."

Jamaica shook her head. "No, not now."

It hurt him that she didn't trust him enough to tell him or feel that she could share with him. He stepped back from her, and tried in vain to create some levity.

"What, are you a man, or something?" he asked with a smile.

Jamaica folded her arms and shifted her weight to one side. "Ha, ha, real funny. Was I a man last night?"

She shook her head and turned away from him. His attempt at levity only angered her. She had too much on her mind right now, for his stupid jokes. But still, she didn't mean to slam the door on him so hard. She smiled at him again.

"You watch too much Springer," she told him.

Tameer laughed, and his laughter became infectious. She joined in.

"Jai, whatever it is that you have to tell me, I'm sure it can't be that bad."

She shook her head. "It's not, trust me."

Jamaica turned away from him. *Trust me*, she thought. He wouldn't be able to do that after she told him who she was. She wouldn't be able to say those words to him any longer, after all of the misleading that she had done. She had lied to Tameer for weeks.

Tameer wrapped his arms around Jamaica again. "I'll wait, but if it's not such a big deal, then I don't see what the big deal is about telling me now. Whatever past you have, whatever mistakes you've made, Jamaica... I love you."

It hurt her even more. Still, she turned and kissed him.

"I love you too," she whispered.

A drop of moisture landed on Jamaica's nose. It was followed by several more drops on her uncovered face. She peered up into the sky.

The snow was thick, moist. It fell in solid clumps of moth ball-sized crystals, thin at first, but it quickly turned into a solid sheet of continuous snowfall. She loved it. He loved it. Quickly, the child came out in both of them.

Jamaica extended her arms out to her sides, turning her palms toward the pinkish-blue, evening sky. She stepped away from Tameer and looked skyward, as the crystals fell onto her face and melted on contact. Her smile was enchanting.

"I love the snow!" she shouted.

"Enjoy it," Tameer told her. "It doesn't happen often around here."

Jamaica stared at Tameer in disbelief.

"Really?" Snow was a given in New York, especially around Christmas.

Tameer nodded. "It happens every eight to ten years. But when it does happen, it's a gift from Heaven. A miracle almost."

Jamaica peered up into the puffy snow-filled sky and smiled. "A miracle." She nodded. "I like that. God's granting us a miracle."

Chapter Twenty-Three

The first snowball she threw landed against the headboard, disintegrating and sending puffs of liquid crystal falling down upon Tameer's face. The coldness startled him into consciousness. He awoke in time only to present Jamaica with a better target for her second snowball.

Tameer's arms flew up to his face after the snowball hit, in case Jamaica had prepared a third.

"Dang it, Jamaica! That stuff is cold!"

"It's supposed to be cold, silly, it's snow!"

"Oh yeah, well, how would you like for me to show you how it feels?" Tameer asked gruffly.

Jamaica smiled like a child about to show their parents their newly captured garden snake. She produced a third snowball which she had hidden inside the pocket sewn into her hooded sweat shirt.

Tameer's hands flew up to block it.

"What are you going to do with that?" he asked. Goosebumps appeared over his shirtless torso, as he imagined the frozen compacted snow striking him.

Jamaica took a step backward toward the door. The wetness from being outside caused her fleece-lined Ugg boots to squeak. Tameer looked down toward the floor where the noise had come from, and the snowball was lobbed.

It landed on the top of his head, and splattered onto the nakedness of his back, causing him to let out a wild Banshee yell.

"War!" he shouted, pointing at a running Jamaica. "You have started a war!"

Tameer leaped out of bed wearing only his polka dot boxers, and pursued a fleeing and screaming Jamaica down the creaking stairs, and out of the front door.

Tameer was naturally faster than Jamaica. Her bulky clothing and hulking jacket made her even easier to catch. He quickly tackled her, and they fell into the dormant, wet grass and soft mud hidden beneath three feet of soft, wet snow, which cushioned their landing. Jamaica's bright red-and-yellow knit bini flew off of her head upon impact, sending her hair flying all over her face. Neither cared.

Jamaica quickly broke away from a nearly naked and freezing Tameer, and was able to form the first snowball. Her quick launch scored a direct hit against Tameer's bare chest. His snowball returned, though with much more force, and scored a direct hit on Jamaica's now frozen forehead. They laughed and screamed, and they engaged in an impromptu snowball fight, with only the screaming red convertible Mustang in between them.

"I'll show you!" shouted a ducking Tameer. His teeth chattered in mid sentence.

"I don't think so!" came Jamaica's reply, as she ducked and headed around the corner toward the rear of the vehicle.

Tameer knew Jamaica. He changed directions quickly, and headed for the rear of the vehicle as well. He knew she would try to catch him behind with a juicy cold shot to his back. He was right.

They bumped into each other on all fours at the rear of the Mustang. She screamed in surprise, and he tackled her.

Tameer was the more athletic of the two, thus, he was able to quickly maneuver himself into a dominant position. He rapidly pinned Jamaica down onto the ground, using his knees to hold her arms in place. Once finally in control, he nodded and smiled at her.

"I told you I would get you!'

Tameer began stuffing snow inside of Jamaica's sweat shirt, bra, and panties. The coldness of the snow made her wiggle fiercely.

"I'm sorry!" Jamaica shouted. "Aaaagh! I'm sorry, I'm sorry!"

Tameer continued stuffing. "Nope! I'mma show you!"

"You cheater!" Jamaica screamed and wiggled and kicked. "It's cold!"

"No shit! It's snow, it's supposed to be cold. Isn't that what you told me in the room?" He smiled even wider. "I'll bet you'll think twice about lobbing snowballs at a sleeping man again!"

"I quit!" Jamaica screamed.

"You quit?" Tameer asked. He shook his head and kept stuffing. "Nope, say you're sorry!"

"I'm sorry!"

"Say I'm sorry, Uncle Tameer!"

"What?" She stared at him.

Tameer began stuffing even more snow inside of her clothing. "Okay." He shrugged his shoulders. "If you want me to keep going."

"Okay! Okay! I'm sorry, Uncle Tameer!" shouted a freezing Jamaica.

"Say, 'pretty please, with sugar on top'!" Tameer commanded.

"Okay! 'Pretty please, with sugar on top'!" Jamaica repeated.

Tameer leaped up off of her, and ran into the apartment. He shouted back at her from the safety of the doorway.

"Sucker!" Quickly, he turned and disappeared inside.

Jamaica rose slowly, spitting snow out of her mouth, and brushing off her sweat shirt and jeans. Her hair was wet, which caused it to hang long in its normal silky-looking form. Standing in the middle of the yard, she shook her free-flowing hair, tossing it back over shoulders. She was determined to get Tameer. No one would get the best of Jamaica Tiera Rochelle. No one!

Jamaica leaned forward, to lift her snow covered bini from the ground, and her long, wet, silky locks fell forward covering her face. Again, she slung it back over her shoulder. Shaking her bini free of snow, she stretched it into a pouch, and set it down on the convertible's khaki, fabric top. Slowly, Jamaica bent down, and began making snowballs to get her revenge against Tameer.

Shamika had been privy to the whole thing. It made her sick. She had sat in the window and watched the entire despicable affair. The chase, the tackle, the snowball fight, and Jamaica's surrender. Their giddiness was like watching *The Partridge Family*. Or even worse, *The Brady Bunch*. Shamika wanted to spit.

They were obviously in love, however, this was less important to Shamika than being able to see Jamaica without her bini. She knew Jamaica, but couldn't place her. It wasn't so much her face, Shamika thought, it was the hair. She knew the hair.

She wanted that hair. She had discussed it, admired it, praised it, coveted it, and even tried to grow it. Dashawnique had told her that she couldn't get it, because those people spent years growing it, and always under the care of a five-star beautician. *Those people*, she thought. *Hmmmm, those people. They had the time to grow it, and the money to spend on it. Those people.*

Shamika shook her head, because it couldn't be. It couldn't be! What would she be doing in the Courts, sleeping in the Courts, and running around with a boy from the Courts! It didn't make sense. Again, she shook her head. But, the more she watched, the more she realized, that she knew that hair.

Tiera was a mega star, an actress, a model, a songstress, hell, she was a living legend! It couldn't be her, Shamika was certain. Tiera was in New York. Hell, she had just released a new video. Shamika shook her head again. No way, it couldn't be.

Shamika's thoughts were interrupted by the entrance of her niece. The disturbance frustrated her.

"Tai, I told you to go play in the living room!" Shamika yelled. "Do you want me to spank you?"

Tai, a precocious five-year-old, who was for all intents and purposes going on thirty, shook her head in the negative. She, like any other five-year-old, did not want to be spanked.

Shamika pointed. "Then go in there and play!"

"But Auntie, Kenitra broke my doll!" Tai told her. She held up the two pieces of her toy.

Shamika exhaled loudly. "Give it here," she told her niece.

Shamika held out her hand, and Tai held out hers as well. Frustrated, Shamika took the doll's body form her niece's right hand, and the doll's head from her left. After a quick examination, she forcefully plopped the doll's head back onto its plastic body, making it whole again.

The doll's sequined, chiffon outfit had matching sequined high-heeled shoes. Its skin was a polished walnut tone, and its eyes a deep emerald with flecks of almond, were almost catlike in appearance. But it was the doll's hair that did it: long, silky, and honey-brown, it hung down to its lower back.

Shamika turned the doll over and examined its face. It took only a few seconds before she tuned to her niece.

"Tai, did you wet this doll's hair?" Shamika asked.

Frightened, Tai stepped back, looked down, and shook her head. "Yes…"

Shamika nodded. "Did you dip this doll's hair in the toilet?"

Tai shook her head. "No, the sink."

"It's okay, baby. Auntie owes you a big hug!" Shamika wrapped her arms around the child, and embraced her tightly. "I didn't mean to yell at you, okay?"

Tai smiled and nodded. She loved her aunt to death.

Shamika caressed the doll, and looked out the window where a now fully dressed Tameer, and a silky-haired Jamaica, were once again engaged in a snowball fight. Shamika lifted the doll against the window, and shifted her gaze continually between Jamaica and the doll, comparing them. Shamika turned to her niece.

"Tai, come here, honey."

Tai approached, and Shamika lifter her onto her knee, so that she was able to peer out of the window. Shamika pointed.

"Look."

Tai's beautiful doelike eyes flew open even wider, when she spied her heroine outside of their apartment throwing snowballs. Tai covered her mouth with both her tiny hands and gasped.

"It's T... T...Tiera!"

"Are you sure?" Shamika asked.

Tai nodded.

Shamika kissed her niece on the forehead, and gently lowered her to the ground. She turned and stared out the window once more, and again compared a life-size Jamaica to her tiny Mattel counterpart. Tai tugged at her housecoat.

"Auntie, can I go outside and play with Tiera?"

Shamika waved her hand. "Later, honey, right now auntie is busy."

Shamika stared out the window, closely examining Jamaica and the doll again. After several moments, her conclusion was reached.

"You bitch," she said softly first. Quickly her anger built. "You...fucking, mega-rich, snowball-throwing, man-stealing bitch!"

Frightened, Tai ran from the room in tears.

"Grandma, Auntie is calling my Tiera doll bad names!"

Chapter Twenty-Four

"Come on over here, Eddie Lee. I've fixed this for you."

"Jamaica, you always make a fuss over me every time I come home." Eddie Lee waved his hand through the air. "There's no need."

"It's my pleasure, besides, you deserve it," Jamaica told him. "You've been clean for how long?"

"Four weeks," Eddie Lee replied. "Four weeks of pure hell."

He looked up, and Jamaica offered him a half-smile.

"Come on, Eddie Lee, I know it's not that bad."

Eddie Lee offered a laugh. "It's not." He slapped his massive hand against his paunch. "I feel good."

Eddie Lee lifted his fork to his mouth, and sampled Jamaica's cuisine. "Not bad. You're becoming a regular chef-girl-Ardee."

It made her smile. Jamaica sat down upon the tattered arm of Eddie Lee's large recliner. The jaggedness of the taped tears in the faux leather no longer bothered her. She had become used to it.

"And you're becoming a regular Eddie Lee Murphy," she told him. "So what time do you have to be back at the treatment center?"

"I got a pass until four. Can you believe it, they trust me to stay clean for eight whole hours?"

Jamaica folded her arms and laughed. It ended suddenly when her thoughts shifted to someone else. She had been waiting to ask Eddie Lee a certain question for a long time. Since they were now alone, it seemed like the perfect opportunity.

"So what happened between you and Mrs. Harris?" she asked.

Eddie Lee stopped chewing. The question had taken him by total surprise. Slowly, he lifted his napkin, wiped his mouth clean, and stared at the table for several moments gathering his words. Finally, he lifted his head and turned to Jamaica.

"I don't think it was because she stopped loving me. I think it was because she stopped loving our life together."

Jamaica nodded. She understood the difference.

Eddie Lee cleared his throat.

"She wanted another life, a life I couldn't give her, and a life we could no longer have." Eddie Lee leaned back in the rusting, folded, metal chair, and nervously tightened his fist, crumbling the napkin it held. "She didn't want a family; she didn't want the responsibility, the commitment. And… And I love my boys, both of them. My boys were, and still are, everything to me. I was angry at her for not wanting this life, for not wanting our two magnificent children."

His weary eyes looked down at the metal card table, and conveyed a sadness that was radiating, infectious. Jamaica wanted to rush to him and offer comfort, but she paused for lack of words. Eddie Lee continued.

"Jamaica, I… I… I tried to make her stay. I used my fist to try and make her stay. I thought that if she just stayed and gave things a chance, she would eventually like it. I ended up driving her away even faster."

Jamaica rose and began her journey toward Eddie Lee. She was embarrassed, ashamed. She wanted to learn more about Tameer, but instead she unlocked the demons of Eddie Lee's past. She had opened the flood gates to the pain which his heart soundly held.

"It's okay, Eddie Lee," she told him as she rubbed her tiny hand across his broad back. "It's okay."

"Jamaica." Eddie Lee looked up from the table, and placed his hand on top of hers. "It was a long time ago. I can't say that it no longer hurts, because I'd be lying. But what I do say is, I want you for a daughter."

Jamaica laughed nervously.

Eddie Lee waved his hand toward a nearby chair, motioning for her to sit. She did.

"Jamaica, I really like you. I like you a whole lot better than that Dashawnique girl."

Jamaica frowned, tilted her head to the side, and nodded. "I'll take that as a compliment."

"Well, it was meant to be," Eddie Lee replied. He reached out and took her hand in his. "Know what you want before you involve others. Know what plans you have, and tell your partner about them. Be honest up front, and don't let other people get hurt."

It was Jamaica's turn to look down and stare at the center of the table. She was embarrassed, ashamed. It was as if Eddie Lee was reading her soul. It made her seriously wonder if he knew about her deception. It was her not knowing, that made her so uneasy.

"If my son ever lays a hand on you, and I doubt that he will, but if he does, you run. You run away, far away from him." He shook his head, and shifted his glance away from her. "My wife did nothing wrong when she did that," he said softly.

Jamaica looked up from the table. "Is that why…"

"Yeah," Eddie Lee answered. He looked down again. "Yeah, that's why I turned to alcohol and drugs."

Jamaica rose and leaned forward embracing him tightly.

He laughed.

"What's an old man done to deserve one of these?"

Jamaica kissed him on the cheek. "You're so sweet."

"Why, thank you." He touched the spot on his cheek where she had kissed him.

"Are they going to let you come over for Christmas?" Jamaica asked.

"Oh, I'm sure they will." Eddie Lee smiled at her. "But I tell you what, let me do the cooking."

Jamaica folded her arms and leaned back. "What are you trying to say about my cooking?"

Eddie Lee's gigantic, ever-ready smile appeared again. "Nothing, it's just that I don't know if you're ready for Christmas dinner yet."

"Oh Eddie Lee!" She slapped him across his massive, ironlike shoulder, and then rose from the table. "At least let me make the cookies for the carolers."

"The what?"

"The Christmas carolers," she answered. "When I was a little girl, that was one of my favorite things about Christmas."

Jamaica closed her eyes and inhaled deeply as she reminisced. "Going door to door and singing. My favorite was 'O'Silent Night.'" Jamaica opened her eyes and spun. "Eddie Lee, I used to tear that song up!"

Eddie Lee laughed heartily. "I'll bet you did used to tear that song up," he told her. "Your Christmas sounds wonderful, Jamaica, but…Christmas is a little different here in the Courts."

"Different, how different can Christmas be?" she asked. "Christmas is a time for snow, and snowmen. It's about carolers, Christmas trees, lights, and toys."

Jamaica stared at Eddie Lee and smiled. "Lots of toys!"

"Well, it sounds like you were a very lucky little girl." He turned in his chair and faced Jamaica. "Jai, most of the families in the Courts are barely eating during the rest of the year, forget about Christmas. A Christmas tree?"

Eddie Lee raised his massive arms and shrugged his shoulders. "Who has money for a Christmas tree? And toys, yeah right!"

Jamaica's face went from incomprehension, to comprehension, to horror. Then came anger, and finally, determination.

"Eddie Lee, are you telling me that most of the families out here aren't going to have a Christmas dinner, most of the apartments won't have trees, and most of the children won't get any toys?"

Jamaica was furious. Children without toys, and nobody was doing anything about it! Children wondering why Santa didn't come to their home, thinking that they may have done something wrong, but deep down knowing that they had not. Children without a smile on Christmas day! Jamaica began turning red.

"Yeah." Eddie Lee nodded slowly. "It's sad, isn't it?"

"Sad?" Jamaica shouted. "It's impossible! Kids should have toys, at least on Christmas! Dammit, Eddie Lee! At least once a year, these kids should have a magical experience. Every child should!

Jamaica's anger was seething, her nose began flaring. "Eddie Lee, where's the telephone?"

Eddie Lee turned back to the table and lifted his fork again. "It's over by the table, next to the couch."

Jamaica rushed to the couch, where she slung pillow cushions and throw pillows around, until the cordless was located. The number to the motel was dialed before she even stepped foot outside onto the porch.

"China?"

"Yes. You could at least say hello first," answered LaChina. "Especially since you've…"

"There's no time for games!" Jamaica told her. "Don't play with me, play with your boy toy!"

"I was!" LaChina countered.

"Well, stop!" Jamaica was embarrassed. "I had meant later, play with him later. I've got a job for you."

LaChina exhaled loudly, and pushed Troy off of her. She sat up.

"Yes, Your Highness." Her voice turned gruff. "What is it now, Jai?"

"Toys, food, Christmas trees, and decorations!"

"Okay," LaChina replied. "I'll be sure to tell Santa what you want. Can I go now?"

"China, this is serious," Jamaica whined. "People here aren't going to have a Christmas tree, a Christmas dinner, or Christmas toys. We've got to do something!"

LaChina exhaled. "Alright, Jai, calm down." She slapped Troy's hand away. "I'll call the supermarkets, the toy stores, and some of the local tree farms."

"Decorations!" Jamaica shouted into the receiver. "The kids will need decorations. We'll bag them up and pass them out with the trees. One bag for each tree."

"Jai, I know that you speak French, honey, but don't mix it with English. You said *we*."

"China, I need you!" Jamaica shouted. "I need you to help me pass the stuff out!"

"No."

"But, China!"

"No."

"Where's your Christmas spirit?" Jamaica asked.

"In New York."

"Remember that old lady who lived in that big, creepy mansion at the end of your block?" Jamaica asked.

"Mrs. Devonshire? Yes, why?"

"You're acting just like her."

"Am not!"

"Are too! You're going to be mean, old, and alone just like her. I hope your cats bite you in the…"

"Alright, Jai, alright!" LaChina exhaled loudly again. "I'll call Jemia and see if she can scrounge up any help."

"Thank you, LaChina!" Jamaica bounced up and down. "Thank you! I knew there was a reason why I loved you!"

"I hate you, Jai."

"I love you too, Sis."

"Bye, girl."

"Bye."

Chapter Twenty-Five

The ten trucks were large eighteen-wheelers, with massive cargo holds. One truck carried the still bundled, but bulky Christmas trees, while another carried bags of Christmas tree decorations. Two of the eighteen-wheelers carried bags of toys, while the remainder carried food.

LaChina had the stores pack each bag of tree decorations so that it included everything needed to decorate one seven-foot Christmas tree. The grocery stores happily obliged, by packing in every four bags, enough food to make an abundant Christmas dinner for twelve. The set included not only a twenty-five-pound turkey, but cans of corn, string beans, cranberry sauce, bottles of three-liter sodas, and boxes of stuffing and cake mix. She even threw in all of the ingredients to mix and make all the items, as well as a roll of cookie dough for the kids.

The toys were bagged according to gender and age group. Half of the toys were donated by local toy stores, which had been a miraculous feat this close to Christmas. The total bill for the trucks, the workers, and the merchandise surpassed one hundred thousand dollars easily, though one would not be able to tell by watching Jamaica. She handed out bags of goodies with an enthusiasm and cheerfulness that would have made Santa himself envious.

The trucks were lined in a row, in the middle of one of the Courts' busy, snow-covered intersections. The tenants themselves were lined up in an orderly row as well. Their line mimicked that of the trucks, allowing them to move from trailer to trailer, and receive their goods in an efficient manner.

The chill of the morning air did little to dissipate Jamaica's warm smile, as she stood bundled and wrapped on the back of one of the food trailers, handing out bags of turkeys. She turned to LaChina.

"Isn't this fun?" Jamaica asked.

LaChina, bundled in a fur-lined Bomber jacket, stopped handing out bags of canned goods, and stared back at Jamaica.

"Yes, Jai, just wonderful, peachy, fantastic. I feel like a damn elf, are you happy now?"

"You're a scrooge, a Mrs. Grinch."

"I am not." LaChina shook her head. "I agree with what you did, Jai, but we could have hired someone to pass these things out."

Jamaica hugged her friend. "Oh, China, this is what Christmas is all about!"

LaChina stood up straight, and stretched her back. She placed her hands onto her hips and leaned forward for several moments, and then reversed the process, by leaning backward. When finished she turned and stared at Jamaica again.

"Jai, this is what Christmas is all about, but what about next year? What about when you are no longer with Tameer, or when you've gone back to New York and when you're traveling and being Tiera again? What's going to happen then? This is a commitment, Jai, a big responsibility. You can't rush into people's lives thinking that you're going to make it better, and then forget about them next year."

Jamaica stopped passing out bags and stood erect. She stared at her friend.

"China, I thought about that. I didn't think about it when I first called you, but I thought about it later. There's a playground here that I've been going to. There's some little girls that play at that playground every day. I talk to them, I push them on the swings, I push the merry-go-round for them, and I catch them when they slide down the slide. I see us, China. I see me, you, Naivasha, Jemia, Tamara, Arriana, Porsche, Teremesha, Brittany, Germany, all of us, when I look at them."

Jamaica nodded her head slowly, and stared off into space. "They're going to college, China, all of them. They are going to go to private school, and then college, on me. They're going to make it."

LaChina smiled, leaned over, and embraced her friend.

"Well…" LaChina blinked several times and sniffled. "There has to be a new generation of the Sisterhood of the Treehouse Chipmunks."

LaChina and Jamaica shared a laugh, and embraced each other tightly. LaChina rocked Jamaica slightly, from side to side.

"My sister, my dear sweet sista." She released Jamaica, leaned back, and examined her. "What's happened to you? What in the world's happened to you?"

LaChina waved her hand over Jamaica's body. "You're dressing different, you're talking like you're from the hood, and you're caring. You really care about what happens to people."

LaChina lifted her hand and placed it on Jamaica's forehead, where she pretended to check for a fever. It made Jamaica laugh.

"I ran away with a spoiled little star, and I'm bringing back a woman. A mature, elegant, socially concerned black woman. My sista!"

Again they embraced.

"If you hoes are dikin', then what you need my man for?" a voice called out from the street.

Jamaica and LaChina quickly turned in the direction from which it came. It was Dashawnique accompanied by Shamika and LaShay.

Sensing trouble, LaChina's aunt Savanna approached from the neighboring trailer. She was followed closely behind, by her daughter Jemia.

Jamaica jumped down from the trailer, followed by LaChina. Dashawnique approached Jamaica.

"Yeah, bitch, what's all that shit you was talking?" Dashawnique asked, pointing her finger in Jamaica's face. "You've got to give the people what they want? Well, I'm here."

Jamaica's palm flew up, stopping just in front of Dawshawnique's face. "You can talk to the hand, because I don't have time."

"That's what I thought," replied Dashawnique. "You scary bitch!"

Jamaica shook her head. "I'm not going to be too many more bitches."

Dashawnique's hand flew to her hip, as she leaned her face into Jamaica's. "Bitch!"

LaChina grabbed Jamaica, and pushed her back against the trailer. Savanna approached them.

"What's going on here, young ladies?" Savanna asked. "If there is a problem, I'm sure that beautiful, intelligent, mature young ladies like yourselves, can all sit down and talk about it."

LaShay's hand quickly flew to her hip. "Ain't no problem, bitch, unless you want it to be one."

Savanna's hand flew to her face and covered her mouth.

"Oh my goodness," she exclaimed. The language and disrespect was shocking to her.

Jemia turned to LaShay. "Did you just call my mother a bitch?"

LaChina turned and rolled her eyes at LaShay, who had offended her aunt. LaShay's head began moving from side to side as she spoke.

"You heard me, yeah, I called her one!" answered LaShay. "I'll call you one, your momma one, your daughter one, and your grandma one, if the bitch was here."

Savanna grabbed Jemia's arm. "Jemia, don't worry about that, let's go." Savanna turned to Jamaica and LaChina. "Let's go. The people from the church can finish giving out the rest of the stuff."

Jemia pulled away from her mother, and reached for LaShay. "You called my mother a bitch, that was all I needed to hear!"

Jemia's first slap landed directly on LaShay's left cheek. It was quickly followed by a left hook to LaShay's right eye.

Jamaica, free from LaChina's restraint, lunged forward and grabbed Dashawnique's braids with both of her hands. She pulled with all of her strength, bringing a screaming and swinging Dashawnique's head down to her waist, where she started slinging it to and fro.

With Jamaica engaged, and Jemia giving LaShay an old-fashioned Texas-style thrashing, it left a smiling LaChina, staring at a wide-eyed Shamika.

Savanna, frightened at the melee erupting around her, ran to gather her sons, and some male parishioners from the other trailers.

The fight between Jemia and LaShay was beyond one-sided, it was a slaughter. Jemia punched, pounded, ducked, dodged, punched, jabbed, moved, and punched some more. LaShay's eyes were blackened, and her lower lip was split.

Jamaica's hold on Dashawnique's hair was broken, when she could no longer find any more braids to pull out. Standing on a snow-filled street, surrounded by dozens of synthetic micro braids, the girls clawed, scratched, bit, and fought.

"And I'll...teach...you...never...to...call...my...mother...a...bitch... again!" Jemia's sentence was interspersed with solid smacks across LaShay's cheeks with her fist. LaShay was desperate.

"Shamika!" screamed a bloody LaShay. "Help me! Shamika, you bitch! You better help me!"

LaChina folded her arms and leaned back against the tractor-trailer. She smiled at Shamika. Together they listened for several moments to LaShay's desperate, crying, screaming pleas for help. LaChina nodded her head in LaShay's direction.

"She's calling for you," she told Shamika. It was a dare.

Jamaica pulled some of Dashawnique's real hair out as well. Her four solid smacks to Dashawnique's face, were the last blows of the free-for-all, as the men from Savanna's church finally arrived and pulled everyone apart. Dashawnique spied her braids strewn all over the ground, and quickly covered her head in embarrassment.

"You bitch!" Dashawnique screamed at Jamaica. "You fake bitch!"

Dashawnique's tears dropped into the slushy snow, joining her fallen tracks.

Jamaica, still being held by the meaty hands of a very large church deacon, replied in kind.

"I'm fake?" she shouted back at Dashawnique. "My hair is still on my head!"

No one held Jemia, as no one had to. Her opponent was sprawled out in the snow being treated.

"Leave Tameer alone!" Dashawnique screamed. "You don't need him!

Go be with your superstars! We're just regular people, why are you messing up our lives!"

Dashawnique's hands were released. She used them, not to attack Jamaica, but to cover her tear-filled face. The crowd's silence became a screaming vacuum that served only to amplify Dashawnique's sobs.

"You can have anybody," Dashawnique told Jamaica. "Just let me have him."

Jamaica's eyes watered and she felt two inches tall. Although she was not sure, she felt as though the crowd's glances now fell scornfully on her. She wished that she could disappear.

Crying heavily, Dashawnique approached a confused Jamaica.

"We're real people, not toys," Dashawnique told her softly. Her trembling hand reached out to Jamaica, wanting to touch her, wanting to caress her face. It never made it. Dashawnique's hand moved to her quivering lip, where it continued to tremble in unison.

"You're beautiful," she said softly to Jamaica. "Just let me and Tameer get back together. If you leave us alone, we'll be together."

Jamaica's mouth fell open. She wanted to comfort the pitiful creature that stood in front of her, but didn't know how.

Dashawnique's face fell into her hands again, and again, she began to sob. "Please...please..."

Chapter Twenty-Six

Jamaica's sensuous laugh resonated throughout the living room. She wore very short tights, which exposed her silky, flawless, mocha legs. They were stretched across Tameer's lap, and he watched them intensely, while caressing them softly. She could feel him throbbing underneath the back of her legs and this caused her outburst of laughter.

"You want some of this, huh?" she asked, smiling at him tauntingly.

Jamaica raised her legs into the air, and rubbed them gently, only inches away from his face. His eyes followed her slow-moving hand along her legs, and again, she could feel him throbbing beneath her.

Tameer wanted her. He wanted her bad. The dryness of his mouth caused him to swallow hard.

"Okay, so you want to tease, huh?" he asked. Tameer reached over Jamaica, and grabbed the ice pack cloth from her right hand. "Give me my rag, and my ice. See how funny and sexy you are with a hand that looks like a melon!"

Jamaica removed her legs from Tameer's lap, and sat up next to him on the couch. "So, are we going to do it or what?"

A smile shot across Tameer's face, and he quickly went for Jamaica's neck. "Yeah! That's what I've been wanting to hear!"

Jamaica pushed his head back. "Not that, silly. Are we going to go visit your mom and my dad?"

Tameer folded his arms, and leaned back in the sofa. "I want to, but I just don't know." He shook his head. "What if she doesn't..."

"Tameer, she's your mother," Jamaica interrupted. "She'll be glad to see you."

Slowly, he nodded in agreement. "I guess you're right. I'm just nervous." Tameer turned and stared into Jamaica's eyes. "I haven't seen her in a long time."

Jamaica reached out to him. Gently, she placed her arm around his neck and pulled him close.

"I know you're nervous, but I'll be there with you." She leaned forward to kiss Tameer on his forehead, but right before her lips were about to touch him, he raised his head and locked lips with her. She pulled back.

"Tameer!"

"Shhhh!" was his reply.

Tameer pulled her close again, kissing, rubbing, pulling, maneuvering. After a moment, Jamaica found herself lying back on the couch, with Tameer inside of her.

"Oooooh, Jamaica."

"Oooooooh, Tameer."

The trip to Houston took over three hours. Jamaica's penchant for fast driving, along with the scarcity of traffic on Interstate 10, allowed them to arrive sometime around noon. The actual navigating of the massive city, choked arterial roadways, and their unfamiliarity with both, resulted in a three-hour search for Cherice Harris' home. It was nestled inside of the Tony River subdivision, one of the city's premier addresses. When they finally arrived, their initial enthusiasm had given way to nervous apprehension.

Jamaica placed her arm onto Tameer's shoulder, and stroked the side of his face gently. "So, what do you want to do?"

Tameer didn't know. It was for a lack of a better plan that he decided to go through with the meeting. Slowly, he turned to Jamaica and shrugged his shoulders.

"Well, we're here now," he answered. Tameer exhaled loudly, and his gaze shifted toward the car's floorboards. "Might as well go in," he mumbled.

Jamaica offered an encouraging smile, and then took the first step by unbuckling her seatbelt. Nervous and shaking visibly, Tameer followed suit.

The home of Cherice Harris was massive, brick, imposing. It was nestled deeply with a spacious, wooded, corner lot. The home's massive Doric columns, gigantic floor-to-ceiling celestial windows, and grand symmetric balconies which overlooked the wide, pristine street, caused it to exude a formal posture.

The lawn was green, unusual for this time of year. It sat well manicured, filled with decorative shrubbery, and active flower beds of red, white, and pink. Interspersed within this neatly clipped domain, rose numerous, spindly, twisting, turning, knotted oaks, which stood majestic, like sentries guarding a medieval castle. To say that the home was impressive, would be an understatement.

Tameer was deeply hurt, as he examined the setting on both sides of the twisting, turning, winding pathway to the door. It hurt to know that his mother lived in this manner, while her family lived amidst the violence and poverty of the Courts.

The doors were made of a solid dark wood, with several massive beveled-glass inlays inserted within, as well as surrounding them. They were flanked by a pair of fancy brass lighting fixtures of French design, which matched the fancy brass door handles jutting out from the massive double doors. It was very clear from the residence, as well as from the S600 Mercedes and convertible Jaguar XKR convertible sitting in the driveway, that Cherice Harris had money. Lots of money. It hurt Tameer even more.

It was Jamaica's tiny fist that knocked first. Tameer found the doorbell.

"Who is it?" a voice called out from behind the massive doors.

"It's Tameer."

"Who?"

"Tameer."

The door opened to reveal a tall, slender, elegantly dressed woman in her mid-forties. Cherice Harris had aged gracefully, they saw. Her hair revealed only a light, yet dignified, streak of silver, which twisted with the rest of her hair into a tightly done French roll. Cherice wore a long, white, sleeveless vest and pants suit, which bell-bottomed at the cuff to reveal a pair of matching white Manolo pumps. Her hands caressed a loose string of Mikimoto pearls hanging from her neck, revealing an expensive manicure with French tips. Cherice leaned slightly forward.

"May I help you?" she asked the strangers at her door. Her gaze shifted inquisitively from one to the other, demanding an answer. Tameer cleared his throat.

"Uh...yea, ma'am, I...I'm your son Tameer Harris."

Cherice's left hand left her pearls, and pressed down upon her chest. "Oh...my goodness, I see." She shook her head slightly, as if to rid herself of a daze. Her hand waved toward her home's interior. "Well, please, come in."

Jamaica knew things were wrong. The lack of a hug, a smile, or any type of affectionate greeting, aroused her suspicions. She knew that she had to maintain her silence, yet she also knew that she would have to remain alert.

Cherice led them into her formal living room, which was larger than Tameer's entire apartment in the Courts. She waved her hand, offering her guests a seat. They took the couch; she chose the love seat across from them. Seated, Cherice crossed her legs and smiled at her son.

"So how are you?" she asked him.

Tameer quickly shifted his gaze from the upstairs balcony, which overlooked the living area, back to his mother. His heart was palpitating rapidly.

"I...I'm fine," he answered. Quickly, he turned toward Jamaica. "Mom, I'd like you to meet my special friend, Jamaica."

"How do you do?" Cherice rose briefly and extended her hand toward Jamaica.

"I'm fine, thank you," Jamaica greeted, as they clasped hands softly. "Nice to meet you."

Cherice nodded. "Likewise." Her finger rose, and she shook it slightly toward Jamaica. "It seems like I know you from somewhere. You look very familiar."

Jamaica adjusted her bini. "I get that a lot. But I don't believe we've met."

Cherice shook her head. "I don't believe so, either."

Tameer leaned forward nervously. "Mom, I've just wanted to come and see you. I mean, how are you?" It was not what he wanted to say, but his nervousness made him reluctant to express his true feelings. She was so... so formal.

"I'm fine," Cherice replied. "And please, call me Cherice."

Tameer's eyes blinked rapidly at her reply. *Call her Cherice*, he thought to himself. It was crazy. It disturbed him greatly. *I'm here so I may as well press on.*

"Savion and I have always wondered how you've been. I mean ever since the day you left." Again, he swallowed hard. "I know that...well, I have so many questions, so many things to say."

Cherice rubbed her top lip using her index finger, and sat up straight.

"Tameer, I know that you have some questions, some I may be able to answer, some I may not." She paused for several moments, and leaned forward. "It was not your fault and it was not your brother's fault; the fault was with me. I want you to know that. I hope that you didn't blame yourselves for my leaving. You were wonderful children."

It made Tameer smile and lean forward also. "No, Mom... I mean... Cherice. We never blamed ourselves, and we never blamed you. Savion and I both understood why you left, it was Dad's fault."

Tameer balled his hand into a tight fist, and clenched his teeth. "It was his abuse, his punches." He pounded the air slightly with his fist. It hit Cherice hard.

Cherice closed her eyes, and leaned back into the comfort of her plush white love seat. *My God*, she told herself, *Eddie Lee has not told them. After all of these years, Eddie Lee still has not told them the truth.*

"Tameer," she spoke softly, almost a whisper. "I was gone before that."

Her voice cracked and caused her to swallow hard. "I was still there in the physical sense, but I had long since made up my mind to leave."

Tameer's mouth fell open, and Jamaica, having heard the story previously, closed her eyes and bit down upon her lip. She, too, now realized that Eddie Lee had not told his son the truth. Tameer's dreams were once again shattered, and she could do nothing to stop it. In fact, she had brought him to this place, she had played a major part in coming to this house of broken dreams. Jamaica wanted to grab Tameer, and race to the car before Cherice could say anything else. She wanted to cover her ears, cover his ears, cover Cherice's mouth, do anything to stop this conversation from taking place. She shivered when she heard him ask the question that she knew he needed to ask.

"Why?" Tameer asked his mother.

"Tameer, I…I…I didn't want children," Cherice blurted out. "I didn't want to be married to your father, I wanted another life."

Cherice shook her head fervently, and grew very emotional. "I didn't want two kids, a big, white house with a picket fence, and a dog. I didn't want to become a soccer mom, a PTA member, or …or one of those people who look back on their life forty years and fifty pounds later, and say I should have, or I could have. I'm …I'm sorry."

Tears had formed in the corners of his eyes, but Tameer managed to hold them back for the sake of his manliness. *Real men don't cry*, he could still hear Eddie Lee shouting. *Real men don't cry!* The crackling inside of his voice was another matter entirely. Eddie Lee never covered that.

"Why?" Tameer asked her. "Why did you have us? Why didn't you tell us, why did we have to come home from school and find you gone? Why did you just leave!"

"Tameer, I was young! Eddie Lee wanted children, I gave him children, then I left. I ran here to Houston, I got my MBA, and I started my own company. This is the life I wanted, this is the life I have!"

Cherice Harris rose quickly from the love seat, and removed a slim white cigarette from a crème-colored pouch lying on her stone-and-glass coffee table. She lit it, inhaled, and exhaled, in what appeared to be to be one smooth flowing motion. She shook her head.

"Tameer, I didn't ask you to come here. You, your brother, and your father are part of a life I no longer have, or even want. Please show your-self to the door, and I ask you kindly, do not return." With that, Cherice Harris turned and exited the room.

Tameer was the first one up. He raced for the door, and quickly headed for his car. He was crying.

"Tameer, wait!" Jamaica called to him. "Tameer! Tameer!"

She continued to call to him from the front door, but he continued to his car. Jamaica watched from the entrance as Tameer climbed into the car over the door sill, and leaned his head on the dashboard. She could tell by the way his body was shaking that he was bawling like a baby. Quickly, she wheeled around, and walked back inside the home.

Jamaica walked through the massive home, searching each room until she found Cherice Harris, who was sitting in her bedroom using the tele-phone. Jamaica strode over to the bed where Cherice was sitting, reached over her, and hung up the telephone.

"How dare you!" Cherice shouted at her. She rose quickly from her king-sized bed. "I thought that I asked you to show yourselves out!"

Jamaica folded her arms, and shifted her weight to one side. "Oh yeah, I'm about to show out alright."

Cherice rolled her eyes toward the ceiling. "I suppose you've come to accost me now." She returned her gaze to Jamaica. "You want to fistfight me or something? Leave my home!"

Jamaica pulled off her bini hat and ran her hands through her hair. Cherice's eyes went narrow as they examined her.

"You...you're the singer." Cherice pointed at her. "You're Tiera!"

Jamaica nodded. "That's right! So you know that I didn't come here to fistfight you. I'm not from the ghetto, the hood, the Courts, or whatev-er the hell you want to call them. But you know what, I wish I was. I've met more people there with...with fortitude, dignity, and more class than you'll ever have! How dare you lord your life over your son! How dare you tell him that this cheap, material shit, is more precious to you than his life! How dare you tell him that he is not wanted! I want him! And you know what? Bitch, I can buy you, and I still want him!"

Jamaica unfolded her arms, and extended her finger into Cherice's face. "There are ways to say things to people, and there are ways to tell things to people. You had no right saying those things to him like that. No right! But I'm glad that you left them, because Mr. Harris was able to raise two of the most wonderful men I have ever met. And while we're on the subject, I'm glad that you left Mr. Harris. He's too good for you! He had more dignity, more class, and more kindness and sincerity in his little pinky finger, than you have in your whole damn body!"

With that, Jamaica turned and stormed out of the room, leaving a stunned Cherice Harris in silence. Cherice turned, and slowly sat back down onto her pillow-top mattress, her mind, focusing on what she had just been told. She was staring at the floor when Jamaica stuck her head back through the bedroom door.

"And I'm calling the fashion police too! White, this far after Labor Day? I don't think so!"

Chapter Twenty-Seven

J amaica sat inside of the car and held Tameer for over an hour, before they finally left from in front of his mother's house. She caressed his head, and she sang to him, while wiping away his tears. When finally they left the residence, they decided to head straight to Oakdale, Louisiana, home of Federal Correctional Institute Oakdale. F.C.I. Oakdale, in turn, was home to Paul Jon Luc Rochelle, or P.J., for short. P.J. Rochelle was Jamaica's father.

Jamaica and Tameer rented a room in one of the town's many cheap motels. Oakdale, like many other small prison towns, was filled with them. The town was host to many things; prisons, guards, and inmates weren't the only inhabitants. They shared the community with mosquitoes, alligators, and encroaching swamp, and thick, walking globs of humidity.

F.C.I. Oakdale was a large institution. It housed over twelve-hundred inmates, and consisted within its razor-sharp, wire fences, was a virtual city. The institution was flanked on all sides by massive armed guard towers, staffed by trained sharpshooters. The perimeter of the institution was constantly patrolled by roving pairs of trucks, which circled constantly, like buzzards around a carcass. This institution was for the big boys. The sight of it all, made Jamaica shiver.

Tameer's and Jamaica's entrance into the prison, transferred them into another world. The guards wore white button-down shirts, with gray slacks, burgundy neckties, and dark-blue sports coats. The prisoners were clothed in dark-brown work suits, with their last names and inmate numbers sewn over their shirt pockets.

The visitation room was fairly large, about fifty feet by seventy feet. Its walls were stark, as they were covered in a dull, non-reflective white. The floors of the room fared no better, as they were covered by thin, well-worn, brown industrial carpeting. The walls were lined with snack machines, interspersed with soda, and change machines. The microwave ovens, water fountains, and restrooms occupied only the right wall, which they shared with the trash receptacles, and the painted backdrop for the numerous family photos which were taken during the five-day visitation week. A massive, large-screen television set off to itself against the far wall of the room, and it had already attracted a large and still growing audience. It was tuned to a cartoon station.

The room itself was a cacophony of people talking, children playing, and babies crying. Tameer and Jamaica chose an area to the far of the room, near the rear, where they waited patiently for her father.

When P.J. entered into the room, he was recognized instantly. She never could have forgotten his rotund appearance, his pale skin, and his large, round jowls. His features set him apart from most others. P.J.'s fat cheeks were splattered with massive brown freckles, and his ever-ready smile was deemed by many, to be wider than the Mississippi River, where he played as a boy. His hair was long, thick, wavy, and jet-black. He wore it slicked back over his head and allowed it to hang freely down his shoulders. Like his daughter's eyes, his were of the light-green, emerald-colored variety. They were alive, bright, sparkling. P.J.'s eyes were eternal.

Jamaica quickly stood, and waved for her father to come over.

"Daddy! Daddy!" She bounced slightly, smiling as she called to him.

P.J. frowned at first. Then, he quickly tuned and looked behind himself. Seeing no one to his rear, he turned back toward Jamaica. His eyes flew wide. He couldn't believe it, it was his little girl. P.J.'s smile grew wider, with each of his steps toward Jamaica, until finally they embraced.

P.J. was a large man, he easily lifted his daughter into the air and twirled her around.

"What in heaven's sake are you doing here?" he asked. His accent was thick, syrupy, Cajun. It bordered on Patois.

"I snuck here," Jamaica answered. "Mommy doesn't know."

P.J. nodded. "I know your Mammy doesn't know, cuz, gal, she'd tan yo hide!"

Tameer could barely follow their conversation. P.J. sounded as if he were from the islands. His broken English was spoken in rapid-flowing, almost melodic tones. It seemed to be a combination of French, island Creole, and Louisiana Cajun speak, but oddly spoken in English words. He was shocked to hear Jamaica use some of the same kinds of words that her father was using, and even more shocked that she could understand what her father was saying.

P.J. waved to the cheap, plastic chairs that surrounded the equally cheap plastic table.

"Bunny, have seat," he told her.

Tameer's eyes met Jamaica's. *Bunny?* he mouthed to her with a smile.

"Forget you heard that," she told him. She turned back to her father. "Daddy, this is Tameer."

Tameer extended his hand, and P.J. took it.

"Nice to meet you, Mr. Rochelle."

P.J.'s forceful grip caused Tameer's expression to change slightly.

"Good to meet ya, son, the name's P.J. Everybody calls me P.J. The warden calls me P.J., the judge calls me P.J., the governor calls me P.J., the president calls me P.J., hell, the Speaker of the House calls me P.J., and I don't even like her!"

It made them all smile.

P.J. turned to Jamaica. "What in the hell brought you down here, Bunny? I mean, it's a blessin', but it's a surprise blessin'."

"Daddy, I've always wanted to come and see you. Mommy just wouldn't ..."

P.J. nodded and smiled. "I know, Bunny, your Mammy wouldn't let you." He reached out and caressed his daughter's face. "It's alright. Bev thought she was doing right. Now, don't you go an' hold it against yo mammy. She just wanted to protect you, from all a my bad doings."

Jamaica nodded. "I know, Daddy, she told me some things, but she kept some things secret."

P.J. knew what his daughter was getting at. Like any normal person in this situation, she had questions. And he knew that she deserved answers. P.J. leaned back carefully in the small, white, plastic chair, and placed his hands over his massive paunch.

"What all did Bev tell you?" he asked.

Jamaica looked over at Tameer, and then back at her father. She wished that Tameer weren't sitting right there with them. She was embarrassed about her family's history.

"Well, she told me that you were sentenced to thirty years, but that you would be out in twenty."

It was more of a question than a statement. P.J. nodded in acknowledgment, and Jamaica continued.

"She told me that it was some investment scam, involving you, China's dad, and Germany's dad, and a whole lot of others."

P.J. nodded again, this time interlacing his fingers, which remained rested on his paunch.

"Well, Bunny, I guess you're old enough now." He exhaled forcibly. "Me, and a bunch of other fellows, including China's dad, Mickey Anderson..." P.J. paused, and squinted his eyes, while staring at Jamaica. "Do you remember your Uncle Mickey?" he asked her.

Jamaica nodded.

"Well, we all sold a lot of bad bonds. They called them junk bonds, Sweetie. Well, we got busted, and the Feds came after me, Mickey, Cameron, and Bruce real bad. They gave all the white boys who were doing it, a slap on the wrist, and they all got out a long time ago."

"Why did they make you, Uncle Mickey, Uncle Bruce, and Cam do so much time?" Jamaica asked. She wanted her father home now. She wanted him home long ago.

P.J.'s easy smile appeared. "Well, Bunny, they also want some bad money that got laundered, and I wasn't givin' it up." He sat up in his chair. "They let me keep the measly two hundred million from the junk bonds, but they wanted the two billion in laundered money from our friends down south, which they can't have. That money is now mines!"

The numbers made Tameer swallow hard. Jamaica leaned forward to speak intimately with her father.

"Daddy, did you really launder the bad money?"

P.J. leaned back. "Of course I did! Everybody did it back then. Just because I invested my profits well, and they can't trace them, they are pissed off at me. I mean, that prosecutor was hotter than a hooker in a…well, let's just say he was mad, Sweetheart." P.J. blushed.

"So when are you getting out?" Jamaica asked him.

"In about three, maybe four, years." His smile appeared again. "I'm going to throw the biggest bash Switzerland has ever seen!"

It was now Jamaica who leaned back in her seat.

"Daddy, what do you know about Switzerland?" Jamaica had long thought that Switzerland belonged to her and her friends.

"Bunny, that's where a lot of the cash is. I was going to Switzerland before you were born. Why do you think your mother takes all them trips there?"

Jamaica's mouth flew open. "Mother's been helping you?"

"Of course!" P.J. told her. "Your mother loves me, we're partners. Jai, how do you think we paid for the karate lessons, the piano lessons, the singing lessons, Juilliard, the art lessons, the Porsche for your sixteenth birthday, the Ferrari for your high school graduation, the house in the Hamptons, the vacation home in Oak Bluffs, the apartment in Manhattan, the Château in Brittany, the town house in Paris, the ranch in Mexico, the …"

"Daddy!" Jamaica shouted. "How do you know all of these things!"

"Why, Bev," P.J. told her, "Bunny, your mammy kept me up on everything you gals ever did. I got pictures of you from the day I left, up until your last con…"

Jamaica's hands flew to her father's mouth, and she quickly turned her head toward a confused Tameer.

"Could you go and use the restroom real quick?" she asked him. It was obviously a command.

Tameer nodded. He knew that she needed to speak to her father in private for a few moments, and he wouldn't deprive her of that. Besides, he needed to splash some water on his face, anyway. He was not bewildered by Jamaica's hands over her father's mouth, but by P.J.'s wealth. Yeah, a splash of water would suit him just fine, he thought. Quietly, he rose, and departed for the restroom.

Jamaica removed her hands from her father's mouth, and again, P.J. smiled.

"That was absolutely the sweetest hand that I have ever tasted," he told her. Together, P.J. and Jamaica shared a laugh. He turned to the restroom door, which Tameer entered.

"He doesn't know about you, does he?" P.J. asked.

Jamaica shook her head. "No."

"He brought you down here from New York?"

"Texas."

"Texas!" P.J. exclaimed loudly. "What in the..."

"It's a long story, Daddy," Jamaica interrupted. "I'll tell you some other time, I promise. Please don't tell him."

P.J. leaned back inside the chair, and shifted his marblelike eyes toward the ground.

"Hmmmm, some other time?" He glanced up at Jamaica. "Does that mean I'm going to get more visits from my Bunny?"

"At least once a month." She nodded slowly. "Nothing can keep me from you now, Daddy."

Jamaica rose, and hugged her father tightly. "I love you, Daddy."

"I love you too, Bunny."

Jamaica sat back down, and quietly began to study her father. She resembled him in many ways, yet in many ways she also resembled her mother.

P.J. smiled at her. "Bunny, I think that you are one of the luckiest people on earth."

"Why is that, Daddy?"

"Because, if that there fella likes you, and he don't even know that you are some big star, then you have a chance at true love."

It made her smile.

"He loves me, Daddy, and I love him."

P.J. slapped his knee. "Then it's a match!"

Tameer exited the restroom wiping his hands. He quickly made his way across the room, and rejoined them.

"Is it okay for me to come back now, Bunny?" he whispered into Jamaica's ear.

Jamaica pinched him on his side. "You call me that again, and I'll punch you."

P.J. reached over, and slapped Tameer across his knee. "So, young man, what are your intentions with my baby?"

It made Jamaica smile.

Tameer swallowed hard. "Well, sir...I mean, P.J., I really love Jamaica. I want her to be a part of my life forever."

It was a decent answer, P.J. thought to himself. The kid's a charmer. It didn't matter anyway, charmer or no charmer, Bunny was in love. P.J. shifted his glance toward his daughter.

"Well, that's wonderful. Has Bev set to making wedding arrangements?"

Jamaica squirmed. "Well, Daddy, she hasn't met Tameer yet."

P.J. broke out into a bellowing laughter, as he thought of Bev's face when Jamaica finally took this boy home to meet her.

"Well...," P.J. said to Jamaica. "You be sure to have a camera ready when you break the news to Bev. That is an expression I certainly must see!"

After several more chuckles, P.J. turned to Tameer. "Where are you from?"

"San Antonio," Tameer answered uncomfortably.

"Texas, I see," P.J. replied. He now knew for sure that Tameer was in trouble. The fact that he was not from New York, would be a major strike against him.

"Well, what do you do for a living, son?" P.J. inquired next, hoping, almost praying that Tameer was a doctor.

"I'm still in school," Tameer answered. It was the wrong answer.

P.J. knew that Beverly was going to go ballistic. *Maybe the kid is studying to be a doctor.* He decided to ask.

"Majoring in?"

"Business, and literature," Tameer answered.

"Business and literature? I take it you must come from a very influential family, to choose those two."

"Well no, sir." Tameer's head fell to the floor.

The kid was broke, P.J. knew from the look upon Tameer's face. But still, he didn't know Bunny had money, either. *They are going to be starting out just like me and Bev did, when we were younger. Well, actually they aren't,* he remembered, *because Bunny had money. The kid can't be all bad, if Bunny likes him.*

"I see," P.J. told him. "Well, son, when I was a young man growing up in southern Louisiana, there were times when I didn't have a pair of shoes. My family was so poor, we lived in a four-room shack, using oil lamps for light, and a hole in the backyard for plumbing! We didn't have two nickels to rub together, but we had each other, and we kept our good name. My daughter has her own money, and I have made sure that she will never want for anything. So, she doesn't need a man with money. What Bunny needs, is a fine young gentleman, who will love her and cherish her. Can you do that?"

Tameer lifted his head, and his eyes locked on to Jamaica's. "With all of my heart."

"Good!" P.J. told him.

He saw they were in love. He could tell by the way Tameer looked at Jamaica, and by the way his Bunny stared at this young man. But Beverly, Jamaica's mother, wouldn't see that. No matter what it was in life, she had always wanted the best for her daughters. To Beverly, Tameer certainly would not be the best. P.J. watched the way she smiled at this Tameer fellow. How she pinched him, played with him, and gazed at him. Bunny was definitely in love.

P.J. had always known his daughter to be a trendsetter, a leader, always outgoing. Throughout her life she had been right on the money in most of her calls. P.J. trusted her judgment. If Bunny saw something special about him, then by God, there was something special about him. But Beverly... Beverly. She would crush all of that once she met him. She would crush everything they had, everything they wanted. He knew that they would not stand a snowball's chance in hell with his wife. He decided to help them.

"Bunny, you two remind me of your mother and myself when we were your age. Bev came from a large, rich, landed family down near Saint Martinsville, just west of the Miss."

P.J. laughed, causing his cheeks to flubber, and his belly to juggle like Jell-O. "They absolutely detested the Rochelle family, because we were considered poor, lower class. Her father had chosen for her a young beau from the Deverraux clan, and forbade her to see me."

P.J. swallowed hard, and leaned forward with outstretched hands, telling his story. "So one day, they had this large family gathering of Bouchairds, your mother's clan, and they invited all of the finest Bayou families to attend. Naturally, mines was not invited. But, I borrowed my granddaddy's finest silk ribbon tie, I put on my brother's brand-new school trousers, my daddy's white, cornstarched shirt, and my uncle's bright-red suspenders, and headed over. Well, needless to say, when I walked up, the music stopped, the dancing stopped, and the entire crowd gathered behind Bev's grandfather, your great-grandfather, Yves Bouchaird. So, here I am on one side, and the entire gathering on the other side, facing me. I knew it was going to be a lynching that night. I mean, I was so nervous, I could pee my pants! Well, old Yves tells me that he has forbidden me to see his granddaughter. Your granddaddy, and your uncles Marc, Luc, Peter, Jon, Girard, Antoine, Jacques, Stephon, and Yves III, are all standing around holding these big, long shotguns."

P.J. exhaled loudly at the memory. "So, I placed my thumbs underneath my suspenders like this here, and I straightened my back, cleared my throat, and looked directly at old Yves. I said, 'Sir, I know that you think that I'm not good enough for your granddaughter, and well...I think you are right. I am not good enough for Beverly, in fact, no one is. Not the ancient kings of France, not the great warrior chiefs in Africa, nor the angels in Heaven! I know that I don't have two thin dimes to rub together. But I guarantee on my honor, that Beverly will never know it, not suffer from it!' Your great-grandpa Yves squinted his eyes just so, looked at me real hard for a couple of minutes, and then turned and spit out his chew. I tell you, those were the longest two minutes of my life! But I stood straight, and I stood my ground. Finally, your great-grandpa said, 'Son, I think your balls are bigger than your brains. But courage is the foundation upon which true gentlemen are built. Come,' he said. 'Come and dance with my granddaughter.' Two years later, I married your mother, and we both left to attend Harvard."

Chapter Twenty-Eight

The visit with P.J. lasted for seven hours. In that time, Jamaica learned things about her mother and father which she never knew, nor even suspected.

Beverly and P.J. had graduated from Harvard together, along with LaChina's and Jemia's fathers. Beverly then went to work and supported the family, while P.J. went to business school, and then Harvard law. Her mother then returned to school and received her M.B.A., while P.J. worked. They had truly been partners their whole lives, and up to this day, were still madly in love with each other.

Jamaica now knew how truly wealthy her parents were, and why her mother had kept her father away from her, and out of public scrutiny. The funny thing, she learned, was that while at Harvard, her mother drove an old banged-up Volkswagen, and her parents had survived off Chinese food from the restaurant which they lived above. More importantly, she found out that her mother still visited P.J. Rochelle every month, and had been faithfully waiting for the return of her husband, the skinny little boy, with the borrowed, silk ribbon tie, from the swamps of southern Louisiana.

Jamaica felt sorry for Tameer, as her visit with her father went so well, while his with his mother did not. She loved Tameer, and she desperately wanted to ease his pain, yet she didn't want to risk saying the wrong things. Tameer spoke first, anyway.

"I'm never going to abandon my kids," he said to her. "I'm never going to treat them like refuse, I'm never going to hurt them like…" His sentence trailed off, but Jamaica knew the rest. He turned and faced her.

"Jai, I'm going to love my kids. I'm going to always tell them that I love them. I'm not going to push them, or make them do things that they really don't want to do. I'm going to let them live their own dreams, and not make them live mines."

Tameer shifted in his seat, as did Jamaica. He had said a mouthful. It made her think of her mother, and how she had thrust her into show business. She had wanted other things out of life, but those dreams had been squashed a long time ago. Tameer swallowed hard, and turned to Jamaica again.

"I'm going to be a different dad. I want to go to PTA meetings, I want to fly kites in the park, I want to push swings, and bandage scraped knees. I'm going to teach them how to ride bikes, and I'm going to be there to catch them when they fall. I want to help them with their homework, and get up on Sundays and take them to church."

"It sounds like a good plan," Jamaica told him. She kept her eyes forward, staring at the empty road.

Tameer clenched his fist, and pounded the air. "It's not a plan!" he declared. "It's a promise! I swear to God, I'm going to be better than my parents. I'm going to do things right."

Jamaica nodded. "I believe you." This time she looked at him, and offered a comforting smile.

Tameer dropped Jamaica off at her motel room at about six p.m. The road trip had been long, and she had driven the majority of it, but Jamaica was not tired. She found herself energetic, invigorated, renewed. Seeing her father had given her a new outlook on life. As a result, she flounced inside of the motel room, without even noticing the large, black, S600 Mercedes parked outside of the front door.

When Jamaica opened the door to the motel room, she found an unexpected visitor lying on top of LaChina's unmade double bed. Quickly, she cried out.

"Kenya!"

Her younger sister stood, and they embraced. Jamaica was all smiles. "What are you doing here?"

Although one year apart, she and Kenya could almost pass for twins.

"I came to visit Jemia," answered Kenya. "The sorority sisters are meeting here next month, but I wanted to come down early and spend some more private time with her first.

Kenya tilted her head to the side, and lifted her hands into the air. "Plus, I came to warn you, that Mother is on her way."

Jamaica's eyes flew open wide. "What?"

Kenya nodded. "Bev is on her way."

"How?" Jamaica asked. Her arms flew out to her sister's shoulders. "How did she find us? As far as she knows, we're in the Caribbean by now!"

Kenya shook her head slowly. "Uh-un, receipts, credit card bills. *Expensive* credit card bills!"

Jamaica's hands flew to her face and she covered her mouth. "Oh, shit!" She turned and stared at LaChina.

LaChina smiled and shrugged her shoulders. "Ooooooops."

"Mom's furious," Kenya told them.

"When....I mean, how long do we have?" Jamaica asked her sister.

"Two days, three would be stretching it," Kenya answered.

"Twenty-four hours is too quick, she'll need that long just to pack."

Kenya nodded and stared off into space. "Yep, I'll say two days is a safe bet."

The knock at the door was more frustrating than startling. Tameer was not expecting anyone, nor did he want to see anyone. Not Savion's friends, not his friends, not even Jamaica. His mind was still on Houston.

He rose slowly from the couch, and headed for the door. His intentions were to get rid of whomever it was, and do it quick. The visitor, of course, had other ideas.

"Dawshanique!" Tameer called out in surprise. He was surprised to see her, but still, he didn't feel like being bothered by her, either. However, he did have several questions that he wanted to ask: what was she doing here, and why did she start the fight with Jamaica. She spoke first.

"Tameer, I want you to know why I did what I did, why I left. Tameer, I knew that you loved me, and I loved you. I still do." Her voice was calm, soft, serene, yet it had a distant crackle in it, as though she had been crying. Slowly, Dawshanique eased her way inside of the apartment.

"I wanted the best for you, I wanted the best for us. You had so much potential."

Dawshanique walked past Tameer, who was still standing near the entrance, and she sat on the couch. She was in.

"I wanted you to live up to that potential, I wanted you to have the best, and be the best. So...so I thought I could get you to play football, if I threatened to leave you alone forever." Dawshanique's head fell toward the floor, just as she had rehearsed all morning. "But it backfired, and I ended up losing you, instead of helping you." Her tears began to fall.

Tameer folded his arms, and shifted his weight to one side. He knew Dawshanique better than that, and he wasn't buying it.

"Dawshanique, that's not what you said. You said that you wanted to marry a professional athlete, whether it be me, or someone else. You said that you were going to marry one, and get the hell outta these Courts."

Dawshanique stood. "Tameer!" She stomped the ground hard. "That's not what I meant!"

Dawshanique turned away from Tameer, and began weeping again.

"I know that I can't express myself like you, because I didn't go to college." She turned and faced him with tears running down her cheek. "And I know that I'm not some glamorous movie star, mega singer like she is, but I still have feelings! I love you, Tameer. I know you've found your ticket out of here, and I don't blame you. But we were supposed to get out of here together. You remember our vow?" Dawshanique broke down into tears again.

Tameer unfolded his arms. He thought she was crazy, or on drugs.

"Dawshanique, what the hell are you talking about? You know I hate it when you're drunk."

She stomped the ground again.

"I'm not drunk!" she shouted. "And you know what I'm talking about. I'm talking about Tiera, your little girlfriend who started the fight with me! I'm talking about the one who's always wearing your clothes, driving your car, and sleeping in your bed! It hurts, Tameer...it hurts!"

He was frustrated, and confused. The hurt from his mother, and now the argument with Dawshanique, only served to aggravate him even more. Quickly, he reached out and grabbed Dawshanique's arm, and began pulling her toward the door.

"I think you should leave."

"I know I can't act, I know I can't sing, and I know I'm not rich and famous, but Tameer... I love you!"

He stopped. "Dawshanique, what in the hell are you talking about?"

"Tiera!"

"Jamaica?" he asked.

"Her name is Tiera! Look!" Dawshanique reached into her pants pocket, and pulled from it a CD case with Jamaica Tiera Rochelle's picture on the front of it. It stunned him.

Tameer snatched the CD case away from Dawshanique's hand, and quickly turned away from her. He carefully examined the cover of the CD. It said "Tiera" in bold letters beneath the picture, but it was Jamaica. He was sure of that much. *Yes*, he told himself, *it is Jamaica*.

His movements and his expression gave him away. Dawshanique knew him, she had studied Tameer like a book. She now knew, that he had not known.

"Son-of-a-bitch!" It slipped out. Nonetheless, she went into attack mode.

"Tameer, you mean you didn't know?" she asked him, already knowing the answer.

Tameer ignored her question. He walked slowly over to the couch, all the while staring at the picture on the CD case cover, and sat down.

"She's been deceiving you all along!" Dawshanique said out loud. It was more a second revelation, a sought-after confirmation, than it was a statement. It was confirmed by his silence. Dawshanique could barely contain her smile.

"All of the hip-hop magazines say that she is going to be appearing in this new movie. It's one of those 'in the hood' movies. She's using you, Tameer! She's using you as research for her next role. She doesn't love you, you're just a toy! You're a project, a play thing, like a gerbil, or hamster. When she's through, she'll go back to her world, and she'll make millions of dollars on her next movie. But you and I...we'll still be here."

Her delivery had been perfect. The seeds of destruction had been planted, and her mission was complete. Dawshanique knew when to exit. She wanted him to be alone, so that he could feel alone. He could sit in silence and think about the witch's deception.

Finally, Dawshanique left him. She intentionally left the door open on her way out, so that Tameer could feel the cold striking him as he sat. *Cold and alone*, she thought, as she strutted down the streets of the Courts. *Cold and alone. Perfect!* Dawshanique skipped and smiled the rest of the way home.

Chapter Twenty-Nine

The drive to the record store had been a short one. Ten minutes in average traffic, fifteen in heavy. Today, the traffic had been surprisingly light.

The record store was crowded, but not more so than any of the other establishments, with it being so close to Christmas. Tameer's determination had waned significantly since Dawshanique's revelation, and he now found himself plodding slowly through the aisles of the store.

He wanted to know, but then again, he didn't. Maybe it was a mistake, he told himself. Maybe it was a coincidence. Her name was Jamaica, he knew, while the girl's name on the CD case was Tiera. A look at some more CDs would provide a world of insight. He hoped that this Tiera person, whoever she was, had more than one CD. To see her photo from different angles, maybe wearing different garments, would surely allow him to rid himself of this silly suspension. Tameer wanted to put Dawshanique's silly accusations to rest and go home. That was what he would do, he told himself. And then he could tell Jamaica about the whole silly thing, and they could laugh about it for weeks. Then, he would call and try to get Dawshanique some help, he thought. Surely, he owed her that much.

Tameer arrived at the section which contained the T's. He began to feel his stomach perform the dance of the butterflies. In the instance, the butterflies were doing the Lambada.

The first CD belonged to Tamara, the second Taral, the third Temia. The fourth and largest group of CDs belonged to a songstress named Tiera.

There were five CDs in this group, and he pulled the first. Examining the picture on the cover of the CD caused him pain. He knew it was Jamaica.

The hair, the smile, the pear-shaped face, along with the haughtiness in her pose, all screamed Jamaica. The second and third CDs that he examined, only cemented his opinion. There was no need to examine the fourth or fifth. He brought them all, anyway.

"Will that be all, sir?" asked the young woman behind the register.

He gave her a solemn nod.

She pointed toward a large, life-sized, cardboard cutout poster which stood near the exit.

"You know we have our Tiera videos on sale," she told him. "They're next to the big poster."

Tameer turned and looked. It was Jamaica smiling, or this Tiera person, or whoever the hell she was. She was smiling…no, laughing at him. The poster was laughing at him. Tameer could only turn and smile at the salesgirl. He did it to keep his tears from falling.

"Thank you," he told her when she finished ringing up the merchandise. He turned, and walked straight to the poster. It was her.

He gazed at it, not knowing what to say, what to think, or what to feel. The main thing on his mind, was why? Why did she choose him, why did she have to use him, he thought.

Tameer lifted several of the DVDs containing Jamaica's numerous music video hits, and returned to the cash register. His purchasing of the videos concluded his transactions for the day. His journey past the poster upon exiting the store brought tears to his eyes. He could no longer hold them inside. Why did she have to play games with him, he wondered. Why him? He was hurt, he felt betrayed, revealed. He had opened himself up, laughed, and shared his dreams to a lie. It was all a lie. He shook his head slowly, and the tears fell.

"China, I keep calling, but no one will answer," Jamaica said to her friend as she hung up the telephone. "I know that it was him that answered the phone and hung up when I said, 'hi.'"

Jamaica turned and met her friend's eyes. "Do you think that bitch is over there?"

LaChina, who was seated at the cheap motel desk that had been provided for them, crossed her legs and shook her head.

"Jai, I don't think so. Tameer's not trifling like that." *At least I hope not,* she didn't say aloud.

Jamaica turned, and sat on the bed next to her sister. "I know, but why won't he answer the phone, or his damn text messages!"

"Jai, I've never seen you like this over a guy before," said Kenya, who leaned over and hugged her sister. "What's gotten into you?"

Kenya peered across the room to where LaChina was seated. LaChina stuck out her tongue and wiggled it around, to answer Kenya's question. Jamaica caught her.

"You're so crass!" Jamaica shouted, lobbing a pillow at her friend.

LaChina and Kenya laughed heartily.

"Jai, he's probably on the road, and can't pull over to call you back," Kenya told her.

"Yeah," LaChina agreed. "Hell, he's probably on his way over here."

"You think so?" Jamaica asked. "I mean … he usually would have called by now. I haven't heard from him since the day before yesterday."

Jamaica exhaled loudly and stood. "Something's wrong, I'm going over." Jamaica strode over to the desk, where she searched for her car keys. "China, have you seen my keys?"

"Jai, sit down," LaChina told her. "I'm sure he'll call."

Jamaica folded her arms. "China, where are my keys?"

"Jai, I understand you like the boy, but chasing him around…"

LaChina did not get to finish her sentence, as Jamaica extended her finger to LaChina's lips shushing her, and turned to her sister.

"Let me use the Benz," Jamaica asked.

"Jai, China is right," Kenya told her. "Let him call you."

"Are you going to let me use the car, or do I have to call for a taxi?"

Kenya exhaled, shook her head, and went inside of her purse. She tossed Jamaica her car keys.

"Thank you," Jamaica answered, snatching the keys out of the air. She turned, and headed for the door.

Upon opening it, Jamaica was surprised to find someone standing in the doorway. It was her mother, Beverly Bouchaird Rochelle. Jamaica screamed, causing LaChina and Kenya to look toward the door, and upon seeing Beverly, they too screamed.

Tameer hung up the telephone. The local radio station's regular DJ was off today, but the fill-in told him that there had been no new car give-away in the last month. In fact, that radio station had never given a car away, he told Tameer. And in case Tameer happened to locate a radio station with that kind of budget, the DJ asked that he give a call, so he could quickly submit his resume. In other words, the contest had been a fake.

The first music video was uneventful. The second, however, showcased Jamaica dressed in an elegant, long, white, form-fitting, evening gown. Her neck glittered from an exquisite layered piece from Harry Winston, and her sparkling earrings which hung elegantly from her mocha ears, were from the same. Her high-split, Dior evening gown, sparkled like her jewelry, as the lighting illuminated the thousands of platinum-colored sequences which were sewn into it. Jamaica was stunning.

The crowd cheered wildly for her in this video, and it made him feel even more stupid. He must have been the only one in the entire world, who didn't know who she was. But the one thing that he did know, he recognized the song which she sang for the crowd on this video. It was the song she sung to him, while she caressed his head as it laid inside of her lap, in front of his mother's home in Houston. Tameer sat silently and listened to the words again. It took only two choruses, before his tears began to fall.

Chapter Thirty

Beverly pointed her finger at Jamaica. "I don't want to hear it, the conversation is closed!" she declared forcefully.

Jamaica exhaled loudly and jumped onto the massive king-sized bed. "You're treating me like a child!" she shouted at her mother.

Beverly slowly walked across the plush, cut pile carpeting of the grand suite to the bar, where she began fixing herself a drink. The suite was on the top floor of the five-star LaCantera luxury resort hotel. It was a two-thousand-dollar-a-night suite.

"Jamaica, I must treat you like a child, because you continue to act like one!" Beverly told her. She lifted the crystal glass of twelve-year-old Scotch to her lips and sipped.

"Never have I been able to trust you. Never!" Beverly sipped from her glass again, and then continued. "I allowed you to leave New York alone, to do a quick one-day promotional, and then depart for a relaxing Caribbean vacation."

Beverly turned and walked quickly to her large, lime-colored Hermes Kelly bag, where she rumbled inside, and then pulled out a hand full of credit card bills and bank withdrawal slips.

"Instead, I received these!" She turned and waved the bills and bank slips at Jamaica. "Ten thousand-dollar cash withdrawal, twenty thousand-dollar cash withdrawal, thirty thousand dollars to Toys-R-Us, seven thousand dollars to The Tree Shop, fifteen thousand dollars to Albertson's grocery store, thirty thousand dollars to Kroger grocery store, forty-eight thousand, nine hundred and fifteen dollars, and thirty-three cents, to Northside Ford, and two thousand, seventeen dollars to the Athletes Foot, and so on, and so forth!"

Beverly wheeled toward her daughter. "Where's the car, Jamaica? Where's the food? Where are the clothes? Where are the toys?"

"I gave the food away to people who needed it," Jamaica answered softly. "And the toys and Christmas trees were for the kids."

"What kids?" Beverly demanded

"The kids in the Courts!"

"Courts? What are Courts?" Beverly asked. "What are you talking about?"

"Projects, mother. Housing projects. Low-income housing tenements!"

Beverly clasped her chest, and immediately sat down upon one of the plush, crème-colored, leather sofas inside of the suite.

"Oh my God! My daughter has been traipsing around inside of a low-income housing settlement." Beverly took several shallow breaths, and then rose and walked to the telephone. "I know, I'll call Dr. Burkes, he'll know what to do."

Jamaica leaped to her feet and rushed to the telephone. "Mother! I'm not crazy, I don't need a shrink!" Jamaica snatched the telephone from Beverly's hand, and placed it back down inside of its cradle.

Beverly placed one of her hands on her hip, while the other rubbed the lower half of her face. Soon, she placed her hand on Jamaica's chin and squeezed her cheeks.

"Jamaica, you do need help," Beverly told her. "You have been racing around this place, wearing hooded rags and mountain boots, using terrible grammar, and traipsing around in what I could only hope to describe as impoverished tenements."

Beverly caressed Jamaica's face. "My poor, poor baby needs help."

Jamaica stomped. "Mommy! I'm not crazy!"

Beverly reached for the telephone. "We'll let Dr. Burkes be the judge of that."

Jamaica wheeled, and ran to the wall outlet, where she yanked the telephone cord out of the socket.

Beverly's hand flew to her mouth. "Oh my God! Jamaica, honey, plug the phone up for Mummy."

Jamaica rose, and folded her arms defiantly.

Beverly extended her arms. "Bunny, come to mother. You and Mummy will go for ice cream and talk."

Jamaica exhaled, and then recrossed her arms.

"Jamaica, don't be stubborn. Mummy will even let you drive. We can ride in your little Ford thing."

Jamaica's eyes flew wide, and she quickly glanced at LaChina. Beverly looked at LaChina also, and saw that her eyes were even wider than Jamaica's. Beverly then turned toward Kenya, who was fidgeting nervously in the recliner, next to a wide-eyed LaChina. It told her enough. She turned back to Jamaica.

"Where's the car?" Beverly asked her.

Jamaica unfolded her arms and quickly strode to where her mother was standing.

"C'mon, Mummy, let's go for ice cream," she said in her most girlish of voices. She clasped Beverly's arm. "We can take the Benz."

Beverly lifted her hand, stopping Jamaica in her tracks.

"Where's the car?" Beverly asked again. "You paid forty-eight thousand dollars for a car that you do not need, and would normally not be caught dead in. Now where is it?"

Jamaica lowered her head as she mumbled the answer.

"Excuse me?" Beverly asked, not understanding the answer. She stepped closer. "Speak up, dear, I can't hear you."

"I said... Tameer... has... it."

Beverly shook her head, and cupped her hand around her ear. "I'm sorry, it sounded like you said that some boy had it?"

"I... did," Jamaica answered. It was almost a whisper.

"Oh, so you've hired another assistant?" Beverly asked.

Jamaica shook her head in the negative.

Beverly quickly lifted her glass of Scotch from the end table, and this time, she did more than sip.

LaChina leaned forward in her seat. "Aunt Bev, it's my..."

Her sentence was interrupted by Beverly's raised hand. "LaChina, you will always be like a daughter to me, but you are fired. Fired, fired, fired!"

"You can't fire her!" Jamaica shouted. "She works for me!"

"Jamaica, enough of this foolishness!" Beverly said sternly.

"You're right, enough of this foolishness," Jamaica shot back. "Mother, you're fired!"

Beverly choked on her Scotch, spitting it from her mouth. She quickly set her glass back on top of the end table. "Jamaica, you can't fire me, I'm your mother!"

Jamaica stomped the ground hard. "I didn't fire you as my manager; I fired you as my mother!"

The room was silent for several long, awkward moments, before Jamaica's poked-out bottom lip, and childlike pouting, caused Beverly to laugh. Her laughter was followed by Jamaica's, then LaChina's, and finally Kenya's. Beverly extended her arms toward her daughter.

"Come here, Jamaica."

Jamaica walked to her mother and they embraced.

"Come back to New York with me, and get some rest."

Jamaica shook her head. "I can't, I want you to meet him first."

"Meet who?"

"Tameer."

Beverly exhaled forcibly. "Jamaica, there are many wealthy, eligible, young bachelors on the East Coast. Forget about him."

Jamaica lifted her head from her mother's shoulder and stared at her. "I can't, I really..."

"Jamaica, he wants you for your money," Beverly interrupted. "There are many wealthy, young..."

Jamaica pulled away from her mother. "He doesn't want me for my money."

Beverly lifted the credit card receipts for the car.

"He thinks that he won the car from a radio station," Jamaica told her. "He doesn't know who I am."

Beverly turned. "Oh, Jamaica, please! You are the biggest R&B and pop music star in the world. You're the most sought-after young actress on the entire planet. It's virtually impossible for anyone to turn on a television and not see you, or a radio and not hear you. Everyone knows who you are. LaChina makes sure of that."

"He doesn't. That's why I dress like this, that's why I have the knit bini hats," Jamaica explained. "He doesn't know who I am, he doesn't want my money, my fame, or anything else. He just wants me, Mummy, me!"

LaChina adjusted herself in her seat. "Bev, he doesn't know."

Beverly peered down at her love-stricken daughter and shook her head. She still did not believe them, but still, if it would get Jamaica to go back to New York immediately, then she would meet this con artist. Beverly exhaled loudly once again.

"And this boy is from the tenements, the flats, the..."

"The Courts, Mother," Jamaica corrected her. "It's called the Courts."

She moved closer to her mother and clasped her hands together. "Please come with me and meet him. Please..."

Beverly recoiled. "I will not do any such thing! I will not venture into any such..."

"No!" Jamaica shook her head fervently. "We'll go to his job."

"His job?" Beverly asked in surprise.

"Yes, he has a job."

"I don't suppose he's a young United States representative, or an exceptionally young junior partner at a massive law firm?" Beverly asked.

Jamaica shook her head. "No."

"Tell me he works at a hospital...where he's a dashing young surgeon?"

"A shoe store..." Jamaica told her. "Where he's a dashing young shoe salesman."

Beverly turned and quickly lifted her drink from the table.

Chapter Thirty-One

The store was empty, which was usual for this time of the day, especially during the work week. Tameer, and two other salespersons, were gathered behind the counter wearing their usual striped referee jerseys, and black work trousers. They were watching an old DVD of Tyson, who was pulverizing one of his opponents in the ring.

Jamaica waved upon entering the store. "Hi, honey!"

Jamaica was followed by LaChina, Kenya, and Beverly. Upon seeing them, Tameer turned to his co-workers.

"Give us a couple of minutes," he asked them. They obliged, by retreating to the rear stocking area of the store.

Jamaica strode behind the counter and wrapped her arms around Tameer. He didn't return her embrace.

"So, why haven't you called, or answered any of my text messages?" Jamaica asked.

Tameer grabbed Jamaica's arms, and removed them from his shoulders. Jamaica recoiled.

"What's gotten into you?"

Beverly frowned at her daughter's grammar. Tameer grabbed a DVD from beneath the sales counter, turned, and ejected the boxing disc from the combination TV/DVD that hung suspended on the wall. He inserted the new disc, and watched quietly as it automatically began to play.

Tiera, live in concert, appeared on the television. Jamaica closed her eyes and lowered her head. She listened silently, as the song that she sang to him in front of his mother's house, played on the television.

Jamaica remembered that concert, the live taping in Vancouver. It had been a magical night for her. Her performance that evening had been flawless. They were able to raise over ten million dollars for war victims in Darfur because of that concert. It had truly been a special moment in her life. Jamaica wished that she could keep her eyes closed, as she would much rather reminisce on the pleasantness of that evening, than open them to the harsh realities of this one. But, she knew that she had to face him; she knew that she had to open her eyes.

"I was going to tell you," she said softly. It was almost a whisper.

Tameer's back was toward her, as he was still staring at the television's screen. She could feel the intensity of his gaze, which was fixated upon her image on the screen. She wanted it to be over, she wanted this terrible moment to be over. It hurt her more so, because he had not yet turned to face her.

"When?" Tameer asked, still watching her performance on the monitor.

"I..." She could only stammer.

"After you were through using me for research for your next movie?" he asked.

She was confused. "Tameer, what are you talking about?"

He turned and faced her. "C'mon, Jamaica... I'm sorry, I mean, Tiera. Your next movie. Your next hood movie."

His smile hurt. It was devastating, because of its genuineness. It was genuine in its bitterness. He was already convinced that she had purposely deceived him, and she knew that there was nothing that she could really say. Tameer folded his arms in finality. Jamaica told herself, that she still had to try. She at least had to give it one more try.

"Tameer, I wasn't using you for anything."

He shook his head. "Your role, the one in *Poets and Gangsters*, about the rapper from the hood. I know all about it...Tiera."

Every time he called her that, it pierced her heart like an icicle. *Tiera*, she thought. It had rolled off his tongue like a ball of poison. She hated it.

"I haven't even started shooting that movie yet!" Jamaica protested. She didn't even know if she ever would.

Tameer's arms unfolded, and he pointed his finger at her accusingly. "Because you're still researching your damn role! You used me! You lied to me!"

Jamaica's hands flew out and clasped Tameer's arms. He stepped back, and pulled his arms away from her.

"Tameer, I didn't use you!" Her arms hung in the air, wanting to grab him, wanting to hug him, but unable to. They trembled nervously.

"Everything I felt was real! Everything I said to you was real! I fell in love with you, Tameer, and that was no acting, and it wasn't for any damn movie! I... love you."

"Which one of you, Jamaica or Tiera?" It was cold.

"Both! God dammit, Tameer, both of them!" Jamaica's hand flew to her forehead, and using her thumb and forefinger, she gently massaged her temples.

"I am one person," she told him calmly. "I am Jamaica Tiera Rochelle."

"Well, I'm pleased to finally meet you." He patted his shirt and pants pockets rapidly. "I wish that I had something for you to sign."

Tameer searched inside of a drawer behind the counter and found a pen. He placed it in her hand. "I'll tell you what. Why don't you go back to the motel room, look inside of your chest full of play things, and autograph my heart for me. When you get through playing with it, send it back to me, will you?"

Jamaica shook her head. "Tameer, don't."

"Don't what? Don't tell the truth? Don't tell you that I fell in love with you, and that you were the best thing that ever happened to me?"

"Tameer, I'm still that person. I'm still that same person."

Tameer shook his head slowly. "No, no, you're not. The person who I thought I knew, I could trust. I trusted her, I shared my life with her, I shared my dreams with her, I let her into my home!"

Tameer slapped his hand across his forehead. "My God, you've been to my home!" He turned back to Jamaica. "I'll bet you have fun describing it to your little friends!"

"Tameer, it's not like..."

"I'll bet you laughed real hard about old Tameer. The washed-up athlete, with the quacked-out mother, and the crackhead dad! I can see it now." Tameer lifted his hand to his ear, as if he were talking on a telephone. "We have to change the script. I want to add a dysfunctional mother, and a crackhead father to the movie."

Tears rolled down Jamaica's cheek as she shook her head. "That's real fucked up, Tameer. That's real fucked up."

Tameer turned toward LaChina, and withered away her scathing glance with one of his own. "You were in on this too. You're no better than she is. Is this what they taught you at Spelman? That we're no longer real people because we're poor? That we're play things to be toyed with and manipulated at your pleasure?"

"You know it's not like that!" LaChina told him.

"The only thing that I know, is that I fell in love with a lie!" Tameer turned toward Jamaica. "It was a great big one. You hurt a lot of people. You came down to our world like some high and mighty goddess, bestowing gifts and favors, manipulating people, and interfering in people's lives. You know what, when you're gone, we'll still be here. We'll still be struggling, still be trying to survive, still be trying to get out of the Courts. Leave me alone. I don't want your damn gifts. *We* don't want your damn gifts!"

Tameer reached into his pocket and pulled out his car keys. He tossed them across the counter to her. "Go back to your world!"

Jamaica turned and flew from the store in tears. Kenya ran after her sister, leaving behind a smiling Beverly, and a guilt-ridden LaChina. Beverly stepped forward and spoke first.

"Impressive. Most impressive," she told him, while clapping her hands in a slow, methodical, almost sinister applause. "Well, young man, you have done me a great service. Maybe now my daughter will understand, that there are elements in society which one simply does not have contact with. She will now return with me to New York, where she will soon forget about you, and this God-forsaken place, marry successfully, and then continue with a long and prosperous career. For your service, you may keep the Ford thing."

Beverly pushed the keys back across the counter to Tameer. They flew off the counter and landed on the floor near his feet.

"If you do not tell the tabloids of your relationship with my daughter, I will give you one hundred thousand dollars. It is more than they will wish to pay. Consider the car a bonus. The check will be forwarded to you in the mail."

Beverly turned away from Tameer, smiled and strutted off. "Good day, young man."

LaChina turned, and followed Beverly out of the store.

Chapter Thirty-Two

The empty carton which once contained some thirty-five chocolate Bon-Bons, landed near the trash receptacle, joining the four other empty Bon-Bon cartons that preceded it. Crying, Jamaica rolled over onto her stomach and began opening another carton. LaChina continued to rub Jamaica's back.

"Jai, you're going to get fat."

"What difference does it make?" Jamaica asked.

"You won't be able to do all of your own steps in your videos anymore," LaChina replied.

"I'm not doing any more videos."

LaChina tilted her head to the side. "Jai."

"I'll use a body double!" Jamaica pouted.

Kenya sat down on the bed next to her sister. She too began to pat Jamaica on her back.

"Use a body double walking along the French Riviera in that two-piece," she told her. Kenya leaned forward and grabbed the carton of chocolate-covered ice cream balls from Jamaica. "Or, try using a body double for the two-piece string you're going to be wearing on the beach in St. Kitts."

"I'm not going to the beach," Jamaica told them.

"The ship ports, Jai," LaChina told her.

"I know, but I'm still not going ashore," Jamaica replied. She turned to LaChina. "Do you think the ship sells Bon-Bons?"

LaChina stood, turned, and extended her arms. She waved her fingers, motioning for Jamaica to rise. "Come here, sister."

"No."

"Come here," LaChina repeated.

Jamaica rolled over and sat up. LaChina leaned forward and wrapped her arms around Jamaica. She began to rock Jamaica from side to side.

"It's going to be alright, Jai. Kenya has called all of the Chipmunks, and sent out the broken-heart distress signal. When we get back to New York, all of the sisters will be there, and we'll start the Chipmunk heart-healing process. We'll have slumber parties, and we'll go out to all of the clubs and get drunk. We'll introduce you to lots of handsome, eligible, young men, and you'll forget all about your broken heart."

"I don't want any handsome young men, I want Tameer!"

Kenya and LaChina laughed. Jamaica joined them in their laughter.

"That's not what I meant," Jamaica told them. "He's handsome... You know what I meant."

Across the room, Beverly placed the suite's telephone back inside of its cradle. She exhaled loudly, and then turned to them. "I used every means at my disposal, and I was finally able to secure you two a pair of first-class cabin suites aboard the Empress of the Sea. She departs tomorrow evening from Miami, so you'll have to fly out tonight."

Jamaica's head fell to LaChina's shoulder, and LaChina caressed it gently.

"It'll be alright, Jai," LaChina said softly. "It takes time."

Tameer pressed the off button and tossed the cordless telephone onto the couch. He turned to Savion. "Save, I just got a call from New York. They say that I won some big poetry contest!"

Savion shrugged his shoulders. "That's cool. How much ya win?"

"They really didn't say. They were mainly talking about me publishing a book of my works." Tameer sat back down on the couch. "Wait a minute, I'll bet you it's Jamaica again. She probably had some bum off the street call..."

"Nope!" Savion interrupted. "That's not her style."

Tameer shot his brother a look. "What do you mean, 'not her style'? Since when did you become so familiar with her 'style' any damn way?" Tameer stood.

Savion stopped eating his cereal and peered across the table at Eddie Lee. They shared a quick smile. Savion turned back to his brother and exhaled forcibly.

"Are you going to pace the floor again all day?" Savion asked.

"If I do, what business is it of yours?" Tameer snapped.

"Touchy, touchy. Your whole little world came crashing down on you, and now you want to snap at me," Savion told him.

Tameer nodded. "Sorry, but you are being a smart ass today."

"I'm not being the ass, you're being the ass," Savion replied.

Tameer stopped pacing. "Didn't we have this conversation last night?"

"Jamaica entered you into the poetry contest, if you wanna know," Savion said flatly.

"How do you know?" Tameer asked.

"I was here when she did it. Hell, I helped her."

Again, Tameer stopped his pacing and stared at his brother. "Whose side are you on? Great! That's just great!" Tameer threw his arms into the air. "Who else is conspiring against me?"

Savion pushed away his now empty cereal bowl. "No one has to conspire against you, you'll always screw yourself up."

"And what's that supposed to mean?" Tameer asked angrily.

"You figure it out," Savion replied.

Tameer threw his hand into the air again. "Savion, I told you what she did!"

"I know what she did. She said her name was Jamaica, which it is. She just didn't tell you that her middle name was Tiera."

Her middle name? How did Savion know...

"Whose side are you on?" Tameer exploded. "Dammit, Savion! You knew! You knew, didn't you?"

Savion smiled. "Of course, I knew."

Tameer pointed his finger at his brother and started toward him. "You knew, and you didn't tell me!"

"You didn't ask. Besides, Tameer, you were happy!"

"I was lied to!"

"By who? Who lied to you, and what was the lie?" Savion asked. "Did you ever ask her if she was a damn R&B star? Did you? No! You only saw what Tameer wanted to see. That's how you are! You live in Tameer's world, and not the real world! It's always about what Tameer wants, and not about what anybody else wants!"

Savion rose from the table and approached his brother. "Did you ever think to ask her, or ask yourself, why she didn't tell you? Look at the way you're acting! Can you blame her for not telling you?"

Tameer turned away from his brother and smashed his fist into the palm of his other hand.

"Dammit, Savion, it's not that simple!" He turned back to his brother. "She shouldn't have lied in the beginning. She should have been truthful."

"What lie did she tell you? That she loved you? You know that wasn't a lie. When she slept with you, was that a lie? Do you really think that somebody would go through all of that, give me money for college, buy you a car, give away toys and Christmas trees to kids, and food to families, just to rehearse for a damn movie role? Think, Tameer! And don't just think about things from your perspective; think about things from everyone else's. She loves you, and you love her. You need her. She got you out of that slump, that stupid 'I'm not worthy mentality,' that you used to run around here with. Jamaica brought out the best in you. I hadn't seen you like that since Dawshanique. Hell, she even fought for you!"

Savion swallowed hard and stepped closer to his brother. "She believed in your poetry, Tameer. She believed in you. The worst thing you could ever do is leave her alone because she loved you. She loved you so much, that she had to hide who she was, just to keep you."

Slowly, Tameer lifted his head, and he stared into his younger brother's eyes.

"Perspective? Mentality?" A smile appeared. "Have you been messing around in my dictionary again?"

The brothers shared a good hard laugh for several moments, before Tameer nudged Savion's shoulder with his own.

"Savion, when did you become the big brother?" Tameer asked.

"I'm not." Savion smiled. "I thought about what my big brother would say to me, if the situation were reversed."

"Come here," Tameer told him.

The brothers embraced.

"Tameer," Eddie Lee called out to him.

Both Savion and Tameer turned in the direction of their father. Eddie Lee cleared his throat.

"I know that...well, seeing you two boys together makes me think sometimes, that I didn't do too bad after all."

It made them smile.

"I... sons, I... I know that I haven't been the best father to you, and I put you through some changes. I loved your mother, and well... I ran her off with my fist..."

"No, you didn't," Tameer interrupted his father. "She was leaving, anyway."

Eddie Lee sat up straight in his chair. "Who... who told you that?"

"She did," Tameer told him. "I went and visited her in Houston last week. She left us, Dad. She left all of us. It wasn't your fault. Dad, you stayed here, and you raised us by yourself. You kept food on the table, clothes on our backs, and a roof over our heads."

Tameer looked down and shook his head. "You drove us hard, Dad. I mean, *hard*." He lifted his head slowly, and once again met his father's eyes. "But neither Savion nor I have ever sold nor used any drugs, and neither of us has ever been to jail. I'm graduating with honors from college in a semester, and Savion's on his way to college with a full scholarship next year. Thanks... Dad."

Eddie Lee had never been a man of many words, and he didn't have any now. He had always driven his sons hard, because he wanted them to be men. He wanted them to be able to withstand the harshness of the real world. He wanted them to be fighters, guys who never quit when things got tough. He always knew that part of living was learning. And part of learning was falling. Eddie Lee wanted his boys to always get back up after a hard fall.

As part of his rigorous discipline, Eddie Lee had often told his boys that real men don't cry. That is why it took them by surprise, when he lifted his big, meaty hand and wiped away a tear that had escaped his eye, and ran down his fat, wrinkled cheek. Eddie Lee sniffled quickly, and then rose from his chair.

"Tameer... don't you let that girl get away, you hear me, boy? Don't you let Jamaica get away." Eddie Lee smiled at his son. "And that's an order, son!"

Tameer quickly brought himself to attention, and gave his father a crisp, military salute. "Yes, sir! I won't, sir!"

Chapter Thirty-Three

The motel room had long been empty. It was a fact that made Tameer's heart feel as though it had fallen into his stomach. Jamaica's beat-up Volkswagen sat abandoned in front of the now empty motel room, giving rise to some semblance of distant hope—at least until he realized that Jamaica had left the vehicle, because she no longer had any need for it. It had served its purpose, it had protected her identity, it had shielded its owner's deceptions. But still, it had to be registered to some address and location. He would find her, he told himself. Be it in New York, Switzerland, or visiting her father in Louisiana, he would find her. He needed to write down the car's license plate numbers, and start from there.

Tameer patted his pockets frantically, searching for a pen. There was none to be found. He didn't trust his memory enough to leave without writing down the car's license plate numbers, so he had to find a pen, a pencil, a marker, or anything that he could use to write down the numbers. He knew that the motel's office would have something to write with.

The large cow bell that hung above the glass and steel doors of the office entrance announced his presence. There was no need. The clerk had been watching Tameer suspiciously since his arrival.

"Noticed you were looking at the red VW over there, Mister," the clerk told him. "Are you interested?"

Tameer frowned. "Interested in what?"

"In buying," the clerk said, as if it were obvious.

"I know the owner of that car. How are you going to sell something that's not yours?"

"It is mine," the clerk replied. He quickly reached beneath the counter and pulled out a stack of papers, and set them on top of the counter in front of Tameer. He lifted the document on top of the stack. "See, I have the title."

Tameer quickly reached for the piece of paper. "Give me that!"

The clerk snatched the paper from the air. "Nope."

Tameer frowned and leaned forward. "Mister, I need to find the owner of that car!"

"I'm the owner."

Tameer examined the clerk for a moment. His disheveled clothing, missing tooth, scruffy beard, and alcoholic breath told him much of what he needed to know. He was getting nowhere, and he knew that it was only going to get worse. The clerk spoke only one type of language, and Tameer was angry with himself for not recognizing this in the first place. He reached into his pocket and pulled out a twenty-dollar bill. He held the money up in the air, directly in front of the clerk.

"I'm looking for the former owner of that automobile, sir," Tameer said politely.

The clerk snatched the twenty from Tameer's hand. "Sir? I like that. I haven't been called sir since... Well, hell, I ain't never been called 'sir'!" The clerk let out a high-pitched gasping laugh.

Tameer folded his arms. "Where is she?"

The clerk scratched his head. "Well, son, if I remember correctly, they left here, and said they were going to some fancy pants hotel. She said, 'Here, Mister, you can have this here car, if you forget ever seeing any of us.'"

"Which hotel?" Tameer demanded.

"Well, I forgot!" The clerk again let out his high-pitched alcoholic laugh, and began slapping his hands together.

Tameer pulled out another twenty-dollar bill.

"Which hotel?" he asked again.

The clerk straightened up. "Son, I'm a man of principle. The lady asked me to forget they were here, and I agreed. Now, for you to come in here, pull out some money, and think that I'm going to compromise my principles for a measly twenty dollars..."

Tameer pulled out a third twenty.

"Well, she did say to forget they were here." The clerk slowly slid the twenty-dollar bill from between Tameer's fingers. "But she never told me to forget where they were going. She had me forward all of their business calls and correspondence to another address. Hold on, I'll get it for you."

The La Cantera was something that Tameer had never seen the likes of before. He had seen advertisements in magazines, and once in a while, he had been able to catch episodes of *Lifestyles of The Rich and Famous*, but nothing could ever have prepared him for what was now sprawled before him.

The grandeur of the lobby, which shot up several dozen stories, was breathtaking. On each floor, balconies overlooked the massive lobby, and the gigantic, marble water fountains, which stood imposingly throughout the lobby. Water sprouted from the fountains, several stories into the air, all of it neatly falling back down into the fountain's base, daring not spill a drop. There were massive silk floral arrangements throughout the lobby as well. They were set inside of humongous vases of intricately carved stone. He surmised that one of the vases would cost twice his annual salary, after he finished college!

The carpeting in the lobby was so thick, that each of his steps reminded him of walking on top of a pillow of cotton. The seating spaced throughout the lobby, was leather covered, with intricately carved legs of wood or gold. Massive silk tapestries draped several of the walls, and legions of uniformed servants fanned throughout the establishment, catering to their guests' every whisper.

The guests, of course, were the beautiful ones. Tameer thought them to be lifted straight from the pages of *Vogue*, *GQ*, *Essence*, and *EM*. The women were young, gorgeous, designer, and toned, while the men were older, conservatively suited, and sported distinguished gray streaks in their immaculately trimmed sideburns.

The young blonde behind the massive marble-and-cherry service desk was exceptionally friendly. Once he told her his name and asked for the Rochelle party, she acted as though she had been expecting him.

"Yes, sir, the Rochelle party is here, and I've been instructed to have you shown up to their suite as soon as you arrived. Hold on for just one moment, while I buzz a concierge."

It was the motel clerk, Tameer thought. It had to have been. The little weasel must have called ahead and warned them. Beverly was smart.

The elevator was speedy enough, slightly slower than the arrival of the concierge at the desk after the blonde called for service. His instantaneous appearance made it appear as though the establishment employed genies of some sort.

The double doors to the penthouse suite were of the massive, solid, light-pecan-shaded variety. Their beauty was accented by the highly polished, gold, French-style door handles and gold hinges. To Tameer's surprise, the doors swung open to reveal a smiling Beverly. She quickly handed his escort an undetermined amount of money, causing him to disappear as quickly as he had appeared downstairs. Beverly waved for him to enter.

"I've been expecting you," she told him, as he stepped inside of the massive suite.

"Is Jamaica here?" Tameer asked.

Beverly ignored his question.

"I garnered that you would probably not let go that quickly, that easily. My daughter was quite distraught, and judging by your anger at her deception, you were quite hurt. Therefore, I take it, that you have some type of feelings for my daughter."

Beverly motioned her hand toward a love seat, offering Tameer to sit. He accepted. She turned to a nearby table and lifted a crystal tanker of Scotch, and poured herself a glass. Never one to be impolite, she offered her guest a drink as well. Tameer waved her off.

"No, thank you, ma'am, I don't drink. Is Jamaica here?"

Beverly sat uncomfortably close to Tameer on the love seat, and began to sip from her glass of Scotch.

"How much will it cost me, to have you forget about my daughter?"

Tameer shook his head and looked down. "I don't want your money, ma'am."

"I see... you are a hard bargainer." Beverly nodded slightly. "I'll tell you what, you name your price, and I'll write you a check here, right now."

"It's not about any money. I love Jamaica."

Beverly threw her head back in laughter, and chuckled in a demeaning manner for a moment, before sipping from her glass of Scotch again.

"What is your name again?" she finally asked him.

"Tameer."

"Tameer, you are from a low-income housing development, are you not?"

He nodded.

"Jamaica was basically raised in Europe, and in the Hamptons. You wear clothing from a rack; Jamaica's clothes are usually designer originals. You drive a Ford; my daughter is a Ferrari."

Beverly smiled at Tameer. "My dear son, you are from two different worlds. Remember what you said to my daughter? To leave you alone and go back to her world? Let her go back."

"I was angry, I was hurt," Tameer replied. "Mrs. Rochelle, I was wrong. I love Jamaica."

Beverly shook her head. "But you don't even know my daughter. How can you love someone you don't even know?"

"I do know Jamaica. We talked, and talked, and talked. We shared our dreams, our past, and we very much want to share our future. We want to make one together, Mrs. Rochelle."

"You knew her? You shared your past? Young man, you did not even know who my daughter was, until a few days ago."

"I didn't know her name, but I knew who she was. I didn't know of her fame, but I knew about her dreams. I got to know Jamaica on the inside, the real Jamaica. Not the TV Jamaica, or the Jamaica on stage, but the

Jamaica who throws snowballs, rides roller coasters, and dances around sombreros. I got to know the Jamaica who cares about people, who cared about me. I love that Jamaica, Mrs. Rochelle."

Beverly leaned back against the love seat, and sipped on her drink. She shook her head slightly as she examined Tameer.

"You are a smooth one. No wonder you were able to get my daughter to fall for you." Beverly turned and stared at the coffee table for several silent moments, before turning back to Tameer. "You know, I'm willing to let you write an obscene amount on one of my checks."

"I don't want your money," Tameer told her again.

"Why not?" Beverly snapped. "Why are you doing this to my daughter?" She turned away from him and exhaled forcibly. "Why can't you just let her be happy?"

"That's what I want. I want to make her happy!"

Beverly turned and faced him again. "What makes you think that *you* can make Jamaica happy?"

"Because I've done it before. I've made her happy, and she's made me happy." Tameer locked eyes with Beverly. "You know she loves me."

Beverly closed her eyes for several seconds, and then took his hand into hers. "Sometimes, if you really love someone, you have to let them go. Sometimes, you have to sacrifice your own happiness, for theirs. Sometimes, you have to love someone enough to let them go on with their life and be happy."

"I've heard the song."

"Don't be selfish," Beverly snapped.

"I love her," Tameer replied.

"Why?" Beverly asked him again.

Tameer stood, and began to pace around the floor of the suite.

"Because she makes me happy." He balled his right hand into a tight fist and pounded the air in front of him. "Because Jamaica makes me whole."

Beverly sipped on her glass of Scotch again, and stared at him.

"You're a shoe salesman?" she asked condescendingly.

Tameer nodded. "For now. I'll finish college in May."

"Really?" He had surprised her. "What is your major?"

"Business. Business and literature."

Beverly recoiled. "Why?"

"Because I want to get a good job. Because one day I want to own my own business."

"Why literature?"

"I love poetry."

"Do you write?"

He nodded. "Yes."

"Well... let me hear some poetry."

Tameer shook his head. "No."

The answer startled her.

"No?" she repeated. No one had told her *no* in a long time. "Why?" she demanded.

"Because I'm not in the mood."

Beverly wanted very much to call him an arrogant bastard, but Tameer was a heathen. You do not lose your temper with heathens, she reminded herself. They could react in some very unpredictable ways. She settled for asking him a different question.

"What type of business do you want to have?"

"Financial services. I also want to open up a small shop, and import African art."

"What kind?"

"Masks, Sub-Saharan masks. Sculpture also, and some plate carvings, and paintings as well."

"What areas, what tribes?"

"Any and all. It's all beautiful."

Beverly sipped from her glass again, and then sat up. "I'll give you the money to start your business."

Tameer turned to her and stopped pacing. His hand caressed a silk flower that was part of a massive floral arrangement sitting on top of a desk, in the corner of the expensively decorated suite. He knew what she wanted, and what the offer would entail. He asked her aloud, anyway.

"If I leave Jamaica alone?"

Beverly sipped from her glass. "Those are the terms."

Tameer stared at Beverly, locking eyes with her. "What have I done, to make you despise me?"

Beverly shook her head slowly from side to side. "I don't despise you. You seem to be a nice, educated, attractive young man, with a bright future."

"But?"

"But I love my daughter." Beverly leaned forward in her seat. "Do you have any children?"

Tameer shook his head. "No, ma'am."

Beverly placed her glass on top of the coffee table before her.

"When you have children, you will understand what I am about to say." She leaned back into the love seat, crossed her legs, and placed her hands over her knee. His attention was drawn to her fingers, where her rings sat forth prominently, displaying their various diamonds of extremely high quality.

"When you have a child, you want the best for that child, always. I have always given my children the best, and raised them to expect nothing but the best. I didn't raise my daughter to marry a shoe salesman, and live in tenements. I want the best for her, do you understand?"

Tameer walked silently to the oversized leather chair, adjacent to the love seat. He sat down slowly, and stared off into space while rubbing his lower lip with his index finger.

"I see," he said to her, while shaking his head. "You feel I'm not good enough for Jamaica."

Beverly slowly lifted her glass of Scotch and sipped. "It's nothing personal, Tameer, I'm a mother."

She was right, Tameer told himself, he wasn't good enough for Jamaica. He had nothing to offer her, nothing at all. He was from the Courts, he was poor, and he had always been poor. Jamaica had wealth, stardom, beauty, everything. Like Beverly said, Jamaica wasn't raised to marry a shoe salesman, and live in tenements. Jamaica was raised in Europe, and the Hamptons. She had always been wealthy, and always would be. Jamaica would marry well, she would marry someone who had as much, or even more, to offer. Someone from... a fine family...

Tameer smiled. He couldn't help but smile. He now knew what P.J. had done. Slowly, Tameer's head rose, until his eyes once again met Beverly's.

"I know that you think I'm not good enough for your daughter. I think you're right. I'm not good enough for your daughter, in fact, no one is. Not the great kings of France, not the warrior chiefs in Africa, nor the angels in Heaven."

Beverly began reciting the verses along with Tameer. They were the words that a young man with a borrowed silk ribbon tie, had spoken to her grandfather some thirty years earlier. She knew them by heart.

"I know that I don't have two thin dimes to rub together, and I may never have two thin dimes to rub together. But I guarantee on my honor, that your daughter will never know it, nor suffer for it. And I swear to you, that I will love her for the rest of my days."

Tameer's glance fell to the coffee table, while Beverly placed her drink down on it. Her tiny fist furiously pounded the air in front of her.

"Goddammit, P.J.!" she shouted. She quickly turned to Tameer and pointed her finger at him.

"That was a low blow. A low blow! And you know what, that man... ooooh, that man!" Beverly burst into laughter. "My God, I love that man!"

She turned to Tameer again, and nodded her head slowly. "He kept his promise. He loved me, he still loves me, and I have never suffered. Never!"

Beverly rose quickly, and wiped her moist hands onto her black Chanel pants legs.

"It wasn't that long ago, you know? Before you were born, but it doesn't seem that long ago." She lifted her glass from the coffee table and took a long drink. Visibly shaken, she smiled at Tameer. "P.J. and I were so poor, we shared a Volkswagen while we were in school. He cleaned floors, and I waited tables. But I loved that man so much, that I never actually knew just how broke we really were."

Beverly's shaking hand rubbed her quivering lips.

"Goddamn you, P.J.!" Again she turned toward Tameer. "He told you that on purpose, you know that? That smart bastard! He knew... he knew, that's why he told you that."

Beverly exhaled loudly, and took another long drink from her glass of Scotch. Her thoughts drifted to a small apartment in Cambridge that rested above an equally small Chinese restaurant. She recalled how her clothing constantly reeked of stir fry and soy sauce, and how she would stay up at night studying, using the light from the brightly lit neon sign outside of their window. It all made her smile.

The apartment was always cold, and stayed empty. But it hadn't mattered then, the emptiness gave them more room to dance. P.J. would grab her, twirl her around, and hold her close as they listened to the latest Motown hits out of Detroit. They had a special spot on the floor that creaked just so, with every rock and with every twirl. P.J. got a splinter in his knee when he knelt down and proposed to her a second time, on that cold, knotted, splintered floor. Beverly smiled, as she thought of the yellow marble that P.J. had glued to a base that he had fashioned out of a piece of tin. He promised to replace that ring with a real one someday, and he did. He did. He kept his promise, and he loved her. She had never suffered.

"My daughter's in Miami boarding the cruise ship, Empress of the Seas. Go to her." She turned to Tameer, and exhaled again. "Go and dance with my daughter."

"What?" Tameer asked. He wasn't sure if he had heard her correctly.

"Go to her," Beverly repeated. She pointed her finger at him. "But you better love her! You better..."

"I do, and I will," Tameer interrupted.

"You don't have much time," she warned him.

"I... I don't have the money to fly there, and I sure in the hell don't have any money for a cruise!"

Beverly walked to the telephone, lifted it from its cradle, and began dialing. "Tameer."

"Yes?"

"Hand me my purse."

"Yes, ma'am."

Beverly gripped the telephone tightly and shook it. "Damn you, P.J.!"

Chapter Thirty-Four

The ship's massive horn blew a thunderous honk across the docks of the disappearing port. The once large crowd of family, well-wishers, and gawkers, slowly began dispersing and returning to their work-a-day lives. Jamaica, standing alone on the balcony outside of her cabin, slowly turned and rejoined LaChina inside.

"Well, we've put to sea," Jamaica told her.

LaChina peered up from her game of Solitaire. "That's what ships do, you know."

Jamaica sat down upon the king-sized, pillow-topped bed, smashing LaChina's spread-out cards. She exhaled loudly, to emphasize her boredom.

"Hey, fat ass!" LaChina cried out. "You've smashed my cards!"

Jamaica gave no response.

"Okay, that's it. That's it!" LaChina sat up from her prone position on the bed. She stood, and quickly walked around the bed to the side where Jamaica sat.

Jamaica stared into LaChina's eyes. "You mean, we aren't having fun yet?"

LaChina tilted her head to the side. "Ha, ha, you're a barrel of laughs. Well, at least I know you're still breathing."

LaChina turned and lifted the ship's entertainment guide. She scanned it briefly.

"Perfect!" LaChina tapped her hand across the open guide book. "It says that they are having a comedian tonight in the lounge. That's what you need, some good jokes to make you laugh."

"I'm laughing already," Jamaica told her.

A knock at the cabin door startled them both.

LaChina smiled and nodded her head toward the door. "You answer it. It may be your next Prince Charming."

Jamaica gave her friend a quick, but fake smile, and turned to answer the cabin door.

"Hello, or rather good evening, ma'am," said the uniformed gentleman outside of the door. "I am your private concierge. If you should desire anything, I am at your service twenty-four hours a day. I'll be conducting a tour of the ship tomorrow, and giving you all of your briefings on safety, expense accounts, the islands where we'll be making ports of call, the activities we'll be having on board the ship, as well as the activities available at the island ports. I'll let you settle in now. If you should have any questions, please ring me."

He handed Jamaica a plastic card. "This is your ship's charge card. Pay for everything with this, as no cash is accepted on the ship. Your bill will be presented later. Your PIN number is on the card's holder. Good evening, ma'am."

The ship's lounge was large, thoroughly modern. Massive black marble columns, with blue florescent lighting, along with highly polished chrome fixtures and railings, gave the lounge a futuristic appearance. The stage itself was black, surrounded again, by aqua-blue florescent lights. The mural that provided the stage's backdrop, consisted of two futuristic clown faces, painted in a variety of colors. Along with the paint, the colors in the clown faces came from shards of colored glass, marble, crystal, and a variety of other materials, which together created the clown montage.

Jamaica and LaChina sat patiently in the back of the lounge, and waited for the appearance of the first comedian. The dimming of the lights allowed Jamaica the privacy to take her eyes away from the stage without LaChina's interference. Her gaze shifted to her glass of club soda.

"You know how when things are going too well, you have to pinch yourself to kind of give yourself a reality check?" The voice from the stage asked the audience. It was a familiar voice. It caused Jamaica to glance toward the stage. She knew that it was him.

"My life was something like that, and I gave myself a reality check," he told the audience. "But, in doing that, I lost the one person who made my life so good. I...I used a petty excuse to back away from this person, and I hurt her. My own insecurities made me push her away, and you know what? I found out that I couldn't live without her. I don't want to live without her." He shook his head. "Yes, I love her that much."

He switched the microphone from his right hand to his left, and slowly descended the stage's black, marble stairs.

"I saw her walk into the room tonight, but the lights dimmed before I could find her." He swallowed hard. "Jamaica, I understand if you don't ever want to speak to me again. You have every right. But I hope you hear me. I hope you believe me when I say... I love you. Jai, I need you."

His hand slid into his blue jeans pocket, and he produced a small, purple, felt box with gold trim. He held it toward the audience that he knew existed, but which the bright spotlights prevented him from seeing, and opened it. Inside of the box, set amongst a breathtaking five-prong, platinum-base ring, was a flawless, round, five-carat, canary-yellow diamond.

"Jai, will you please forgive me?" he asked. "And if you can forgive me, would you do me one more favor? Could you do me the honor of becoming my wife?"

With that, Jamaica could no longer remain seated. She rose so quickly, that had it not been for LaChina's quick reflexes, the small table at which she had been sitting, would have fallen to the floor. Jamaica shouted across the room.

"Tameer, I love you! I forgive you! And of course, I'll marry you!"

Jamaica started toward Tameer. He searched desperately in the direction from which her voice had come, but the glaring, disabling brightness of the spotlights prevented him from seeing her.

"Over here!" she shouted to him. "Over here! I'm coming!"

Jamaica rushed to Tameer and they embraced. Her legs flew around his waist, and she wrapped her arm around his neck, gripping him tightly. He held her in his arms, kissing her, and turning her through the air slowly.

The crowd clapped and cheered, some even offered a few whistles, but Tameer and Jamaica could not hear it. To them, this was their world, and they were the only ones in it. They kissed passionately, all over each other's faces. Their tears mixed, becoming one, but they quickly kissed those away as well.

"I love you, Jamaica"

"I love you so much, T," she replied. "I'm so sorry that I hurt you."

"I'm sorry." Tameer grabbed Jamaica's hand, and dropped to his knee. Slowly, he placed the ring on her finger. It was a perfect fit. "Will you..."

"Of course!" she shouted, interrupting him. "What took you so long!"

Tameer rose, and again they kissed.

"How did you find me? And how did you pay for this ring?" She held it up to the light.

"The car, I tracked you down through the car." He kissed her again. "It took care of us, Jamaica. And Beverly..."

His answer made Jamaica recoil. "Who?"

Tameer smiled. "Beverly. The plane ticket, the cruise, the money, the ring, my clothes, everything! She even drove me to the airport!"

Jamaica placed her palm on Tameer's forehead, to see if he were feverish. "Are you delirious?"

Tameer laughed and shook his head. "No, she did everything."

"My mother?"

"A wonderful woman!" Tameer shouted. "She loves you very much." He pulled Jamaica close and hugged her again.

"And P.J.!" Tameer shook his head. "Your father's incredible!"

"Daddy?"

"I'll tell you about it later. That's another story entirely."

"Kiss me," she told him.

"Of course."

And they kissed.

Epilogue

The wind swept across the ship's balcony, blowing her hair into his face. He stood behind her, with his hands wrapped around her waist, holding tightly the blanket which provided them with the warmth on this cool, star-filled Caribbean night.

The ocean was pitch-black, and its waves crashed melodiously across the ship's starboard, creating a soothing rhythm. The breeze caused her to shiver.

"Are you okay?" Tameer asked.

She nodded. "Yeah."

Jamaica turned inside of the blanket and faced him. She gently placed her arms around his shoulders and smiled. "Remember the snow, that magical night? You said that it was God granting us a miracle?"

Tameer nodded.

"Remember the things you told me about your father, and how he treated you when you were young? Remember what you said after we saw your mother in Houston? Remember the promises you made? Remember all of the things you said about how you were going to do things differently, and how you would raise your children differently?"

Tameer nodded.

"Well, you're going to get your chance," Jamaica said softly. "We got our miracle. T, I'm pregnant."

The breeze and the news hit simultaneously, though it wasn't the breeze that caused him to shiver. "Jamaica, why... Why didn't you tell me before?"

She rested her head upon his chest. "Because I didn't want you to think that you were obligated to stay with me. I wanted you to be with me because you loved me, not because you felt you had to."

"I do love you, Jamaica. I do."

"I know, and I love you."

And she did, she really loved him. She truly loved him, as did he truly love her. Together... together they loved each other. They loved each other for the rest of their days. And together, they lived, happily... ever...after...

The End
Thank You, and God Bless
Caleb Alexander

About the Author

Caleb Alexander resides in San Antonio, Texas with his family. He is an *Essence* No. 1 bestselling author and has written *Eastside, When Lions Dance, One Size Fits All, Big Black Boots* and *Next Time I Fall.* The author has also written several television dramas, and the hilarious and touching screenplay, *Finding Gabriel.* He has also penned the action/adventure screenplay *The Team*, a political thriller titled *UNICOR* and several articles for various magazines. The author can be reached via email at Caleb@ calebalexanderonline.com. For more information you can visit the author's website at www.calebalexanderonline.com

IF YOU LIKED "TWO THIN DIMES," READ MORE ABOUT LIFE IN THE COURTS. CHECK OUT THIS EXCERPT FROM

EASTSIDE

BY CALEB ALEXANDER
AVAILABLE FROM STREBOR BOOKS

CHAPTER ONE

Travon smacked his lips. "Man, you're stupid."

"Why?" Justin asked, shifting his gaze toward Travon. "Just because your brother got killed don't mean I will. Besides, it's for the hood."

Travon exhaled, and lowered his head. "I told my brother that he was stupid too, and now he's dead."

The boys continued around the side of the old red-brick school building toward the back. Staring at the ground, Justin haphazardly kicked at gravel spread along the ground beneath his feet.

"Yeah, Tre, but at least Too-Low went out like a soldier," he replied.

They were headed behind the middle school to a pair of old wooden green bleachers that sat across the well-worn football field. They could see the others standing just in front of the peeling bleachers waiting for them. Travon shifted his gaze from the waiting boys back to Justin. He started to speak, but Justin interrupted him.

"Tre, what's up with you?" Justin asked. "You ain't got no love for the hood? Your brother was down; he was a straight-up G. Don't you wanna be like that? Making everybody bar you and catch out when you step on the scene?"

Travon stared at Justin in silence. His silence seemed to only anger his friend more.

"I know that you're still trippin' over your brother getting killed, but he'd want you to ride for the hood!" Justin shouted. "He'd want you to be down!"

Travon halted in mid-step, and stared at Justin coldly. "How do you figure that?"

Like a precious family heirloom, Travon considered his brother, his brother's thoughts and wishes, as well as his memory, to be sacred. They were his and his alone.

Justin paused to formulate his reply, but one of the waiting boys shouted. "Y'all lil' niggaz hurry the fuck up! We ain't got all muthafuckin' day!"

Now filled with even more nervous anxiety, Travon and Justin quickly ended their conversation and hurriedly approached the waiting group. A tall, slender, shirtless boy stepped to the forefront. His torso was heavily illustrated with various tattoos and brandings, while his body was draped in gold jewelry, glimmering brilliantly in the bright South Texas sun.

"So, y'all lil' niggaz wanna get down, huh?" the shirtless boy asked.

Another boy anxiously stepped forward. "Say, Dejuan, let me put 'em on the hood!"

Dejuan, the first boy, folded his arms and nodded.

Travon walked his eyes across all of the boys present. There were six of them, all adorned with large expensive gold necklaces, watches, bracelets, and earrings, and all of them had gold caps covering their teeth. They were members of the notorious Wheatley Courts Gangsters, or WCGs for short. The WCGs were one of the most violent drug gangs in the State of Texas. Their ruthlessness and brutality was legendary.

Travon nervously examined the boys one by one. Those who were not shirtless were clad in burnt-orange University of Texas T-shirts. Burnt orange was the gang's colors, and the University of Texas symbol was their adopted motif. It stood for the location of their home, the Wheatley Courts. It was their municipality, their ruthless domain, their merciless world. It was a place where their will was law, and where all those who disobeyed were sentenced to death.

The Wheatley Courts was a low-income housing project where drugs and violence were the rule, and not the exception. It was also a place where many more than just a few of its occupants had made millions in their professions as street pharmacists. Perhaps worst of all, the Courts were home to the WCGs, a gang of ballers, and stone-cold murderers.

Travon shifted his gaze to his left; Justin had begun to remove his T-shirt. He looked back at the group of boys, to find that several of them were removing their shirts and jewelry as well. The festivities were about to begin.

"Let me whip these lil' niggaz onto the hood!" Tech Nine asked Dejuan again.

Without waiting for a response, Tech Nine walked away from the group and onto the football field, where he was quickly joined by Quentin, Lil C, and T-Stew. Once out on the field, the boys turned and waited for Justin.

Hesitantly, Justin made his way to where Tech Nine was waiting patiently and cracking his knuckles. Once Justin came within striking distance, Tech Nine swung wildly at him. The blow slammed into Justin's face.

"Muthafucka!" Justin shouted. He quickly charged Tech Nine and tackled him. Both boys hit the ground hard.

Lil C approached from the side and kicked Justin in his ribs. Justin cried out and rolled over onto his side. Justin tried to lift himself from off the ground, only to be met by a fist from Quentin. Justin grabbed his bloody nose.

"Wheatley Courts Gangstas, you punk-ass bitch!" Tech Nine shouted, as he charged Justin. "This is WCG, nigga!"

Lil C delivered a kick to Justin's back, just as Quentin swung at Justin again.

"Get that muthafucka!" Dejuan shouted from the sidelines.

Justin was able to roll away from Tech Nine's lunge, but had to take another blow from Quentin. He was able to make it to his feet just in time to receive another punch from Lil C. Although tired and out of breath, Justin was able to sustain the blow and remain standing.

"WCG for life!" Quentin shouted, advancing again.

Lil C swung at Justin again and missed. Justin, however, was unable to dodge a kick from Tech Nine. It landed directly in his groin.

Justin stumbled back, and Tech Nine kicked again, this time missing Justin and striking Lil C.

"My bad, man!" Tech Nine shouted. "I was trying to kick that little muthafucka!"

"Shit! Aw, fuck!" Lil C slowly descended to the ground while clutching his groin.

This brief intermission gave Justin time to recover and go on the offensive. He quickly dropped to one knee and punched Quentin in his groin, just as Quentin was about to swing at him.

"Aaaaaargh, shit! Punk muthafucka!" Quentin fell to the ground clutching his crotch.

Tech Nine maneuvered behind Justin, and threw a hard punch to the back of his head.

"Yeah, muthafucka, this is Wheatley Courts on mines!" Tech Nine shouted.

Justin rose, stumbled forward, and tripped over Quentin's leg. Tired, he hit the ground hard; this time, he could not find the energy to get back up. Tech Nine hurriedly approached and began kicking.

Justin, unable to move, curled into a ball and waited for the pain to be over.

"Punk muthafucka, fight back!" Tech Nine continued to kick brutally. He kicked Justin until he became tired, and retreated to where the others were standing.

Dejuan turned to Tech Nine. "Do you think that's enough?" he asked laughingly.

Tech Nine, sweating profusely, swallowed hard before answering. "I think he can get down. I think he's got enough nuts." He shifted his eyes to Travon. "You lucky I'm tired today, but tomorrow, I'm going to enjoy putting hands on you."

Travon's heart slowed to a semi-normal pace once he realized that they would not be jumping on him today. He quickly walked to where Justin was lying curled in a ball on the ground. Travon dropped down to his knees beside his friend.

"Justin, are you all right?" Travon asked.

No answer.

"Justin." Travon grabbed Justin's shoulder and shook it gently. "Justin."

"Yeah, I'm cool," Justin answered weakly.

"Leave him alone, he's all right!" shouted Lil C, who was slowly rising to his feet again.

Tech Nine shifted his eyes toward his friend. "Say, C, are you all right?"

"Yeah, muthafucka," Lil C answered. "Just watch where in the fuck you kicking next time."

Justin slowly uncurled, and pain shot through his body as he tried to brace himself to stand. Travon helped his friend off the ground.

"Yeah, you WCG now, baby!" T-Stew shouted.

Quentin, Tech Nine, T-Stew, and Dejuan quickly surrounded Justin.

"You WCG for life now, baby!" exclaimed Dejuan.

"Gimme some love, homie!" Tech Nine shouted.

"It's all about that WCG!" Justin declared weakly.

"Yeah!" T-Stew shouted. He extended his right arm into the air and made a *W* by crossing his two middle fingers. Doing the same with his left arm, he cupped his hand and formed the letter *C*.

"Wheatley Courts, baby!" Lil C shouted, as he and Justin embraced.

"Wheatley Courts!" T-Stew repeated, maneuvering into position for his embrace.

Dejuan swaggered away from the group, over to a pile of T-shirts lying on the ground. He lifted up a burnt-orange University of Texas T-shirt and examined it. On the front of the shirt rested a large white *T*. On the back of the shirt, printed in Old English script were the words *Wheatley Courts for Life*. Dejuan turned and walked back to where the boys were waiting, and Travon watched in fear, disbelief, and a slight bit of jealous envy as Justin was given Dejuan's very own Texas T-shirt to put on.

CHAPTER TWO

Weeks Later

Tonight, like every other night since his brother's death, Travon dreamt of him. Sweating profusely in the blistering South Texas heat, he tossed and turned as his last conversation with his brother was replayed inside his head.

"How do you like these Jordans, Tre?" Too-Low asked.

"They're pretty clean." Travon nodded. "Are you gonna let me sport 'em?"

Too-Low smiled at his younger brother. "I gotta stay on the cuts all night, 'cause tomorrow's the first. If I make enough ends, I'll take you to the mall and get you some."

"Cool!"

"So, how are your grades in school?" Too-Low asked.

"They're all right."

"All right? They need to be better than just all right." Too-Low leaned forward and jabbed his finger into Travon's chest. "You better not be fuckin' up in school!"

"I'm not." Travon frowned. "My grades are okay."

"I'll tell you what," Too-Low told him. "I'll spring for some fresh gear for school this fall, if you do well the rest of this year."

"Put me down, and I can buy my own shit," Travon replied.

Too-Low slapped Travon across the back of his head.

"Fuck!" Travon shot a venomous glance toward his bother. "What the hell was that for?"

Too-Low jabbed his finger into his younger brother's face. "Tre, if I catch you anywhere near this shit, I'ma put a foot in your ass! Do you hear me?"

"You're doing it, so why can't I?" Travon replied. "You won't even let me get down with the hood! That shit ain't fair, Too-Low!"

Too-Low kicked a crushed beer can that was lying on the ground near his foot, sending it tumbling noisily across the roughly paved street.

"Fuck this shit, Tre!" Too-Low shouted, once he had turned back toward his brother. "I'm doing this shit so you don't have to! And I already made it clear to everybody that I'll kill anybody who puts you on the hood, and everybody who was there watching!"

"Everybody else is down!" Travon protested.

"Tre, you better not ever join a gang, or pick up any kind of dope. Do you hear me?"

Travon shifted his eyes away from his brother, to a distant spot down the dark and empty street.

Too-Low grabbed Tre by his arm and shook him violently. "I said do you hear me?"

"Yeah, yeah, I hear you!" Travon yanked his arm away from his brother and again stared down the dark, trash-strewn street. All of his friends were joining, and it wasn't fair that he wasn't allowed to. All the girls in school were falling all over the guys who had joined. He would almost kill to be able to wear burnt orange to school.

"This shit is dangerous," Too-Low added. "The first chance I get, I'm getting us the hell outta these fuckin' courts!" When he saw the moisture welling in his younger brother's eyes, Too-Low decided that he had been a little too harsh. He decided to make up for it.

"Here." He reached beneath his burnt-orange University of Texas T-shirt and pulled out his nine-millimeter Beretta handgun. He handed the cold, steel, death black weapon to Travon. "Take this home and put it under my mattress. Go straight home with it, Tre. And don't be fuckin' 'round with it either."

Travon lifted the weapon into the air and examined it. After a few seconds, he turned back toward his brother. "You ain't gonna need this tonight?"

Too-Low shook his head. "No. Lil Anthony, Pop, and Tech Nine are on their way. We all gonna stay down tonight. I know that them fools is strapped, so I don't need to be. 'Sides, if one time runs up on us tonight, I ain't trying to catch a pistol case."

Travon slid the gun into his pants and pulled his shirt down over it. Too-Low reached into his pants pocket and pulled out a wad of rolled-up bills. He counted out fifteen hundred dollars and handed it to Travon.

"Tonight, when Momma goes to sleep, put four hundred dollars in her purse. Don't let her catch you. If she asks you in the morning where it came from, just tell her that you don't know. You can keep a hundred for yourself, so that leaves a thousand. Put the G under my mattress, along with the strap."

"All right, Too-Low, thanks!" Travon extended his fist and gave his brother some dap. "Good looking."

Too-Low roughly rubbed his hand over his brother's head, messing up his waves. Travon smiled, ducked away, and turned and headed for home. Of course on the way to his apartment, he would have to stop by Justin's and show off his brother's gun.

Once out of his brother's sight, Travon turned and made a beeline for Justin's apartment. He cut across the alley, then through the playground, taking the shortcut to his friend's apartment. He could faintly make out the sound of deep bass notes resonating from a stereo system. The notes grew progressively louder until finally a dark blue Hyundai came into view and passed by on the street just *in front of him, silencing its stereo system. Travon watched from the shadows as the car slowed and turned the corner. Moments later he heard the sound of semi-automatic weapon fire crashing through the midnight silence, and quickly decided that he had better head for home.*

Once safely inside his apartment, Travon did as his brother had instructed, and then retired to his bedroom. After awhile, he heard a knock at the front door, which was followed by his mother's screams.

Travon bolted up from his bed. His bare chest heaved up and down, his breathing was hard and labored. Travon wiped away the heavy beads of perspiration from his face, and then tried to focus his eyes. A slow glance around his balmy dark room quickly confirmed what he had suspected. He had, once again, suffered a nightmare.

Seven a.m.

"Tre! Tre!" his mother called out to him. "Travon! It's time to get up and get ready for school, boy!"

"Shit!" Travon swore under his breath and rubbed his eyes as he slowly pulled himself out of bed, then staggered to his bathroom. After washing his face, brushing his teeth, and taking a piss, he headed back into his bedroom. He had just begun to put his clothes on when his mother appeared at his door.

"Travon, I got breakfast waiting downstairs."

"Momma, what are you doing at home this morning?" Travon asked, rubbing the top of his head.

"I had to change jobs, baby. The company I was working for only want to do home health care now, so they need people with cars. I have to work in a nursing home for right now, at least until I can get us a car. And the only positions the nursing home had open were night ones, so I work at night now," she explained.

Travon stretched his arms and yawned. "Oh, I was just wondering what you were still doing home at this time, that's all."

His mother smiled. "You're not afraid to stay at home by yourself at night, are you?"

Travon frowned. "Naw, I ain't scared a nothing."

Elmira rolled her eyes toward the ceiling and crossed her arms. "All right, bad ass. You just better have your butt in the house by ten o'clock."

Travon dropped his shirt. "What?"

She uncrossed her arms. "You heard me."

"I can't even sit on the porch?" he asked.

Elmira stepped into the bedroom and caressed her son's chin. "Tre, you know what happened to your brother. So just bear with me for a little while, okay?"

Travon shifted his gaze to the floor and nodded. He could never forget what happened to his brother. He could never forget the night that his life changed forever.

"Okay," he said softly.

Elmira turned and started for the door. "Now come on downstairs and eat you some breakfast." Quickly, she whirled back toward her son. "Speaking of food, I haven't seen Justin in a few weeks. Where is he?"

"Well, he um, he got himself some new friends."

Elmira tilted her head to the side. "Tre, look at me, and don't lie to me. You and Justin were as thick as thieves, and now he don't even come around anymore?" She placed her hand upon her hip. "What happened?"

"Uh, nothing, Momma. We just don't kick it that much anymore."

"I was born at night, but not last night," Elmira replied. "Justin done joined that damn gang, ain't he?"

Travon's gaze fell away from his mother. "Well, I guess. I don't know, Momma."

"Tre, baby, just stay away from them and find you some new friends. Baby, just as soon as things get better, we'll get the hell outta this place. It's just gonna take some time."

Elmira lifted her hand and pointed out the window. "I don't want those people's welfare or food stamps. I have to do it without those things, so it will take us just a little bit longer to save. But we will get outta here, baby. One day, we will get the hell outta this place!"

With his gaze still focused on the floor, Travon nodded. "Yes, ma'am."